# The Forever Fight

## Ida Heartthrobs Book One

# BETHANY
# MONACO SMITH

First edition floral discreet paperback January 2025
ISBN 978-1-963450-17-0
Editing by Lacey Braziel at On the Page Publishing
Cover Design by Bethany Monaco Smith
For more information about this book, visit the author's website.
www.bethanymonacosmith.com

# About The Forever Fight

*The Forever Fight* is a standalone new adult romance featuring a prominent side character from my *Friends Like This* series. If you haven't read it, no worries! This story gives any and all details you need. It does contain a few minor plot/relationship spoilers related to the *Friends Like This* series, if that is important to you and your reading preferences.

If you're already a *Friends Like This* fan, I'm excited to finally give you Jesse's story. *The Forever Fight* is set at the same time as *Together Like This,* and you may see a few plot point crossovers. Whether you're an old friend or a new reader, get ready for a swoony, angsty, snarky, sweet, and steamy frenemies to lovers romance.

**Are you ready to fall for Jesse and Dani?**

# Meet the Characters

**The charming (former) playboy**
Jesse Wilkinson

**The grumpy-sunshine girl**
Dani Malone

**Dani's family/friends**
Olivia Malone
Weston Malone
Amelia Davis
Mason & Taylor Abbott
Mark Abbott

**Jesse's friends/family**
Joel Wilkinson
Evan Andrews
Garrett
Brooks

Jenna Reilly
Brett Reilly

**<u>The crossover friends/family</u>**
Rae McKinley
Sarah McKinley
Aaron Cooper

**<u>The best grandparents ever</u>**
Pete & Bea Abbott

# Trigger Warnings

If you're looking for possible triggers in this book, this page is for you. If you're not, you can skip this page and dive into the story.

*trigger warnings may contain plot spoilers*

Potential triggers in this book include: Discussion and brief depiction of cheating (not by a main character), depiction and discussion of loss and grief.

Any updates or changes to this information can be found on my website: www.bethanymonacosmith.com/triggers

*For everyone who has been patiently (or not) waiting for Jesse to find his forever girl. His love story and HEA is for you.*

# 1

## Ban Douchey Guys

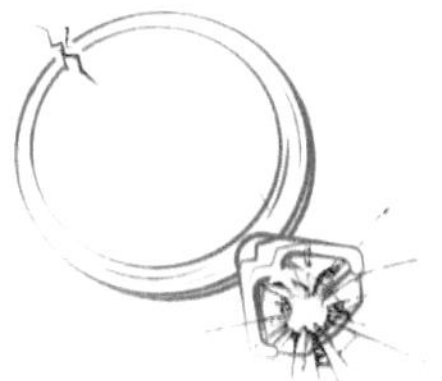

### Dani

LIFE LESSON NUMBER ONE: never fall for a smooth talker. Not for the charming guy who can flash a smile and make the world melt. They will suck you into their world, make you think they care, and then fuck up your heart.

Or in my case, they'll say all the right things, convince you they love you, propose, then suddenly decide they never wanted to get married.

Now that you're up to speed...

"You're a fucking coward!" I seethe at my fiancé—make that *ex*-fiancé—Jason.

He says nothing, which only supports my statement.

"You lied to me!"

"I didn't... lie. I always thought you were pretty, Dani. Sexy. Fun to be around. But I never thought of us as a long-term thing."

"Then why did you *propose?*" I yell.

"It seemed like what I was supposed to do. It's what my family expected of me. What looks better to all those jobs I was interviewing for. I figured I'd give it a shot, but I can't keep pretending I want this."

The bitter truth hits.

It's always been a lie. Every word out of his pretty mouth.

He needed to show he was in a serious relationship to get his trust fund. He needed someone on his arm for all those corporate dinners. All along I've been his fake fiancée, he just didn't bother to mention that to me.

*Fuck romance novels. Where's my happy ending?*

That's another kick in the fucking vagina. He actually *is* good in bed. Makes me scream and beg and see stars.

Is that why I believed it?

"You couldn't have told me? You had to string me along?"

Tears threaten, but I channel my inner Elsa and hide it all away.

"I wasn't—"

I hold my hand up. "I don't care. If this is over, then you can go."

He looks at me like I'm nuts, then turns on that charming voice that makes me want to shove a pair of scissors down his throat.

"Dani, baby, this is *my* condo."

"Call me baby again, and you won't be leaving with your balls attached to your body. And seriously? I decorated this place."

Well, as much as he would *let* me with his bland taste. "I made it a home." And that part is true. I thought it was a home. *Our* home. I made it warm and inviting. Cooked meals. Packed his stupid lunch every day. He'd kiss me before he left. *Thanks for the lunch. Love ya, baby.*

And it was all a lie.

"*I* paid for it."

"Because you refused to wait to sign the lease until I got home from visiting my family in New York."

Jesus Christ. He did that on purpose too.

My eyes dart around the condo, taking in the cream walls and expensive leather furniture. It's modern. *And boring.* It would never be what I want, anyway. As an interior designer, it was zero fun to design this place—the condo that was supposed to be my home.

*Screw this.*

He's talking again, but I'm not listening. I walk to the bedroom, grab my biggest duffel, and pack all my essentials and business stuff.

When I walk back out to the living—sorry, *entertaining*—area, he rises from the couch, but I ignore him, grab my purse, and aim for the door.

Before I get there, he grabs my arm.

"Dani—"

Glaring at him, I wrench my arm away. "Let go of me. There's nothing you can—"

"I need my key back."

I laugh in his face.

"You'll get your key back when my brother comes to pick up my stuff."

He yelps at that. Weston isn't a fighter unless he has to be, but hurt one of his baby sisters and he'll be thrilled to take out some aggression.

"Bye, Jason."

I turn on my heel and walk out of the condo, briefly letting my anger dull the pain of my broken heart.

"Why did I believe him? Am I that stupid? Or naive?" I sniffle as my younger sister Olivia runs her fingers through my hair. I'm in full Lorelai Gilmore wallow mode. Curled up on the couch, my head on a pillow in Olivia's lap.

"No. He was a very good liar."

"Then why does it hurt?"

"Because you loved what you thought you had. Your heart's still broken over that."

"That's stupid," I cry. "I fell in love with a lie. *I'm* stupid."

"No. He was a raging douchebag whose ass is going to get beaten by me and all the Abbott cousins. Especially Mark," Weston says, shutting the door behind him as he walks into the apartment he and Olivia share.

Mark is the same age as me, and like many of the Abbott men, extremely protective of the people he loves. Though we live in Virginia and he lives in New York, we've always been close. As a pro football quarterback, he could probably do some serious damage.

"I'm never falling in love again," I whisper. I don't need to look up to know Livvie and Wes are looking at each other skeptically. Love is the center of our family. Love for each other, and finding the right person to spend your life loving. Our grandparents instilled it in their kids, who have taught us all the same lesson. Open your heart and love hard. When you find love, don't let it slip away.

Where's the guidebook on finding the person who actually loves you and doesn't just play with your heart and string you along?

I should've known it when I met him. All the charm. Everyone in the room was drawn to him. He knew just what to say to keep everyone hooked. All surefire signs that he'd do the same thing in a relationship.

Never again. I need a sweet, quiet accountant who might be a little boring, but comes home from the office thrilled to see me, snuggle on the couch, and then spend the night worshipping me in the bedroom.

I wonder if accountant porn is a thing.

*I wonder if I've crossed the bridge into insanity.*

Weston leans down and kisses my cheek. "I'm going to get your stuff from that asshole so you can completely cut ties, okay?"

I turn to look at him. "Are you really going to beat him up?"

He laughs. "No. He's a whiny little bitch who probably bruises like a peach and would call the cops if I sneezed on him. I'll growl and grumble and give him a few menacing glares. That should be enough to make him shit his pants."

I laugh too. "If he does, please take a video."

"Done. I'll be back. Love you!"

"Love you too," I call after him, the door shutting just after the words leave my mouth. Discomfort replacing my vulnerability, I slowly sit up.

"What are you thinking, D?" Livvie asks.

"I want to dye my hair."

"Okay. I personally think that's a more solid choice than a dramatic breakup cut. Hair dye is more easily fixable."

"Well, I want to get it cut, too, but not dramatically. Just a little shorter. I want something more... me. Jason hated that I dyed my hair, so I stopped. I didn't want him to look bad to his clients or his family for being with a girl with pink hair." My voice falters. *Shit.* It wasn't just my hair. I toned down the vibrancy in every corner of my life, from the clothes I wore to how I spoke to people to my hobbies.

Hell, even my job. Instead of continuing to work as a freelance interior designer, I took a job working for my mom. She's a commercial interior architect focused on helping businesses create a structural design that both effectively utilizes space and represents what the company is. She brought me in to design the atmosphere to go with it. Unfortunately, most of what she does is business with very little excitement. The interior design is bland because the businesses are bland, too. Of course, Mom thinks choosing between sharp angles or an archway is exciting, so it's all fun for her.

Not me. There will always be clients who want a style that's boring or less fun to design for, but overall, that's not the norm. When I was working freelance, people chose me because I liked designing interesting or funkier things. I also love designing living spaces and kids' rooms. I like making things feel like home.

Instead, I've been designing one-note, cold, or boring business spaces part time so I could be at Jason's beck and call when he needed me for a business or family event. I'd been slowly slipping into that beige housewife role he wanted without even realizing it. He didn't want a partner. He wanted someone to look pretty, then blend in with the ugly, boring wallpaper.

*I hate wallpaper.*

My body thrums with chaotic energy, and I quickly stand up, pacing back and forth in front of the couch as I face the ugly truth. I stopped living for me and put myself into the box he wanted me to fit in.

"I'm cutting my hair! And dying it. I want pink again—no, teal. Or maybe purple." My eyes light up. "Ice purple."

Olivia raises her eyebrows, then shakes her head and smiles. "I'll drive. Don't need you crashing in your fit of mania."

I grab my bag and hustle over to the door. It's time to let the color back into my life.

"Oh my gosh, I love the purple, honey. I mean, not the reason you got it. Want me to have him blacklisted from every business I've worked with?"

I smile at my mom. "That could be fun."

To people who don't know her, Sylvia Malone can come off as cold because she's very poised and businesslike, but that couldn't be further from the truth. She's warm and welcoming and the kind of person who likes to drink wine in sweats and a wife-beater and dance around to Taylor Swift. Honestly, she's kind of my hero. My mom has a wild side always waiting to come out and play. In fact, if I had told her I was going to dye my hair ice purple, she probably would've met me at the salon and gotten pink highlights.

Olivia jumped on the bandwagon and got some pretty light blue streaks added to her hair. Given I have light brown hair, it took a lot longer to apply the ice purple color to my hair than it did to add the blue to her bright blonde hair.

"Didn't you help design that dreadfully boring 'men's club' he likes so much?" my dad asks.

My dad describing anything as boring is hilarious. He's straightlaced, especially compared to my mother. Maybe that's why I thought my relationship with Jason would work. Except my dad never tries to change my mom. He embraces her wild side, and when she pulls him up to dance, he dances with her, even if it is very badly. He's not the most exciting person in the world, but he's a good man and he loves us all to pieces.

Mom swats his leg. "Be nice. But yes, I did. I'll make a call." The evil smirk my mom gets makes me laugh. It reminds me of Grandpa—her father. Pete Abbott is deeply loving, great at calling people on their bullshit, and a mischief-maker, much to my grandmother's chagrin. Although, given the feistiness of all the Abbott women, my grandmother has plenty of spice, too.

Mom scribbles a note on a piece of paper, then looks back at me.

I bite my lip, then say, "Is it okay if I quit working with you?"

Mom squeezes my hand. "Of course, honey. I know it's not what you love. I was surprised you said yes to the part-time job. I only mentioned that I needed help, so you could get some extra money here and there if you needed it."

"Yeah, I was trying to do what I thought was best for my relationship."

"That's admirable," Dad says, "but next time, make sure it's someone who would do the same for you."

"And who isn't a smarmy douchebag," Weston says.

"Wes..." Dad sighs.

"Yeah. Honestly. Who says 'smarmy' anymore?" Olivia asks.

"That was not my point." Dad shakes his head.

Ignoring them, Mom looks at me. "What are you planning on doing now? Are you going to go back to freelance work?"

"I don't know. I feel like I'm one of those circus performers who can squish themselves inside a box, and now I'm climbing back out and I want to take up space. I want to *do* something. Live life. Experience things. I think I need a change of scenery."

Mom thinks for a moment. "You know, it's early May, your cousins will be home from college soon, and I'm sure Grandma and Grandpa would love a visit from you. Why don't you go up to New York? Take some time for you. You went to college fifteen minutes from home and lived with Olivia and Weston until shortly before you got engaged. You've never had that exploration period. Go live your life, baby."

I think that over for a moment. "I like the sound of that."

"Go pack some things. I'll call Grandma. I'm sure they'd be thrilled to have you fill one of those empty bedrooms in the farmhouse."

"Thanks, Mom." I look around the room. "I love you guys. Today sucks, but it's also opening up a door to something better, and I'm excited for that."

"You should be," Mom says. "Now go pack."

Smiling, I walk out of my parents' living room and down the hall toward the spare room where all my stuff is. I'm like Bilbo Baggins about to set off on an adventure. I'm taking back my vibrancy.

# 2
# Whiskey Melts Witches

## Jesse

"Is that the last box?" Carrie asks as I set the box I'm carrying down on the living room floor.

"Yep."

"Any chance it contains toilet paper?"

I chuckle at that. "You need to pee?"

"Desperately. And the people who moved out didn't even leave half a roll behind."

She does a little dance as I glance around the room. Planning is not Carrie's strong suit. Though I like to live in the moment, I like having a plan, too. Especially for big things like moving into your first home with your girlfriend. Granted, it's a lease, but it's gorgeous, and it's a big step. Though we slept at each other's apartments over the last nine months in college, this is our first time fully living together. We're in a new town now, just us. It's scary, but it's exciting too.

Finally, I spot a box that reads "extra bathroom crap" and pull it open.

"Got it," I call, fishing a roll of toilet paper out.

"My knight in shining armor," she says, smacking a kiss on my cheek and tossing her phone onto a nearby box as she grabs the toilet paper and runs for the bathroom.

I look around at the living room filled with boxes. There's a squeeze of uncertainty in my chest. I've never lived with anyone before—other than my siblings and parents. Although, for most of my life, I lived primarily with my little brother, Joel. I have two older brothers as well, Jonathan and Jared. Jared, the oldest, is an asshole on a good day. I wasn't exactly crying when he moved out of the house for college when I was twelve. Jon is quieter and fine to live with, but as an introvert, he was always happy to keep to himself. Since I'm a massive extrovert, our personalities clashed. By the time he graduated from high school three years before me, my parents had checked out mentally and often physically. They retired early and can be found traveling around the world like Carmen Sandiego.

That left me with Joel, who is two years younger. Though we drive each other crazy—as brothers do—we're also very similar and have grown closer as we've gotten older. Even he wasn't always around much since he has a group of five best friends who are so attached to each other they all went to college together. Don't get me wrong, they're great, and they're my friends, too, but I went to college to meet people, not hang out with the same ones I've been friends with my whole life.

On a nearby box, Carrie's phone vibrates.

"Carrie! Your phone's ringing!"

No answer. Of course she's taking the world's longest pee right now. She's been waiting for a call from her new job about where to go for her physical, and they've been playing phone tag.

I grab the phone, but as I do, it goes to voicemail.

*Can't say I didn't try.*

But as I look down at the screen, my blood runs cold. On the screen are several missed texts from some guy named Dean. I don't claim to know every person in Carrie's life, but I know anyone who texts her regularly, and I don't know anyone named Dean.

My chest tightens.

*Not again.*

I stare at the screen for a moment, deciding whether to look. You're supposed to trust your partner, right? The thing is, Carrie and I started off strong. We had a great relationship. I was patient with her as she moved on from her ex, and as she opened up to me, we built a strong relationship. Then, out of nowhere, she became secretive and withdrew from me. She ended up breaking up with me, right around this time last year. She wanted to make sure she was done with her ex. It crushed me, but I held on, hoping she'd sort her shit out and come around. She did. By the end of summer, she was done with him and we were talking regularly again. Once we were back at school, we talked, I forgave her, and we moved forward.

At least, I thought we did.

Over the last month, I've noticed she's been quieter and more withdrawn, but she said it was because she was stressed about graduating from college and moving here. I let it go because it is a big change.

*How stupid am I?*

Time to find out.

Swiping up on her screen, I put in the lock code.

I click on his messages, and don't have to scroll back far to get my answer. Their messages confirm the unsettling feeling that's been growing in my gut.

**Dean: I can't wait to finally meet you in person.**

**Carrie: I'll call you this week when I'm settled, and we can find a time.**

**Dean: Does that mean you're finally going to say yes to a date with me? A month of talking, and I'm ready for more.**

**Carrie: Maybe. We'll see how meeting in person goes.**

"Oh, I needed that. I found the boxes with the washcloths in the kitchen and washed my face, too," Carrie says, walking into the room.

My head snaps up, an ugly mix of anger and crushing pain swirling inside me. "Who the fuck is Dean?"

Carrie's face goes white, and she crosses the room, snatching her phone from me. "Just a friend."

"A friend? Tell me, how did you meet this *friend?* On Tinder? Hinge? eHarmony? Whatever trendy fucking dating app there is now? Because there's nothing friendly about you talking to him for a month behind my back. And there's definitely nothing friendly about you considering dating him when you're *moving in* with me."

She bites her lip as tears fill her eyes. I curl my hands into balls, digging my fingernails into my fists and doing everything I can to stop myself from reaching for her. For two years I've given this girl my heart. Now she's ripping it to shreds.

"I'm sorry, I—"

"You what?" I yell. "I moved here for you because *you* found the job you wanted here. I let you pick the rental because I wanted *you* to be happy here. I wanted to start our life together in a place that felt like home, and you've basically been cheating on me for the last month?"

She grabs my arm. "Not cheating—"

"Not physically. I'm sure if I scrolled through those texts, I'd see the signs of emotional cheating." Then something dark hits me. Something I can't believe I never realized before. She did the same thing with me. Before she left her ex the first time, we became friends. She leaned on me. And then she finally broke up with him and spent her time with me. *Oh fuck.* This pattern has been here the whole time. "I'm done," the acidic words form a hole in my chest as I say them, but there's nothing else.

"No, Jesse! Please, I... I was just confused. Struggling with the move. He said the right things. I want—"

"You don't know what you want, but you clearly don't want me."

"Jesse..."

I shake my head. "No. There's nothing else to say, Carrie. We did this once. I'm not doing it again. I'm not interested in being your maybe guy or wasting any more of my time on someone who doesn't love me. I hope you find what you're looking for, but I'm not it, and I'm done letting you pretend I am. If you don't want to stay here, I'll try to get us out of the lease, otherwise, I'm done. Don't call me again. Don't text me. This is over. Not for the summer while you find yourself. Forever."

That word hits me square in the gut. I thought *she* was my forever. I was chasing a future with her I was never going to have.

She clears her throat. "I can't afford this place alone."

I force a breath, wanting to believe she wasn't staying with me for my money. I wasn't born with a silver spoon in my mouth, and other than how much my parents travel, you'd never know how much they're worth, but I have a lot of money thanks to a trust fund my grandpa left me after making millions in New York City real estate in the '80s.

She didn't know all that when she met me, but she's known for a while now. For fuck's sake, I want to believe she's not that awful.

"I'll handle the lease, but you should plan on getting your stuff to a hotel tonight."

"But I—how—Jesse..."

She reaches for me again, but I pull away.

"Why don't you call Dean?"

With that, I turn around, grab a box of my stuff, and walk out of the house, my heart so fucking shattered I can't think straight, except that I need to get the fuck out of here as soon as possible.

"She's a witch. Like one of the green ones with a big wart on her nose and scraggly hair," my best friend Jenna says, sipping on a hard lemonade as we sit on my parents' back deck.

Jenna Reilly—formerly Barone—has been my best friend since we were in kindergarten. One hundred percent pure platonic friendship. There was a hot second when we considered dating—that's what male and female best friends are supposed to do, right? If you ask half of our friends, that would seem to be the case, but it wasn't for us. Despite a deep friendship, we had negative chemistry, and I could not be more grateful. No awkward teen uncertainty, just awesomeness. I've always been able to count on her and vice versa.

"Oh, and ugly twisted toes. Witches always have horrible feet."

I nearly spit out my whiskey at that. My brother Joel coughs on whatever he's drinking as Jenna's husband, Brett, pats her leg, laughing. "Nice one, babe."

"It's true," she insists.

Jenna is a whirlwind. She can be oblivious at times, has zero filter, but also delivers profound wisdom without realizing she's doing it.

I drove the three hours from Albany back to my hometown of Ida, New York, last night. When Joel walked out of the house and saw my Impreza stuffed with boxes, he poured me a drink, then helped me unload. He also listened as I ranted and cried—because I'm a pathetic bastard.

"I have now unfriended her on every form of social media. I didn't delete her number in case I need to call her and give her a verbal bitch slap, but I did change her name to Careless Witch," Jenna says.

I cackle at that. *How much whiskey have I had?* Enough to melt a wicked witch. There's water in whiskey, right?

"Ooh, love that. I'm changing her to Wicked Bitch of the East in mine."

I look up and see Rae McKinley. My neighbor. One of my little brother's best friends. *My* friend. A girl I've crossed more lines with than I should have—and almost destroyed my friendship with her in the process.

She gives me an empathetic smile, then walks over and hugs me. "I'm sorry, J. I'll kick her ass."

"Thanks, Rae Rae," I whisper, smiling weakly.

Aaron Cooper, her boyfriend slash childhood sweetheart slash soul mate slash my friend who I also almost ruined my friendship with, claps a hand on my shoulder. "I'm sorry, man. She's good at playing people."

I nod as Rae's sister, Sarah, leans down and kisses my cheek. "You'll find someone better." Then she turns and walks over to Joel, plopping on his lap and wrapping her arms around his neck. She's his girlfriend, except for the part where she isn't because they're fucking idiots.

Aaron wraps his arms around Rae and a pang of jealousy hits. I want that. That kind of love. They've been through hell to get here. More often than I should've been, I was mixed up in that. In the worst moment, it almost wrecked everything. Yet, here they are now, comforting me when my heart is in shambles.

"So what's happening with the lease? And the job?" Brett asks. Since Brett and Jenna started dating four years ago, we've become good friends. He was a little wary of the male-female best friend dynamic, but once he got to know me and saw us together, he wasn't worried.

"I called the owner and offered to pay an additional month besides the first and last we'd already paid, and he was fine with it. It's a nice house. I doubt he'll have trouble renting it again. I already spoke to the hiring manager at the company I was at. He was pretty relaxed about it. I wasn't supposed to start for two more weeks, so it was mostly fine. I had to return the small sign-on bonus they gave me, but that wasn't a big deal."

"What about witchy tits?" Jenna asks.

Rae does a full spit take at that.

I smile despite the darkness I feel. "Don't know. I made sure she got to a hotel before I called about the lease, then I blocked her number. I don't care how she got stuff to the hotel or anything else. I don't give a fuck." Throwing back the rest of my whiskey, I'm surprised by the lack of guilt I feel. The first time we broke up, I was heartbroken. All I wanted was to get her back. I'd stare at pictures of us and stalk her social media. This time? I never want to see her face again. It's amazing how quickly love can turn to hate when the person who was supposed to protect your heart crushes it.

"So," Jenna says, knocking her elbow against mine. "What's next for you?"

I look down at my empty glass. "More whiskey. Then eventually a plan. A job." I scoff and look at my brother. "Dad is already trying to get me in where he used to work." Until he retired, our father was the CFO of a moderate-sized, extremely successful company that deals with private and government contracts manufacturing vehicles, aircraft, and drones. There are plenty of business sector jobs there, but that's not really what I'm looking for. I was willing to take that kind of job before because I was starting a life with Carrie and I could move on when I found something better. Now? I'd rather find a job I'll enjoy. I have the money to not work for a couple of months while I figure it out. Until then, I'll find somewhere to volunteer. *And probably day drink.* Yeah, day drinking sounds good.

"Sounds like Dad," Joel says, lips pulling into a flat line.

Our parents are kind, generous people. But as parents? They suck. They're never around when we need them, and their advice is often more focused on finances and how to enjoy life than it is on how to get through the hard stuff. If everything in my life fell apart and I didn't have a cent to my name, they'd probably stop into town for a day or two, tell me they loved me, and hand me a nice juicy check. To some people, that probably sounds like the life. For me, I'd rather have an actual relationship, but it is what it is. They love me. It's just usually from halfway across the world.

"Whatever. They're not here. The witch is gone. Here's to getting drunk and moving on."

I grab my glass of whiskey that is somehow full again and raise it up.

"And to burning any remnants of her," Rae says with an evil smile.

"Oh, yes. I second that," Jenna says. "I've never had to do it, but on TV shows, it's always cathartic."

"And I've got some ice cream to help heal the burns afterward. If you don't eat it all first," my close friend Garrett says, walking onto the deck. He runs his own ice cream shop and truly makes the best ice cream I've ever tasted. "Your go-to." He hands me a pint of ice cream and a spoon and sits down next to me. "She was never my favorite, but I truly thought she cared about you. Fuck her for taking advantage of the way you cared for her. You're better off."

"Thanks, G." I open the pint of ice cream—vanilla with peanut butter swirls, chocolate chunks, and Butterfinger pieces—and dig in.

"There's plenty more ice cream for everyone else inside," Garrett says.

I raise my spoon. "Here's to getting drunk, playing with fire, eating a shit ton of ice cream, and then moving on."

*Here, here.*

# 3

# Sunshine Vibes

## Dani

Yawning, I walk down the stairs of Grandma and Grandpa's farmhouse and round the corner into the kitchen.

"There she is," Gram says, bustling around the kitchen. "Morning, Sunny."

I laugh at that as I lean against the counter. As a kid, I was so upbeat, optimistic, and obsessed with the color yellow, Gram started calling me "Sunny."

"I don't feel particularly sunny these days," I say as she pulls me into a tight hug. There's nothing like a hug from Gram. It soothes my soul. She has a deeply calming presence.

"Well, you're still healing," she says, letting me go.

It's been a couple of weeks since the breakup, and while I left town the day it happened, I only got here a few days ago. I took my time exploring along the way. I stopped in a couple of small towns as I made my way from Virginia up through Pennsylvania. I also stopped and spent a few days in New York City with my cousin, Mark, who is the second-string quarterback for New York's top football team, the Bandits. Since it's the off-season, he had plenty of free time, so we hung out, ate tons of good food, and went to a NY Metros baseball game where I only slightly lusted after the hot players, especially pitcher Corey Matthews and third baseman Declan Lowery. Hot with a capital H, O, T.

Now I'm living the cozy, small-town life at Grandma and Grandpa's farmhouse and forty plus acres of property. I've spent most of my time hanging out with them, reading, and exploring the trails through the woods. It's nice to be somewhere surrounded by love.

I sit down at the kitchen counter as Gram slides over a plate of pancakes, eggs, bacon, and some warm maple syrup. "I didn't realize how much of myself I let fade away. I want to feel bold and vibrant again."

I chomp down a bite of pancakes and almost groan. Gram's pancakes are always perfect. So fluffy. Not too sweet. Lots of vanilla.

Gram places a piece of paper and a pencil in front of me. "Make a list."

"A list?"

"Yes, it's what old-fashioned people do. They use that long yellow thing to write words on that white lined stuff." Grandpa smirks at me as he wraps an arm around Grandma.

"I'm familiar with the concept."

"I thought you kids were too busy using your phones to read books and play games and write papers and wipe your ass to do anything else."

"Peter Abbott," Gram chastises while fixing up a plate for him.

"Don't act like I haven't seen your nose buried in *your* phone playing Candy Crush, old man," I tease, handing him a napkin as he sits down next to me.

"Good to see you're getting your spunk back. Don't let that bastard tear you down. You're stronger without him." He taps the paper. "That's what the list is for."

"So, number one should be 'never fall for a charming smile again?'"

"Not quite, girly," Grandpa says. My whole life, Grandpa has referred to all his female children and grandchildren as his girlies. No matter how much sass he might give us, we're his soft spot.

Gram leans over the counter on her elbows. "Don't waste your time making a list of things you're *never* going to do. Make a list of all the things you want to do, the joy you want to find, the life you want to experience. No negativity. Show me your vibrance."

She gives me a wink, then turns around and starts cleaning up.

"Gram, I can do that," I say.

"Hush. I'm not some old lady. My knees try to make me feel like one some days, but I'm perfectly capable of washing a pan or unloading a dishwasher."

I smile at that. For being in their early seventies, my grandparents are pretty spry. Of course, with four kids, thirteen grandkids, and two great grandkids, they have to be to keep up. I'd argue more with Gram, but since my only other argument is that she shouldn't have to take care of me, I don't bother. That one definitely will not fly. Bea and Pete Abbott live for their family.

"Think I should put 'find a job' on this list? Or is that not exciting enough?" I ask, doodling on the paper between bites of pancakes.

"That depends on if you want it to be an exciting part of your future," Gram says, stopping with a load of clean bowls in her hands.

"Speaking of that, I was talking with your cousin Mason last night," Grandpa says. Mason is my uncle Chris's son and the oldest of all my cousins. "He and Taylor are looking for a nanny. Their last one got married and moved away right before Taylor gave birth last month. Next month, Taylor's going to be working part time again and they'll need help. She'll be working from home, but with two under two, she'll need all the help she can get. I know it's not interior design, but it might reinvigorate you while you find the right thing. They're planning to hire someone full time when she goes back to work in the fall, so it wouldn't be forever."

I side-eye Grandpa. "And did you happen to mention that I'm a weary, vagabond traveler trying to reclaim her life and happiness?"

Grandpa chuckles at that. "No. I believe Mark did that for me." Mason is Mark's older brother.

"I'm open to it. Kids are fun and I miss Mase and Taylor—everyone up there. I'd get to spend more time with that part of the family." Though my mom and her siblings were all born and raised here in Ida, New York, both of my uncles moved up north to the Watertown area where there is a second family compound with both of their houses and a guesthouse. Several of my adult cousins live up there as well.

"Give him a call. I'm sure they'd be happy to have you whenever," Grandpa says.

I put on a fake pout. "Are you kicking me out?"

"Not yet," Grandpa says with a wink. "But the minute you start wallowing and not fighting, your tiny little butt is out of here."

"Yes, sir." Gram laughs at that, and I can't help but smile. "No wallowing, I promise. I'm even leaving the house tonight to meet everyone at some new place. The Rooftop?"

"Oh, I've heard it's fantastic. Knowing the girls and their friends, it'll be quite the gathering," Gram says.

"I'm excited. I've missed getting out and having fun."

Knowingly, Grandpa taps the paper next to me.

Though many things are flowing through my mind, I write one thing down.

*Find the sunshine again.*

That's what I want most of all, to find the little things that bring me joy and make me smile. I wasted too much time hiding in the shadows. I'm ready to bask in the sunlight again.

Dressed in a flowy yellow tank top, black leggings, and shimmery silver flats, I make my way up to the top of The Rooftop. The restaurant has four levels. A brewpub on the ground floor. A twenty-one and up club area on the second floor. A private entertainment area on the third floor—available to be rented out for parties and such—and finally, the rooftop bar.

I'm early because I hate not knowing where I'm going. I've spent time in Ida regularly since I was a kid, but not enough that I know the area well when driving around. Giving myself extra time to find the place made me feel better. I don't like feeling rushed. It stresses me out.

Since I'm early, I head for the bar and order a drink. Just a soda. Alcohol and I don't get along most of the time, and I don't feel like being sick tonight. I want to spend time with my cousins—and more than likely all of their friends. Every time I'm around them all, there's so much joy and laughter and shit-giving. I love it.

"Jack and coke," a voice next to me says. It's a voice as smooth as caramel and strangely familiar. Turning in my seat, I instantly recognize why. It's been years since I've seen him, but I'd know that charming smile anywhere. *Jesse Wilkinson.*

I fully admit, in the past, that smile might've done something to me. Not anymore. Don't get me wrong, the cute boy I remember has grown into an attractive man. He still has the mischievous green eyes and the smattering of freckles across his nose and cheeks I remember, but the rest of him is notably more adult. His once shaggy dirty-blond hair is now long on top and shorter on the sides. It's still a little messy, but in a put together way. His jaw is more defined as are most of his muscles, though he's still lean. And that smile hasn't changed a bit, except that it no longer affects me.

I'm over charming smiles, sultry looks, and pretty words. Been there, got the T-shirt, and thankfully, I've outgrown it.

When he doesn't get an immediate smile, he elbows me. "Aw, not even a smile for me? I know it's been a long time since we've seen each other, but I don't recall you hating me. Come on, Dani. Where's the ray of sunshine I remember?"

With an eye roll, I put on an overly enthusiastic smile. "Jesse! It's been too long."

"Wow. So much sincerity."

I nearly snort at that. From what I remember of Jesse, he's a self-proclaimed playboy who uses that grin to melt a girl's panties off, then it's on to the next. Nothing about him screams sincerity.

"I—" before I can respond, there's a voice behind me.

"Hey!" Rae calls, hurrying over to us with her boyfriend, Aaron, and their best friend—Jesse's little brother—Joel.

Rae throws her arms around me, and I hug her back tightly. Despite growing up a few states apart, Olivia and I have always been close with Rae and her sister Sarah.

"Hey, I've missed you," I say.

"I'm glad you're here. It should be a fun night." She glances over at Aaron and smiles. He looks at her like she hung the stars. To him, she probably did. It's hard to deny that true love exists when you watch them. They've been best friends since they were five, and though they went through hell to get here, they're extremely happy now. It would be less nauseating if I wasn't so down on love right now.

"Dani," Aaron says, leaning over to give me a quick hug and a kiss on the cheek. Then he nods at Jesse and smacks him on the shoulder. "Hey, man. How are you tonight?"

Jesse shrugs. "I'm fine. I'd be better if the company actually liked me." He smirks at me, then stands up and flips his hand through the hair at my shoulder. Leaning in, he whispers, "I love the purple." No, I did not feel a shiver when he did that, *thank you very much.* He turns to Rae. "Rae Rae," he says, calling her by the nickname Joel gave her when they were kids.

"Hey, J," she says softly, giving him a hug.

Talk about weird. How Aaron isn't bothered by the charming playboy his girlfriend used to hook up with being here is beyond me. Who knows? Maybe he's being nice because it's Joel's brother.

"Anyone else here?" Rae asks.

"Just grumpy pants over here," Jesse says, throwing his thumb up in my direction.

Rae shoves him, then whispers something to him. His eyes dart to me and his expression softens. Ugh. If Rae just told him I got dumped recently and now he's giving me pity eyes, I'm going to hit someone.

Before I can find out the answer, a bunch of Rae's friends show up, and together they walk toward a large lounge area. There are multiple across the rooftop, along with some booths and high-top tables. The lounge areas have comfy outdoor couches surrounding gas fire pits. The whole place has a relaxed but timeless vibe. I like it, but there could stand to be a little more color. I smile to myself. That design part of my brain never fully switches off, and I love it. Everywhere I go, there's a constant stream of inspiration and excitement. Now, I need to lean into it again.

Rae and Aaron are absolutely nauseating. He can't take his eyes—or his hands—off her. And that's when their lips and tongues aren't tangled up. But hey, if anyone is going to be nauseating, it's the two of them, seeing as they just announced to everyone that they're engaged. I'm not surprised. Despite them only being twenty, it's been years in the making. Even though my heart is wounded and I never want to give in to the soul-crushing power of love again, I'm genuinely happy for them.

"Hey stranger," my cousin Sarah says, wrapping me in a hug. It's funny, of everyone in my family, she hugs the most like Gram and they aren't biologically related. Sarah was Rae's best friend when they were little, and when Sarah's useless mom abandoned her, my aunt Kara and uncle Charlie adopted her. We all loved her right away and agreed she was always an Abbott, even if we didn't know it at first.

"How are you?" I ask as we pull apart.

"Good. I got stuck late at work. I'm glad Rae waited to make the announcement until I got here. It was fun seeing everyone's faces."

"Nobody should have been that surprised."

She laughs at that. "Less surprised and more *finally*."

"Now that I get." Looking around the rooftop, I notice Rae isn't standing with Aaron, she's having some sort of intimate conversation with Jesse, who looks like he might cry any second. "What's the deal with them? Doesn't it bother her *fiancé* that she's being so touchy-feely with a guy she had some kind of sordid affair with? And what's with the sad boy act?"

Sarah lifts a brow. "I love you, so I'm going to give you a pass since you just went through a very shitty breakup, but Rae and Jesse did not have a sordid affair. He and Aaron are friends. And there's no sad boy act. His relationship just ended because of cheating. He feels like shit about it."

My eyes narrow. Did he cheat, lose the girl, and now he feels bad? Hell, it surprises me he was even in a serious relationship. *This* is why you don't fall for the charming smile. I'm sure he'll be happily hitting on a new girl at the bar in no time. And I will happily sit back and sip on my drink because it won't be me.

## Jesse

I thought I was past this stage. After staying constantly drunk for forty-eight hours, I thought I was past the drinking to kill the pain game. Then Rae and Aaron dropped the engagement bomb and I've been surrounded by sickeningly adorable lovey moments.

It's a little more than my bruised heart can take. So, now I'm two double whiskeys in and moving happily toward three sheets to the wind.

"How are you doing?" Aaron asks, dropping onto a stool next to me at the bar.

"Smooth as whiskey," I mutter, shaking the glass and taking another sip.

"Right." He looks down at his own glass. He's not old enough to drink, but the bartender went to school with us and has always been the type to fill people's cups, as it were, even if they're underage. "Look, I'm sorry—"

"Don't. You're allowed to be happy and celebrate that you're stupidly in love, even though I'm not anymore. Rae talked with me. I don't need you over here apologizing to me. It makes me feel even more pathetic."

He sighs. "I know, but..." He clears his throat. "You were there for me when I was in that place. I'm here for you."

I cough on the surprising amount of emotion welling in my throat. "I appreciate that, but I'll be okay. You should go celebrate with your girl." Back in the day, I would've teased him and said if he didn't, I would. But after what happened, I don't even like joking around about that stuff.

Aaron nods, then stands up. "We're all here for you, so don't drown yourself in the whiskey bottle, okay?"

"Yeah."

He smacks my shoulder, then walks back to where everyone else is hanging out.

Spinning on my stool, I look over at everyone else. Plenty of couples. Lifelong friendships. So much warmth, joy, and happiness. Normally, I'd be in the center of it, but right now, it only makes me more miserable. I suppose it doesn't help that I've gone through considerable life changes in the last couple of weeks from graduating from college, to moving two days later, then finding out I was essentially being cheated on, and moving back home on the same day. Now I'm the pathetic drunk asshole sitting on a barstool. No job. Not sure where I'm going. Just sitting alone at a bar while everyone else in my life celebrates.

Jesus. I'm careening toward rock bottom. Whatever, that's fine. I'll hit it tonight and climb up tomorrow. I need to find *something* to do. Get my mind off this and move on with my life. If I were me, what would I tell myself?

*What the fuck was that sentence?*

What advice would I give myself right now if I wasn't a basket case?

*Something better is coming. If she really loved you, she never would've hurt you like that. Focus on yourself.*

Wow, I'm a self-help book.

"That's nice…" I spin and look across the rooftop. Some guy has Dani stopped halfway between where everyone was sitting and the bar. She's glancing around, looking excruciatingly uncomfortable.

Well, fuck that shit.

Grabbing my glass, I walk directly to her.

Her eyes go wide when she sees me, and I get the feeling she wouldn't respond well to me pretending to be her boyfriend, so I go for a different approach.

"Dani! What the hell are you doing here, troublemaker?"

She laughs and shakes her head. "Same thing as you, probably. How have you been, old pal?"

"I'm good," I say, throwing my arm out for a hug.

She leans into it and whispers in my ear. "Thank you."

The guy who was talking to her clears his throat. Letting her go, I turn to him. "You got a problem, man?"

"We were talking," he says, voice tight.

I laugh in his face, then clap a hand on his shoulder and lean in toward him. "Buddy, anyone with eyes could tell you she was not into you. She was leaning away, looking around, and her arms were crossed over her chest. It's clear she was uncomfortable. Next time, choose a willing participant." I smack my hand on his shoulder, then step back, tossing an arm around Dani's neck.

"Whatever," he mumbles, then walks away, grumbling something else.

When the guy is safely out of earshot, I drop my arm from around Dani and look at her. "Old pal? Really?"

She laughs lightly. "I didn't know what else to say. You caught me off guard."

"Should I have walked over and kissed you instead?"

All playfulness fades away as she glares at me. "No. Definitely not."

But the glare just makes me smile. I've known Dani in passing since we were kids. She's always been fun-loving with that tough girl Abbott attitude, but there's something about this guarded version of her that makes me want to both push her buttons and protect her from whatever is out to hurt her.

"I'm not sure if I like your smile or your scowl more," I say, flashing my signature smirk at her.

She rolls her eyes *hard.*

*Oh, babe. You have no idea that's* not *a turnoff for me.*

Wait. Am I turned on by her? I'm too many whiskeys deep and not thinking clearly.

"You don't need to like either one."

"Whoa. Easy, Dani girl. I know we haven't seen each other in a long time, but I thought we were friends. At least, I thought you didn't hate me for no reason."

Her expression softens, and she clears her throat. "Sorry. My anger might not be for you directly."

Leaning closer, I run my hand up her arm and give it a gentle squeeze. "I'm sorry about what you went through. Your ex sounds like a jackass. You deserve a hell of a lot better than that."

Her gaze drifts down to my hand on her arm, some surprise in those sultry wildcat eyes. I wonder if she feels the same heat I do. She definitely feels *something* because she meets my eyes again, then slowly pulls her arm away, that tough facade taking over again.

"Yeah, I do. Thanks for the save, Wilkinson. I'm going to say goodbye to Aaron and Rae and head out. You should sober up. You deserve better than drinking yourself stupid."

Looking more pissed than she was before I intervened, she spins on her heel and walks away, leaving me staring at her, dumbfounded. I don't know the details of what happened, but whatever her ex did, he deserves the ass-kicking of the century for stealing Dani's brightness.

Then again, I can't say much. My ex did a number on me, too. With one last look at Dani, I turn and head back to the bar. I can sober up tomorrow.

# 4
# Occasionally Be Naked

## Dani

"I MIGHT CRY. THIS is... perfect," Elisa, the café owner I've been working with says as she looks around the finished space. "Thank you so much, Dani. It's exactly what I wanted."

"You had a great vision," I say. "You knew what you wanted. I just helped put it all together."

She shakes her head. "I couldn't have done it without you. You get free coffee for life."

"I'll take it," I say with a laugh. "Especially the days when I've been up all night with kids. Nannying for my cousins sounded really fun until I realized how frequently I wouldn't sleep."

"Seriously, anytime," she insists, then gives me a hug. "You do great work, Dani. I hope you continue."

"Thanks," I say, beaming.

This is the third job I've done on the side since I started nannying for Mason and Taylor in mid-June. This was by far the biggest and took a good chunk of my free time, but I loved every second. Elisa was a gem to work with and it was my favorite design style. Eclectic, funky, vibrant, and very connected to Elisa's vision for the café. We tore out all the modern furnishings, sold what we could, and used all that money to repaint, get some new pictures for the walls, and get a bunch of mismatched tables and chairs from the local flea market. Now, the café screams local coffee, food, and products. I think Elisa will do well with it.

"Well, I guess I better get on with my last inventory checks before opening day."

"Of course. Before I go, can I take a few pictures? I want to get a full website up and running, and I'd love to include this."

"Absolutely! I'm going to head into the back and work on a few things. Take all the pictures you want. Just let me know when you leave so I can lock up."

"Will do. Thanks, Elisa."

"Thank you, Dani," she says with a smile as she walks toward the back.

I take ten minutes and snap photos. The sunlight streaming in through the large windows at the front of the building provide the perfect lighting. The colors pop, and the café's warmth exudes through the photos.

After letting Elisa know I'm leaving, I pause at the door and take one last look. It's stunning. And I helped create that. *Damn, I love doing this.*

As I walk down the street toward my car, I text Olivia the final pictures. It's been weird living away from her. Even though we didn't live in the same apartment anymore, we saw each other almost every day. She and Wes were always my go-to supports, and they still are, just from a distance. I miss them, but I especially miss Livvie. Unlike a lot of sisters close in age, we didn't fight much. She was the Anna to my Elsa, and Wes was the older brother we teamed up to lovingly annoy.

My phone goes off with a notification the second I'm inside my Nissan Frontier. Hoping for a text back from Livvie, I flick my phone screen on, only to see an Instagram notification instead. *From Jesse.*

Oh, no. No, thank you. My heart absolutely *did not* just do a little flutter reading his comment.

*Looks amazing. Great job, Dani girl.*

He commented on the before and after picture I just freaking posted. When did he even start following me? *Why do I care?* I shouldn't care. Maybe he's a sweet guy sometimes, but he's also a player—something I don't need in my life. I'm sure we'll be friends or friends-adjacent, maybe even frenemies—if he keeps pushing my buttons—but nothing else.

*Do you hear me, heart? Nothing.*

And yet, I'm in a deep-dive scroll through his Instagram when my phone goes off with a call from Livvie. I quickly close the app, as if Livvie could see me and pick on me, then connect my phone to the Bluetooth in the car and answer her call.

"Hello—"

"Oh my god! It's gorgeous! Dani, you did amazing. Like, I know you're talented, but when I see stuff like that, I'm in awe."

"Thank you," I say softly.

"I'm so proud of you. And I miss you."

"Come visit me. Two months without my sister is too long. Can you come up? Mase and Taylor have an extra bedroom. Of course, the guesthouse is only a five-minute drive from their house if you don't want to be woken by screaming kids."

"Well... I'm working a shitty job, life is unbelievably boring, I haven't seen everyone up there in months, and I miss you. I'm on my way!"

"Really?"

"Yes. I'll quit my job tomorrow. Maybe I can work at that little café you just designed. When does it open?"

"Monday."

"Perfect. I can work there for a month before I go back to school."

"You're a genius," I say with a laugh.

"Well, duh! I've been wanting to visit up there more, but I put it off since I'll be in Ida for Rae and Aaron's wedding in October."

Watertown, where Mason and Taylor, my uncles, and several cousins live, is about two-and-a-half hours north of Ida. It's on the edge of Lake Ontario and absolutely gorgeous.

"I'm so excited to see you. When do you think you'll be here? If you fly into Syracuse, I can drive down and pick you up."

"Oh yes. They probably won't have a direct, but that's okay, it'll be cheaper. I gotta go figure this out. I'll text Mason and Taylor and see if they're okay with me crashing."

I laugh at that. "You know Tay, the more the merrier. Just get ready for nudity. Tay sometimes forgets to put on clothes."

Olivia cackles at that. "I remember when we first met her and she was going on about how she hates wearing clothes, and someday, when she had her own house, she was always going to walk around naked. Mason looked thrilled."

"Now he just rolls his eyes and reminds her that clothes exist. And I'm staying with them. She laughs it off. No shame. I love that about her."

"Hell yes! Okay, I'm going to go. I'll let you know when I have all my flight details. Seriously, amazing job on that café. Love you!"

"Love you too, Livvie. Bye."

We both hang up and I'm smiling like an idiot. I get to see my sister soon, *and* I helped design an amazing new business.

Grabbing my purse, I slide open a zipper at the back and pull out my list—the list I made at Grandma and Grandpa's kitchen counter two months ago—and look over it.

### *The Ultimate Life To-Do List*
*-Find the sunshine again*
*-Try new hair colors*
*-Live my passion*
*-Buy more funky jewelry*
*-Drive across country*
*-Learn to snowboard*
*-Drink espresso & eat a chocolate croissant at a café in Paris*
*-Design a place that heals my soul*
*-Dance in the rain*
*-Wish on a star (too Aaron & Rae???)*
*-Try new foods*
*-Find out if I still hate oysters*
*-Design my dream home*

I smile as I read them over. I haven't done most of them yet. Plucking a pen from my purse, I put a line through *Find out if I still hate oysters.* Fun fact, I do. I also put a line through *Try new hair colors.* As the ice purple in my hair faded, I switched to a deep wine red, which looks even more amazing than I thought it would on me. After this, I'm going for a copper brown. Safe to say, I'll keep having fun with that. I quickly cross out *Buy more funky jewelry.* Taylor is the queen of shopping and jewelry. She found plenty of amazing pieces for me, and I found more at the flea market. Finally, I cross out *Design a place that heals my soul.* Because the café did that.

My life is richer and fuller now than it was a few months ago, and I'm so thankful for that, even if it took being treated like shit to be here. Looking at the list again, I think of where I've been, where I want to go, the café, and my conversation with Olivia. Then I add one more item to the list.

*Be naked more.*

Smiling to myself, I tuck the list and pen back into my purse, then start the car and head for Mason and Taylor's house, driving slowly as I go by the café, feeling like I've gotten a little more of my sunshine back.

## Jesse

"No, Jen, I don't think getting Taylor Swift to play here is realistic," I say to my best friend through the phone. Whenever I need inspiration or a fresh idea, I call her. Her random banter and lack of filter usually leads to some kind of useful idea. At the very least, it takes me down a rabbit hole to the right place.

However, the idea that we could get Taylor Swift to play at a small minor league stadium in a post-industrial town when she sells out the biggest football stadium in each state in like four minutes is highly unrealistic.

"Hey, maybe she'll want to play smaller, more intimate venues to connect with her fans at some point."

"Yeah, not this summer," I say, pulling my keyboard closer and looking up indie music festivals. As usual, Jenna's words have me thinking about what *would* work here.

In my last month as the events, social media, and marketing manager for the triple-A baseball team, the Binghamton Knights, an affiliate of the New York Metros, I've come up with some great ideas for themed nights at the baseball games and ways to draw interest to the team.

*Social media.* Get some young, attractive baseball players dancing in short videos online and suddenly your views go through the roof. I wish I could take credit for the idea overall, but I can't. Damn the Savannah Bananas for that. Or worship them. Because the idea worked. Of course, we've made it our own, but there's nothing like a thirst trap to drive people to the stadium in droves.

Social media is fucking weird.

"What about new or indie singers or bands?" I ask. "Have any favorites? It would be cool to do a big fall festival here with concerts. Maybe some local people as openers."

"Ooh, I love that," she says. "There are a few up-and-coming solo acts I like, but I bet you could even get some bigger indie bands like Guster or The Head and the Heart. Even Death Cab for Cutie. There are a lot of great bands like that. I'd freaking love a lineup like that. They're chill. Reasonably family friendly. You could even have bands or artists during the day that increase in popularity, leading to the bigger concert at night."

I snap my fingers. "You're brilliant." Quickly, I key in the website for a brewery up near where I went to school. They host summer outdoor music festivals with some of the same bands Jenna was talking about.

"Well, obviously," Jenna says with a laugh. "Hey, I've gotta go, but if I think of any more ideas, I'll text you."

"Perfect. Love ya."

"Love you too." She makes a kissing noise, then hangs up, as I deep dive into bands that would be great to get, overall fall festival ideas, and what it would take to pull it all off this year. Then my mind shifts to the holidays. Maybe for planning purposes, the fall festival should be the following year. But this year, we could do something leading up to Thanksgiving. A turkey trot, maybe. Or something family-focused on Black Friday to draw in people who don't want to be out shopping. Maybe we could do a German-style Christmas festival. And I know other stadiums that have put up an ice rink in the winter with a chance to meet players and the mascot.

I'm in the midst of typing up a few bullet points for each of my many ideas—summer movie nights?—when there's a knock on my office door.

"Come on in," I call.

The door swings open, and Jamie Henderson walks in. Jamie is a new addition to the Knights after being drafted by the Metros after his senior year of high school. He's also a close friend of Aaron's and one of the best pitchers I've ever met. Aaron has a knack for coaching and worked with Jamie throughout middle school and high school to help him get to this point. As soon as he was drafted, we knew he'd be coming here. We have several pitching vacancies, and with Jamie being immensely talented, there's a good likelihood he'll be called up to the Metros within a year or two.

"Hey, Jesse," he says. "Or do I have to call you Mr. Wilkinson?"

I grimace at that. "Unless it's a girl with a daddy kink, I don't want anyone calling me Mr. Wilkinson. Sit." I gesture to the chair in front of my desk. "Welcome to the team."

His cheeks flame almost as red as his hair. "Thanks."

Jamie is hilariously humble and sweet. You'd think girls would chew him up and spit him out, but no. They flocked to him and I'm pretty sure he got more girls than I did in high school. Not that it matters beyond his current relationship with Rae and Aaron's close friend, Amanda.

"So, you get to listen to my spiel now about how to behave on social media and among the general population, since you are always a face of this team and the Metros organization. I know Aaron trained you well, so I'll hit a few points and pass you the guideline sheet I give to everyone. Somewhere in the paperwork you signed, you agreed to follow that, so do it."

"Got it," he says, taking the sheet and looking over it as I mention a few key dos and don'ts.

"Last thing to talk about is our social media presence," I say. He grins at me. "You've heard how I've upgraded our social media strategy over the past month. What I have for you is a waiver to sign that you're comfortable being on camera, being used in our social media to attract people to the team and the games, etcetera." I slide him the waiver, and his smile grows as he reads it over.

"Basically, you're not only asking to sell tickets with my baseball skills but with my body?"

I grin back. "Something like that. Hey, I've gone shirtless and joined the guys a couple of times."

He laughs as he signs the waiver and slides it back to me. "Oh, I know. I saw the viral dancing one. Aaron and I were impressed by your moves."

Laughing, I lean back in my chair. "Is Amanda going to be okay with you being a part of that?"

He waves a hand. "She won't care. She says as long as she's the only one who gets to keep my heart and share my bed, she's good."

I jokingly wipe my brow. "Good. I don't need her kicking my ass."

"She could, too."

"Oh, I know. Hey, she's an event planner, right?"

He gets a proud smile on his face. "Yep. A damn good one. She's handling all of Aaron and Rae's wedding stuff, and in the past, she has interned for private planners and event companies."

"Nice. Do you think she'd mind if I called her about some events I'd like to do here?"

He shakes his head, then scrawls her number on the back of one of my business cards. "Not at all. I'm sure she'd love to help."

"Perfect. Thanks, man. You're good to go. Any idea when your first game will be?"

"A couple of weeks, probably, they said."

"Well, I'll be here whenever it is. Let me know if you need anything."

"Will do. Take care." He waves as he exits my office.

I put the card with Amanda's number in my top drawer, and I'm about to get back to work, when my phone lights up with a notification. Instagram. *From Dani.* I assume she's replying to the comment I posted—which she liked—but no. Oh, no. This is *so* much better.

She just liked a post on my account from over a year and a half ago. She went deep diving through my Instagram account like my own personal stalker. A sexy one. I smile to myself, excited to know I have some kind of effect on Dani, and surprised at the effect that knowledge has on me. Maybe it wasn't the drinks I had on the rooftop that night, maybe those stray feelings were a hint of something more. Something I'm hoping I might get lucky enough to explore in the future.

I allow myself another moment to revel in this feeling, then get back to making my list of event ideas.

The inspiration and excitement I feel at this job is more than I could've imagined. Some people think of marketing as boring and social media as dull and tedious, but they're only those things if you make them that way. Getting to test the limits of my imagination and ideation fulfills the creative part of my brain while combining it with my business skills and love for baseball.

Before I found this job, my dad had been pushing me to go work for his old company as a financial analyst. It would've made me a lot of money—his primary argument for taking it. That and growth potential, which honestly sounds a little dirty. Neither were good enough reasons for me to want to take that job. When I told him about this one, he was supportive. Ish. It's clear he sees this as a *for now* job. There isn't enough room to grow, in his opinion—especially financially. I don't give a fuck about the finances. It pays well enough to live off and I have more money than I know what to do with, anyway. And when it comes to growing within this job, social media and marketing are a constant state of change. It never stops. I could work this job for the rest of my life and be doing something new every week. I love that.

This job has also shone a light on how unfulfilled I was in my relationship with Carrie. She wanted a very specific kind of life, and looking back at it now, it wasn't really what I wanted. I was trying to keep her happy because I was scared she'd leave me again if I didn't. Nothing I did ever would've made her stay, and stifling myself for her wasn't healthy for either of us. People can grow together in relationships. I've watched people I love do it. Carrie and I never did. The more distance I have from her, the more I realize we were never the right match. In some ways, that's comforting. It reminds me the right person for me is still out there. In other ways, though, it hurts. I was ready for forever. I was willing to give her that, and in the end, all she gave me was a crushed heart—something I'm still healing from.

For now, though, I'm learning about myself, discovering what I enjoy, and living my best life. I look out at the baseball field below my office. *No better place to find myself than right here.*

# 5
# Ice Cream Leads to Bad Decisions

## Dani

My cousins are ridiculous people. Specifically Rae, Sarah, and all their best friends. It's Rae and Aaron's bachelor/bachelorette weekend and they've taken the word *extra* to a new level.

We were taken by limos—that's right, there were two, one for the guys and one for the girls—to New York City. The girls had a spa day and fabulous sushi lunch. The guys literally played a game against the New York Metros—we got to watch. Then we all spent the night in swanky suites in a New York City hotel.

I don't know who in their life won the lottery, but *damn*. I mean, it was fun as hell. Olivia and I snuck off between the spa and dinner to go to the top of the Empire State Building. Olivia cried. She hates heights. How I got a non-adventure-lover for a sister, I'll never know. I wish I could convince her to go skydiving with me—something I recently added to my list. I really need to find someone who wants to do the things on there with me. Some of it I can do myself, but a lot of it would be more fun with someone else.

As the weekend of shenanigans continued, we limo-ed back to Ida from NYC this morning, then the girls had a tea and luncheon with all the wonderful women who are a part of Rae's life. That was actually very emotional because Gram wrote a letter to Rae and read it aloud and made us all sob. After that, Rae performed a strip show for Aaron, then they snuck off to have sex. Now comes the true ridiculousness. We're getting ready to play a game that they made up as kids, called spy.

Which involves running around the neighborhood with walkie talkies and Post-it notes and trying to tag the other people to get them out until the spy wins or is tagged.

Though most of the guys and girls who were here for the parties have left—including Olivia who was exhausted from drinking, her near death experience with heights, and more drinking on the limo ride back—there are enough of us left that we're pairing up for this silly game. I stuck around because I was curious what my cousins and their friends were like when there were only a few of them here. Turns out, they're nerds.

The pairs end up mostly couples, except for Miles and Mackenzie, who are apparently the only platonic besties of the friend group. Then Aaron and Rae whisper to each other, and suddenly I'm paired up with the charming asshole himself. Jesse Wilkinson. The glimmer in Aaron's eyes makes me think he did this on purpose. What the purpose is, I don't know. Keep Jesse away from his girl? *Whatever.*

As the teams break off and the game begins, Jesse strolls over to me. "Hey, Dani girl." He leans in and kisses my cheek, and damn it, my traitorous body reacts. Heat flushes in my cheeks at the same time it swells in my stomach. *No charming smiles. No players.* No matter how cute he is. "I like the hair," he whispers, twirling his finger around a strand. "The ice purple looked good, but this is so you. Especially with the longer hair."

I loved the wine red I had over the summer, so with my hair longer, I turned it into a wine red to pink balayage. Though it's half pulled back in a topknot, the rest is on full display and I fully admit, looks gorgeous. My stylist did a great job.

But those thoughts are at the edges of my brain right now because Jesse is still in my space. He's acting like we're old friends. Yeah, I've known him for years, but we don't really *know* each other. We met as pre-teens and hung with the same group of people here and there when I was in town, but we never sat down and talked.

"Thanks," I finally choke out, to which he smiles.

*Does he like making me flustered?*

Wait, probably. Isn't that in the player handbook?

"So, are you ready to do this?" he asks, leaning back.

"Do what?"

He raises his eyebrows. "Spy." His face breaks into a smoldering grin. "Unless you had something else in mind."

*There it is.* A one sentence reminder of why I'm not going there.

My eye roll is instant, followed by his laugh.

"In case I didn't mention it the last time I saw you, that eye roll doesn't scare me," he says in a voice that's practically pornographic. His eyes say what his words don't. *He likes it.*

I step back, not realizing I'd moved toward him. What the hell does my body think it's doing? Honestly, this is ridiculous. Am I drawn to this sort of guy? My first boyfriend in high school was nothing like this. My dad is nothing like this. But the first guy I dated in college, most of the ones I hooked up with, and then Jason, were all like this.

Is charming asshole my type?

*Gross.*

What is wrong with me?

"Dani?"

"Hmm?" I snap my gaze back to Jesse, who is staring at me, amused.

"Are you ready to play spy?"

Right. The ridiculous game. I love my cousins. Maybe this would be fun if I'd done it in the past, but the idea isn't that exciting to me, and I'm freaking exhausted from everything we've done in the last thirty-six hours.

"Honestly? Not really. I was hoping for more relaxing and less running around."

He laughs lightly. "No worries. Come with me." He extends his hand. I furrow my brow, and now he's the one rolling his eyes. "Would you just trust me?"

"Fine." I take his hand, which unfortunately is just as hot as his gaze.

He drags me down the driveway, then grabs the walkie talkie and presses the button while pointedly saying, "Let's walk down Front Street. Everyone else should be gone by now."

A moment later, Miles and Mackenzie appear from nowhere and get us out. Jesse hands over his walkie, then he slings his arm over my shoulder and we walk back to the house.

"Okay, that was brilliant."

He chuckles as he leads me inside. "I've played my fair share of games of spy with them. It can be fun, don't get me wrong, but I don't enjoy it nearly as much as they do. Plus, my brother and Rae end up ultracompetitive by the end. It's better to give up now." He strolls over to the fridge and pulls out some kind of fancy beer. "Want anything? We've got a gamut of beer, wine, and hard liquor."

My stomach tightens. "Uh, anything non-alcoholic?"

He glances at me. "Of course. Sorry. My brain is still in bachelor party mode."

I chuckle at that. "It has been quite a weekend. And I'm guessing expensive. Did someone win the lottery, and I missed it?"

He looks surprised or maybe confused for a second before he says, "Not that I know of." He clears his throat. "Anyway, there are all kinds of sodas. Lemon lime, orange, grape, cola, root beer, cream—"

"Ooh, a cream soda float sounds amazing. If you have vanilla ice cream."

He gets a huge smile and pulls the freezer door open. "I always have vanilla ice cream."

I cock an eyebrow as I look at the multiple quarts of vanilla ice cream in the freezer. "Apparently."

"Fun fact about me, I love vanilla ice cream."

"Oh god, are you one of those people who thinks *vanilla* is the best flavor?"

He laughs, a joyful, childlike smile appearing on his face. It makes my heart beat erratically. His charming smirk is easy to deny, but this smile does devastating things to me. Like wearing down the armor I've carefully crafted to protect me.

"No, vanilla isn't the best flavor, but it is the best base. You can add anything to vanilla. Make whatever flavor you want. I have a mild obsession with ice cream, so I always have the best vanilla ice cream in my freezer and a variety of toppings and mix-ins."

"The best vanilla?"

"My buddy owns an ice cream shop. It's the best ice cream I've ever had because he's passionate about making it that way. He's creative and always coming up with new flavors."

"So you keep his vanilla in your house?"

"Yeah..."

"I get it can make all kinds of flavors, but I'm surprised you don't have your favorite flavor in there."

He looks offended. "I can't choose a favorite."

"What?" I say, bewildered. "You're addicted to ice cream, but you don't have a favorite?"

"Do you like to read?" he asks.

"Uh... yeah?"

"What's your favorite book?"

My eyes widen. "That's not fair! There are so many to choose from. And—oh..." He smiles victoriously. "Fine. I get your point, but it's different. Books, music, movies, anything like that come with emotions. You can't pick a favorite because it depends on your mood. Ice cream is different. Your favorite is the one you always go to. You trust it. When you don't know what to pick, you pick that one. Most importantly, it's the one you reach for on a bad day. The one that comforts you. Are you telling me you don't have one like that?"

He stares at me for a moment, then a hint of sadness creeps into his eyes. "Yeah. I guess I do. It's vanilla with peanut butter swirls, chocolate chunks, and Butterfinger pieces."

"That sounds amazing," I say, staring up at him. My body warms as my heartbeat ticks up again. If his joyful smile is devastating, this wistful one makes him irresistible. My hand must feel the same because it goes rogue, reaching for him. I cup his face and run my thumb over his cheek. "If it's your favorite, why do you look sad?"

*What am I doing? Why am I touching him? Why can't I stop? Why do I want to fix the sadness in his eyes?*

He looks down at me, a mixture of hurt and surprise on his face. "I was thinking of the last time I ate it. After my ex cheated on me."

I drop my hand from his cheek, staring into his eyes, surprised by his vulnerability—and maybe by the fact that his ex cheated. I assumed...

"I'm so sorry. No one deserves to go through that. My ex proposed to me, then decided he didn't actually want to get married."

*Shit, why did I tell him that?*

He leans in closer, brushing some hair off my shoulder. "His loss. You're clearly better off without him." We stare at each other intensely, and it's hard to breathe. *What is happening?* He must notice, too, because he takes a half step back and clears his throat. "Anyway, what's *your* favorite ice cream, Dani girl?"

I suck in a breath. Right. Ice cream. Maybe that will cool me off. I need it because right now I am unacceptably hot for Jesse Wilkinson. "Um, raspberry cheesecake."

"Cheesecake pieces and raspberry swirl in the ice cream?" he asks.

"Yep."

"I think I have..." he trails off, rummaging through the freezer before pulling out some frozen cheesecake bites. He grabs a quart of ice cream as well, then pulls some raspberry sauce from the refrigerator. "Homemade raspberry sauce on ice cream is perfection."

He grabs two bowls and starts creating his ice cream concoctions as I yank a cold bottle of water from the refrigerator and chug it, trying to settle myself down and cool myself off because somehow a conversation about ice cream has me all riled up. Except it wasn't the ice cream. It's *him.* This playful and seemingly honest side of him.

He smiles at me, eyes still dancing as he cuts up the cheesecake squares into bite-size pieces. I think I might actually like this side of him. I take another sip of water, my stomach all twisted up because the heat I feel isn't dissipating, it's spreading. To my surprise, it's moving south.

Clearly, it's been too long since I've had sex. Too long since I've felt wanted. The way Jesse gazes at me makes me feel wanted, but then I wonder if he can make any girl feel that way with a look. Or maybe I'm misreading everything. All I know is I need to settle the hell down before I do something crazy, like fall for Jesse Wilkinson.

## Jesse

Let the record reflect, Dani Malone is smiling *and* laughing. With me. She's the happy, vibrant girl I remember, and damn if it doesn't make my blood run hot. All the ice cream in the world doesn't stand a chance at chilling the blood running through my veins.

"So, what's the verdict?" I ask as she finishes the last bites of her ice cream. We've been sitting on the back deck, talking about all the craziness of the last couple of days.

"Pretty good," she says with a nod, setting the bowl aside.

"Pretty good?" I ask, taking mock offense.

"Okay, it was really good, but not as good as my favorite version. I'm kind of an ice cream nerd, too. In fact, one of my favorite things to do is find the best local place to get homemade ice cream wherever I am. My favorite place back home makes the best raspberry cheesecake ice cream ever. Even the base ice cream is cheesecake flavored."

I admit, that sounds fantastic. "I'll talk to my friend about it next time I see him. I'm sure he'd be up to the challenge."

She looks me over as she's done many times tonight, like she's trying to decode my words or the way I'm looking at her.

"Why does this matter to you?" she asks softly. "It's not just about ice cream, is it?"

I pull my bottom lip between my teeth as I take her in. Her messy red and pink hair, those wildcat eyes, the few freckles that dot her cheeks, and the surprising vulnerability written all over her face.

Cupping her cheek, I wipe a smudge of ice cream away from her bottom lip. "I like seeing you smile. I don't know what your ex did to you, but I might need his address so I can go kick his ass for stealing your light."

She stares up at me, breathing heavily. "But why do you care?"

I run my thumb across her cheek. "No one deserves to have their heart shattered." Disappointment flickers over her face. "And..." *Fuck it, why not take a chance?* "Because your smile draws me in. It warms me up, like when the sun finally shines through on a cloudy day. When you're happy, your eyes dance, your face lights up, and joy flows out of you. For that moment, it feels like nothing could be wrong anywhere in the world. I'm kind of a sucker for that smile, Dani girl."

She blinks at me a few times. "Jesse..."

Her eyes lift to mine, then drop to my lips.

I raise my eyebrows, not wanting to push her, not for a second. The corners of her mouth tip up slightly and she pulls at my shirt. My heart is pounding so hard I can barely think. I never used to be nervous around girls, but Dani... God, she's impossible to read. I never know how she feels about me or what she wants. For this brief moment, though, it seems like she wants me, and I'm not going to let this pass.

Slowly, I lean down toward her, stupidly giving her time to stop me, but she doesn't. Thank fucking god, she doesn't.

Sliding my hand around the back of her neck, I pull her closer until our lips brush.

*Last chance, babe. Stop me now or you're mine.*

She fists my shirt, pulling me that last quarter of an inch until our lips collide. Her lips are soft and full as they press into mine. I swallow back a groan at the contact. I haven't felt like this in a long time. Unhinged, like her lips are a drug, and if she pulls them away, I'll go into withdrawal.

I pull her closer, shifting her part way onto my lap. Her chest rises and falls against mine. Her fingers tickle up my forearm before gripping my bicep as she leans into the kiss.

Risking it all, I run my tongue over the seam of her lips, and to my delight, she parts them, letting me in.

And fuck.

I've died and gone to heaven. Her tongue is wrapped around mine, then playfully darting away, flicking at the roof of my mouth, driving me insane. The taste of raspberries lingers in her mouth.

I've thought about Dani on and off for the last few months. She's been there in the background, popping up in my thoughts—sometimes very inappropriate ones. Something about her sucks me in and now I'm getting swept away. Lost in the way she kisses, like she's giving herself over to me. Her fingers curl into my hair, and I want nothing more than to take her upstairs and continue this, but given Dani's hesitance with me, I'm not going to push her.

My dick, however, does not get the message. This incredible woman is kissing me and he wants to enjoy the fun.

Dani makes a *mm* noise, or maybe it's a moan, against my lips, and I instinctively pull her closer. Shit. Hard-on. Bad idea. She takes a sharp breath in when she feels it, pausing with her lips still pressed into mine. She leans in closer and kisses me harder, like she might tear my clothes off and fuck me right here. As quickly, though, she rips her lips off mine and pulls away, scrambling off my lap.

"Dani," I say, a little dazed as I reach for her hand.

She shakes her head. "I shouldn't have done that."

I stand up as her eyes dart around wildly, like she's looking for an escape route. Jesus Christ, I wish I didn't know that look, but I do. Must run in the Abbott genes because I've seen it on Rae's face more than once.

"Hey," I say softly, once again reaching for her hand, but she yanks it back.

"I'm sorry," she mutters, then she hurries past me into the house.

Once the door slams shut behind her, I drop back onto the bench we were sitting on and rub my hands over my face.

I wish I knew what the fuck was going on in her head. Or her heart. She's been hurt before, but there's more to it than that.

A smarter man would give up. Let her go. But I've never been the smartest kid. Most competitive? Fuck yeah. More than that, I'm no quitter. I don't give up because it's hard or I don't know the answer. I keep fighting until the problem is solved. I don't know what it is about Dani that pulls me in, but I'm wrapped up in her now, and I'm not stopping until I unravel all her threads and figure out what's holding her back and hurting her.

# 6
# Don't Be Afraid (to Crush Him)

## Dani

"YOU LOOK GORGEOUS," OLIVIA says, stepping back with the curling iron still in her hand. I chose big, soft curls for Rae's wedding. "Actually, you look hot as fuck." My sister grins at me. "Maybe a certain Wilkinson boy will notice."

I stand up and meet her gaze in the mirror. Her blonde hair is already tucked back in a low bun. She's wearing a rust-colored tank top dress with a cute cropped denim jacket and wedges.

"I'm not trying to look hot for Jesse."

"No. Of course not," she says. "Why would you after you kissed him, then ran away like a crazy person?"

I sigh dramatically as I run my fingers through my hair. No, I'm not trying to look hot for Jesse, but Olivia's right, I look damn good. I'm wearing a shimmery short sleeved dark gray dress with chunky black leather boots. I've got a sexy smoky eye happening, too. I'm usually drawn to bright colors, but there's something about the right pairing of dark colors that's sexy and a little badass. It's nice to feel that way.

But it is *not* for Jesse.

"I want to look hot for me. And for Rae because she deserves nothing but all of us looking fabulous for her wedding day. Besides, why would I want to look hot for him?"

"Because he's obviously into you?" Olivia says, bumping my hip so she can look in the mirror.

"Yeah, and that's just what I want. Rae's leftovers—a guy who uses his smile to charm the pants off women and make them fall into bed with him."

"Wow, when did you become such a bitter hag?" Olivia asks playfully. My face falls. "Hey, I'm kidding."

"About the hag part, maybe. You meant the bitter part, though."

She turns and takes my hand. "Maybe not bitter... but with Jesse, especially, you're being very judgy. I don't completely understand why. Especially since you kissed him. And don't start with him having hooked up with Rae. If all you do is worry about the past, you'll never have a future."

I stare at her for a moment, then bump my shoulder into hers. "I thought I was supposed to be the wise older sister."

Olivia shrugs. "Everything's objective from the outside. I just hate seeing you sideline yourself."

"I'm not trying to," I protest. "Yes, Jesse is cute and can be sweet, but he's not the kind of guy I want to be with."

"Even if your lady bits disagree with that?" I pin her with a glare, but she's not wrong. "Don't look at me like that. You don't want to date him, but wouldn't he be fun to hook up with?"

"I don't know. And I'm not interested in hooking up right now."

"What are you interested in? I mean, what would be your perfect guy at this point?" I stare at her for a moment, smiling, then she rolls her eyes. "Oh no. Really? Still? Fireworks boy?"

I nod. "You asked. That is my answer."

"Because he's the unattainable dream guy. You don't know who he is. I still half think you imagined him."

"I did not imagine him."

"Maybe you read a book like that and applied it to your own life."

I smack her arm. "Stop it. I remember it too vividly for it to be fictional."

"Oh boy. Here we go. Wait, I'll start. It was a Fourth of July party here at Grandma and Grandpa's house when you were nine years old. We'd had fun playing with squirt guns and water balloons and chasing each other around, spitting watermelon seeds at each other. You remember seeing him a couple of times, but never spoke to him. But he smiled at you and it was big and bright."

I roll my eyes, but continue the story. "It was. Big and toothy and genuine. I love a genuine smile. His blond hair was cut short and his skin was tan like he'd laid on the beach for days. After dinner and dessert, I didn't see him and I thought he left before I got to talk to him, but then the fireworks started." For someone who has always loved all things bright and vibrant, fireworks terrified me as a kid. "Even though I was trying to put on a brave face, I was terrified, and went running from the clearing back toward the farmhouse, when one of the super loud fireworks went off. I stopped by the barn and started crying. A moment later, that little blond boy appeared, took my hand, and told me it would be okay. He was so sweet and caring and I felt—"

"Safe," Olivia finishes for me. "I know. Because I've heard the story a thousand times. Whenever you talk about what you want in a dream guy, you talk about him. How he was sweet, caring, and protective." She coughs. "And fictional."

I smack her arm. "He's not fictional. Grandpa saw him."

"Then who is he? No one else knows who the hell you're talking about."

"I don't know. I've never asked Grandpa. I always assumed he was some friend of the family. Maybe one of Aaron's cousins or something."

She grins at me. "Well then, it's a good thing you look hot, because he might just be here tonight." She flips at my skirt. "Now come on, let's go see the bride."

She takes my hand and leads me out of the room as I fantasize about what my fireworks boy might look like now, and if he could be here tonight, dreaming of me and ready to sweep me off my feet.

Talk about a beautiful wedding. I'd expect nothing less from Rae and Aaron. With a love story as epic as theirs, they deserve an epic wedding to go with it. The food—from two of their favorite food trucks parked outside the barn—has been incredible. The toasts were funny, and Sarah and Joel crafted a beautiful slideshow with photos of Rae and Aaron throughout childhood up to this year, with the final part including video of them kissing at the end of the ceremony.

I take a sip of water as I watch them laughing while dancing, happiness radiating off them.

Sadness creeps into my chest. I wanted that. I convinced myself I had it. Only for me to end up a duller, bitter version of myself. I may be reawakening my passion with my career, as I continue to do more interior design projects that fulfill me, but I haven't made much progress in my personal life. No hook ups. No relationships. Not even a dating app. Maybe Olivia was wrong. I'm not bitter, I'm fucking scared. I don't want to fall again. I don't want to get my heart crushed again.

"Hey, you okay?"

*Damn it.* I let my guard down for two minutes and who shows up?

"Hi, Jesse." I clear my throat. "I'm sorry about um... the last time we saw each other."

He sits down next to me. "For what? You not liking the ice cream I made you? Or you running away after kissing me? I'm not sure which I'm more offended by, to be honest."

He gives me a soft smile, and it cuts through my walls. How does he do that?

"I liked the ice cream," I say, trying to lean into some playfulness. "I've just had better."

He chuckles at that, but his gaze on me intensifies. "You didn't answer my first question." My brow furrows. "Are you okay?"

*Right.* "Yeah. Just all this love... makes me emotional."

He stares at me for a moment, like he's trying to figure out if I'm telling the truth. I mean, I sort of am.

"Come on," he says, standing up and taking my hand.

"What? Where?"

"It's a wedding. Let's dance."

I'm standing now, but I plant my feet on the floor. I'm not sure dancing with him is a good idea. When I'm around him for too long, I lose my mind. This isn't the guy I want... right? A player. A charmer. Insincere. Has hooked up with my cousin. That's most of the boxes on my "no thanks" list.

"Uh, I don't know..."

"C'mon. It's just a dance, Dani girl. Besides, I'm the one taking a risk here."

"Oh?"

"Yeah. You might kiss me again and make me a little crazier for you before running off and leaving me all alone on the dance floor."

I shake my head, rolling my eyes a little, but I give in. What is it about him that draws me in?

"Fine."

"Try to dial back that enthusiasm."

"Is sarcasm your only language?"

He scoffs as he leads me onto the dance floor. "No. I thought I was fluent in kissing as well. After you ran away from me, I'm not so sure." He pauses, all playfulness fading as he wraps one hand around my waist. "This okay?" he rumbles.

And *damn it*. That sultry voice sinks into me, twists inside me, and does something to me.

*Stop it, Dani. He's not the guy for you. He'll end up breaking your heart. You know his type.*

"It's fine. As for kissing, maybe we were speaking different dialects," I tease, unwilling to own up to how unbelievably perfect that kiss was, how hot for him I was, or how I almost lost control. Then I realized all I'd ever be is a hookup to him, and I came to my senses.

He dips his head down so his lips are against my ear. "Don't lie to me. You were enjoying flirting with me. I even saw you smile. And that kiss... you can't tell me you didn't feel the sparks."

His other hand moves up my back and into my hair, tucking between the strands and playing with them.

My body lights on fire at the feeling. It's so simple. So small, yet it utterly undoes me. I cannot do this. I can't. I did the devastating heartbreak this year. And when I look into Jesse's eyes, I know he has the power to destroy me. His charming smile will break me. Time to put up my armor.

I shrug. "I was just having fun."

His eyes narrow, piercing into mine and making my heart race. I wonder if he can tell.

He leans in slightly, lips parting before growing into a smile. *He can tell.*

"Why did you run away from me? What are you afraid of?"

"I'm not afraid," I answer instantly. *Lie.* "I've been with guys like you before and you're more trouble than you're worth." *And that's why I'm scared.*

"Guys like me, huh? What does that mean?"

His fingers are still in my hair, and though his eyes have grown more serious, the rest of him is calm.

"Players. Guys who use their charm like a weapon. They flash a perfect smile to get whatever or whoever they want. Then they walk away unscathed, leaving the other person hurt."

He laughs incredulously. Though still in my hair, his fingers stop moving as he takes me in, a flash of disappointment in his eyes. "That's really what you think of me?"

I bite my lip. "I don't know. I've seen you do it. A few words, throw in that charming smile, and girls would lose their minds."

"That may be true, especially when I was younger, but I was never dishonest or underhanded about hooking up." His eyes roll over my face, that slight gaze burning through the armor I'm trying to put up.

Maybe Olivia is right. Maybe I'm being too hard on him. I've seen the sweeter side. A sincere, caring side. At least he seemed sincere. Then again, I thought Jason was sincere, too. Maybe I can't trust myself. Or Jesse.

I swallow down my thoughts and look into his eyes, not sure if I should believe what they show me.

*Do I have him all wrong?*

The thought runs through my brain for a nanosecond before logic takes over. How do I know the truth? How do I trust the facade I see when I don't know if it's real? Falling for it comes with a price—one I'm not willing to pay. I don't want to get hurt again.

*Scaredy cat,* a voice somewhere inside me says, but I try to ignore it.

"I told you what my ex did, but even if I hadn't gone through that, I'm not a liar or a cheater. I don't play games with people."

He's calm and confident as he says it, but anyone can say the words. That doesn't make them true. As I glance over his shoulder, the bitter truth I know tumbles out of my mouth. "No. You're the kind of guy who sleeps with his friend's girl behind his back."

He steps back, yanking his hands off me like I'm burning him. My words probably did. His eyes are brimming with hurt.

I wince as I look up at him. "Jesse, I—"

"Thanks for the dance, Dani," he says through gritted teeth, then he turns and walks off the dance floor, leaving me standing alone.

That's what I wanted, right?

*Bitter hag, party of one.*

Feeling every bit as shitty as I was to Jesse, I make my way over to my table and sit down, rubbing my hands over my face.

"Nice one," a deep voice says. I look up and see Trevor Matteny sliding into a chair next to me.

I smile despite the situation. Trevor was my cousin Sarah's first boyfriend. They dated for years, so I got to know him pretty well. He's funny, raunchy, doesn't take himself too seriously, and has a big heart. He's the kind of guy who'd be great to kick back and grab a beer with.

"Nice what?" I ask.

He shakes his head. "Takes talent to wipe a smile off Jesse's face and make him look like he was just punched in the balls. Well done." His dry words make my brow furrow. "What's your problem with him? He can be a pain in the ass, sure, but he's a good guy, and he seems into you."

"I keep hearing that."

"What did you say to him?"

"Maybe something about him having slept with Rae behind Aaron's back." Trevor's eyebrows shoot up. "It's the truth."

"I know it is. I also know he and Aaron are cool. They're actually closer than they've ever been. And from what Aaron has told me, Jesse has felt guilty about that since the second it happened. No wonder he looked like he wanted to cry. Especially since he seems to like you."

I roll my eyes. "He wants to hook up with me."

"I don't think so, D. Even if he did, who cares? You're both consenting adults."

"That doesn't mean I'm interested in him," I say, rolling out my party line.

Trev leans in, grinning. "See, that's what your mouth says. What your eyes and body language say is something else entirely."

"I don't want to be with a guy like that again," I say, looking down.

"Hey," he says softly. "Listen, I know all about having my heart shattered. Of course, it makes you wary, but that doesn't make everyone else your ex. You're worried about Jesse being a player—presumably because you feel like your ex was one."

"Oh, he played me. It was always a game. I just didn't know it."

"There's a difference, Dani. There are users. People who don't give a fuck who they hurt along the way. Then there are people who play the field. Until recently, I was one of them. Miles is too. Are we bad guys?"

"No," I say quickly. Because they're not. "Jesse's just... different. One second he's genuine, then the next he's overly flirtatious, and it feels like a line or a game." I flip a hand through my hair.

"Or maybe," Trevor says, squeezing my hand, "he gets under your skin because there's something there."

I stare at him, knowing in my gut that he's probably right, and I hate it.

Where's my stupid dream fireworks boy? Why is Jesse the one who sets my body on fire and makes me feel things I don't want to feel?

"I should probably go talk to him."

"Probably. Don't be afraid, D. All that does is hold you back from happiness." He looks up, a smile growing on his face as his girlfriend Chelsea walks over and extends a hand to him.

"Dance with me, baby?"

"Hell yes," he says.

He kisses the side of my head, then stands up and follows her onto the dance floor.

I look around the room. Rae and Aaron are nowhere to be seen. They probably snuck off for a quickie, knowing them. I don't immediately see Jesse, and rather than look around for him, I make my way outside Grandma and Grandpa's massive barn for some fresh air.

When I get there, I find myself drawn to the spot. Leaning against the barn, I close my eyes and think of fireworks boy, wishing someone would walk over and take my hand. Make me feel protected and safe like he did that day. Then I flash my eyes open. It's just a stupid fantasy.

Olivia was right. So was Trevor. Probably everyone but me is right at this point. Living in the past or out of fear isn't going to get me anywhere. Not anywhere I want to go, at least.

I think of the list tucked away in my purse inside the house. It's all about living. Being strong and bold and... naked. I haven't been doing that.

"Hey, what are you doing out here?" Rae asks, walking down from the house.

I smirk at her. "Better question is what were *you* doing in there?"

She gives me a coy smile. "I have no idea what you're talking about."

"Mhm."

She walks over and loops her arm with mine. "Come on. Let's go dance."

Can't deny the bride on her wedding day. We walk back into the barn together, and a moment later, we're surrounded by damn near every girl at the wedding as we dance and laugh like we're living our best lives. Exactly what I should be doing.

## Jesse

I'm nursing a beer and feeling sorry for myself as I walk around tables, avoiding the dance floor. Dani put a nice dent in both my ego and my heart, so I have no desire to go back over there. Especially since she's still out there, laughing and dancing with the girls like nothing happened.

Seeing my brother and Aaron at the back of the room, I head in their direction.

I didn't realize how deeply I felt for Dani until I saw her practically crying at the table tonight. I knew there were feelings there—undeniably so after that kiss. I didn't understand why she stopped it and ran off, but since she seemed to feel bad about it, I tried not to worry. My attraction to her grew as I thought of the passion and desire in that kiss.

Then she looked so sad tonight and all I wanted was to cheer her up. I didn't realize she hated me. I said I wouldn't give up on her, but I'm not sure there's anything left to fight for. I spent two years loving someone who didn't actually want me. Now I've been wasting my time chasing a girl who apparently thinks I'm scum.

Aaron throws his head back, laughing, as I walk over to him and Joel. "You know you almost said something profound. Then you had to give me shit."

"What fun would it be if I didn't give you a little shit on your wedding day?" Joel smiles warmly. "Congrats, man."

"I second that. I'm happy for you guys," I say, a small smile appearing on my face as I extend my beer bottle to him. No matter what just happened with Dani, I am happy for them.

"Thanks. I'm glad you're here," he says sincerely, clinking his bottle against mine.

"You know I'd never miss this."

He nods. One of many moments of understanding passing between us. If you looked up the words "good man" in the dictionary, you'd probably see a picture of Aaron Cooper. He's kind, forgiving, and would do anything for the people he cares about. I'm lucky to be one of them. For a while, I thought I wouldn't be again. Nothing like making a dumb decision after drinking and sleeping with your friend, who your other friend happens to be in love with. He looked at me like he wanted to hit me for months after that. Eventually, we talked, and he said we were good, but I didn't really believe him. And truthfully, I felt like trash. Had it been me going through it… well, maybe I'm not as good a guy as Aaron is.

Earlier this summer, he got tired of me being weird around him and not teasing him and giving him shit like normal, so we spent an afternoon getting day-drunk and airing any grievances. It was good for both of us and we're better friends because of it.

I take another swig of my beer as we stare at the dance floor. The girls are having a blast. Rae spins Sarah around, then Dani grinds against her for a moment, laughing before doing a spin. I internally reprimand myself for thinking she's adorable. *That girl is so not into me.*

"Hey," Aaron says, elbowing me. "There something going on with you and Dani?"

I snort at that. "Nope. Other than her hating my guts for existing."

"Do I wanna know?" Aaron asks.

"Nope."

"Okay then," Joel says.

"Probably for the best," Aaron jokes. "Those Abbott girls are more trouble than they're worth."

"Tell me about it," a voice says from behind us.

We turn and see the girls' cousin, Mark—a pro football player who had a game earlier today and originally said he couldn't come—standing there.

"What are you doing here?" Aaron asks.

"Finished the game and came straight here. I was hoping I'd be able to, but I didn't want to get her hopes up in case I couldn't."

"Mark!" Rae yells, running over and jumping into his arms.

I smile as I watch them. They have an amazing family with a deep bond. Rae drags Mark and Aaron to the dance floor, and a moment later Rae and Sarah are praising their grandparents for the beautiful family they've built.

Joel steps closer as *Buy Dirt* by Jordan Davis starts playing.

"Beautiful family," my brother says.

"Yeah. Must be nice."

"We'll have it one day because we'll create it ourselves."

"I think you're a step closer than me," I say, nodding toward where Sarah is waving to him from the dance floor. They still aren't officially together, but everyone knows they're meant to be.

Joel pushes off the wall, then smacks my shoulder. "Maybe you're closer than you think," he says, nodding toward Dani as he walks away.

Her eyes are on me, and it's too fucking much. I'm staring down all the things I want but don't have.

A big, loving family. Parents who are actually parents, and not people you see four times a year because they're too busy traveling to show up otherwise. I love them, but I'll never be able to stand up and give a speech about the legacy of family and love they built.

While I'm grateful to even be on the periphery of the Abbott family and know that many of them would still show up for me if I needed them, it's not the same. And that only becomes clearer as I watch my brother dance in the mix of them all. Familial and romantic love entwined together. It's beautiful, and it makes me feel wholly alone.

Pushing off the wall, I walk out the doors at the side of the barn that lead to the large clearing where the wedding ceremony was.

Leaning against the barn, I look out at the clearing. It's a perfectly clear night. Even the weather cooperated for Rae and Aaron. I'm surprised they didn't have blankets set up out here to make wishes on stars. That's always been their thing.

"Jesse?"

I glance to the side as Dani walks over, but don't turn my head. Taking another swig of my beer, I turn my gaze back to the dark

October sky. It's chilly tonight, but in that perfect fall kind of way. Makes me wish there was a bonfire I could go stand in front of. There's nothing like staring into the flames to soothe the soul.

"I'm sorry," Dani says softly, leaning against the barn next to me.

"It's fine."

"No, it's not. I—"

I shove myself off the barn and turn to look at her. "It's okay. I get it. I've been pushing this, and I shouldn't have been."

"It's not that—"

"It is." I gulp down the rest of my beer and step closer. "That night at The Rooftop, I told that guy that it was obvious you weren't into him and he needed to read the room. I didn't follow my own advice. I'm sorry if I made you uncomfortable at all. I thought…" I run a hand through my hair. "Doesn't matter. Either way, I'll leave you alone now."

"No. Jesse…"

Leaning in, I whisper, "Take care of yourself, Dani." Then I walk back inside, thankful to see that Aaron and Rae are getting ready to make their escape. That means I can too. I need a break from all this nauseating romance. And Dani.

I made the mistake of thinking she wanted me. Maybe I was projecting my feelings onto her. Either way, I know her nannying gig with her cousins is almost over, so she'll probably be heading back to Virginia soon. It wouldn't have worked out with us, anyway.

We were never meant to be, and I need to stop trying to force something that's never going to happen.

# 7

# I Wanted to Lick You

## Dani

THERE'S NOTHING AS MAGICAL as a snowy afternoon spent by my uncle Chris's fireplace as family slowly trickles into town for Thanksgiving. As I look out the window next to the fireplace, a tingle rolls up my spine. *I love this time of year.*

I take a sip of hot cocoa, then look back down at my phone. When I flick the screen back on, I have Instagram pulled up. *Why?* Oh yeah, I was going to stalk the author whose book I just finished. Before I can, though, I notice the picture at the top of my feed.

*Jesse.*

It's been a month since I last saw him. *And ruined any chance I had with him.* I don't know for sure that I want a chance with him, but I can't get him out of my head. I think of him often, and he's even infiltrated my dreams. Sometimes completely innocuously. Other times? My cheeks flush as I think back to the dream I had about him last week. The way he owned my body. It was a fantasy wrapped in a dream, but I'm not sure when he became my fantasy. Now that I'm working to push all the fear aside and the anxiety telling me not to trust him, I'm starting to wonder what could have been.

*What could be?*

I don't know why I'm bothering. I have no idea where I'm going to be living in the new year, and even if I was going to be somewhere near him, I was a bitch to him on the dance floor and he barely looked at me when I tried to apologize.

A glutton for punishment, I click on his profile and look at the last couple of pictures he posted. One of a campfire. One teasing an event he's planning at the stadium. And the one from today. A bedhead selfie of him making a dramatic thinking face.

My thumb hovers over the like button, but I don't click it. Instead, I scroll back up and click the button under his name that says "message." My messages—or lack thereof—with him come up. I stare at the blank chat. The only words are the ones I'd typed in but never sent. Every so often, I do this. Try to find the right words to truly apologize to him. No matter what I want or if I trust him, what I said was unnecessary and mean.

*What do you say when you've messed up a sort of friendship with someone you know but don't really know at all and kissed once before running away?*

I stare down at my phone, then backspace what I wrote last time and start again.

*Jesse, I wanted to apologize again for what I said at Rae and Aaron's wedding. I was hurting and took that out on you.*

This is where I always get stuck. What do I say next?

*I want us to be friends? I wanted to keep kissing you? I wanted to lick you instead of the ice cream?*

Sighing, I flick the screen off again. I don't know what I want. What I'm hoping for. Do I just want to make amends? Be friends with him? More? More still feels like insanity and an extremely stupid decision.

Speaking of extremely stupid, I'm still staring at my blank phone screen when the front door opens and Grandma and Grandpa walk in. Throwing my phone down, I hurry over to them and throw an arm around each of them.

"Well, it's good to see you too, girly. And good to know you've missed us," Grandpa says with a wink as we pull apart.

"I think I miss you more now that I see you more often. That probably doesn't make sense."

"I think it does," Gram says. "The more you see someone, the more connected you feel to them, and the more you want to see them."

"You knew just the right way to say it, as usual," I say as she pulls me in for a solo hug.

"How are you, Sunny?" she asks, holding me tightly.

I love Gram's hugs. It's not just her arms that wrap around me, it's her warmth, too. And when she pulls away, that warmth stays, like she leaves a tiny part of herself with whoever she hugs.

"I'm okay," I say honestly.

"Just okay?" She lets me go as Uncle Chris comes to greet them. It's the Friday before Thanksgiving, so all the younger kids are at school. Grandma and Grandpa are the first to arrive, but my parents will be here over the weekend, and so will some of my cousins.

Mason and Taylor are both off work starting today. Since I didn't need to nanny, I decided to spend the day at Uncle Chris's house—which is more of a family gathering place—and just relax.

"I don't know. Still... finding myself, I guess. And I also need to find a job since Mason and Taylor's new nanny starts the week after next."

"About that," Grandpa says with a smile.

Uncle Chris laughs. "Oh boy, I know by now when Dad smiles like that, it means he's got something up his sleeve."

I poke his arm. "What are you hiding up those sleeves, old man?"

Grandpa's smile grows. "Well, *young lady*, I was talking to a friend in town the other day. He runs a construction company, and he's looking to hire an interior designer to work with them. I mentioned I had a granddaughter who does just that, and he told me to pass his info along to you. It's a family business, and I know he likes to keep it that way—even if it's not his family specifically." Grandpa pulls out a card. "His name's Leo Barone. Give him a call and find out the details if you're interested."

I take the card and look it over. "You want me to move back to Ida?"

"We want you to find the path that makes you happy. This is just one option," Gram says. "If it's the right one for you, you know you'll have a room at the farmhouse as long as you need it."

"Thanks," I say, turning the card over in my hand.

"Follow that heart, girly," Grandpa says, kissing the side of my head. Then he and Gram follow Uncle Chris into the kitchen to get some lunch.

I watch them for a moment, then grab my phone and laptop and head into the office just off the living room.

I didn't have much of a plan about what was next for me. I had considered staying up here and going back home. I was leaning toward going back home because I miss Olivia, Weston, and my parents, but with this option in front of me, it's impossible not to dream about a small-town life in Ida with weekly dinners at Grandma and Grandpa's house.

*What the hell?* I might as well see what this is about.

Plopping down in the oversized office chair, I pull out my phone and dial the number on the card.

He answers on the second ring. "AB Construction, this is Leo Barone."

"Hi, Mr. Barone," I begin, trying to sound professional. "My name's Dani Malone. My grandfather, Pete Abbott, gave me your card and told me I should call you about a possible interior design job."

He chuckles. "Dani. Good. I ran into him a couple of days ago and mentioned I was considering hiring an interior designer. He mentioned you—not by name—but I assumed it wasn't one of the local girls or he'd have said so. It wouldn't be a full-time gig, more of an independent contractor. I'd say maybe a third to half of the projects we book ask if we have a designer in-house. If that's still something that interests you, I'd love to jump on a video call with you. I like being able to see the person I'm talking to. It gives us a better read on each other."

"I fully agree. Honestly, that sounds like something that would be a good fit for me. Let me give you my email and you can send me a link to video chat."

"Perfect."

I give him my email and a few minutes later, we're off the phone and on a video call.

When he comes on the screen, I'm a little surprised. By the way he spoke, I was expecting a businessman in a fancy suit, but instead, I'm greeted with a bearded, muscular guy in a T-shirt with his company's logo on the upper chest. He's got graying dark brown hair and a warm smile. From the edges of his sleeves, I catch a few tattoos popping out.

"Dani, good to see you."

"You as well, Mr. Barone."

"Oh god. Please call me Leo. I might be a grandpa, but Mr. Barone always makes me feel extra old unless I'm in a formal setting or I need to command respect. Otherwise, I hate it."

"Leo. Got it."

"So, you're Pete's granddaughter?"

"Yep."

"Where are you from?"

"Virginia originally, but I'm living in Watertown right now. I just finished up being an interim nanny for my cousins. I've been working some design jobs on the side. I've been considering what I wanted to do next, and this fell in my lap."

He smiles. "Gotta love when fate throws something in your path. Obviously, this is an off-the-cuff conversation, so I'm not expecting a résumé—actually, I hate résumés, anyway. Anyone can lie on paper or spin the truth. I prefer word-of-mouth references for that reason. It's how we've built a reliable crew here. Obviously, I trust Pete, and I know he wouldn't have mentioned you if he didn't think you'd be a good fit, but if you have any kind of portfolio or anything you could send me, I'd love to see some of your work."

"I don't have a full portfolio put together, but I'm emailing you the link to my website, which has all my recent projects. I'm also sending a link to my Instagram account where you can find older projects if you scroll back a bit."

We chat more as he looks through my website and Instagram, complimenting me on a few things and asking some questions. I ask him some, too, trying to get a sense of what the work environment and clientele are like. Overall, Leo seems great and so does his description of the company. I like the idea of working in a family friendly environment, having a variety of clientele, and still being able to run my business on the side where I can be choosier with jobs and find ones that fulfill me.

I agree to send over a list of references, and we set up a meeting in Ida after Thanksgiving, but for now, I have a tentative offer on the table.

When I hang up, my heart's beating fast and my shirt is soaked with adrenaline sweat. I never thought I'd be considering moving to Ida, but the more I think about it, the more excited I get. I unlock my phone again, excited to text my mom and Olivia, but then realize my phone is open to Instagram.

*What was I doing?*

Right. Trying to apologize to Jesse. I stare at the half-written text again. If I'm moving to Ida, there's a good chance we'll be a semi-regular part of each other's lives. I need to apologize to him. I stare at the blinking cursor in the message for a moment, then grow a set and type the best words I can come up with. I put my phone away, determined to let it go. The ball is in his court now, and I have something else to focus on.

I'm going to celebrate my new job offer.

# 8
# Trash

## Jesse

I LET OUT A sigh, staring at the photo my brother just sent me. It's a group selfie he took with Sarah and Rae on one side of him, Aaron on the other, and Mark and Dani standing behind them. They're all smiling and laughing.

Even Dani. She's probably off living her best life. I wish I didn't care. I never used to fucking care. Then I got a taste of love, and I fucking crave it now. I want to be loved the way I deserve to be. *Fuck, I'm pathetic.*

And to add to that, I flip over to the message Dani sent me almost a week ago. I read it and read it again. Hell, I've probably read it about five hundred times by now, but I can't come up with a response.

**Dani Malone: Hey, Jesse. I wanted to apologize to you again for how I treated you at Rae's wedding. I was hurting, and I took it out on you. You didn't deserve that. We were just getting to know each other, and I don't want to ruin a potential friendship with you. Anyway, I hope you have a good Thanksgiving. Maybe we'll get to see each other at some point over the holidays. Take care.**

I stare at the words again, sighing. I need to reply. I'm sure she knows I read it, though she probably doesn't even care. She's probably just trying to keep the peace. I have no idea why it even matters. I thought she was going back to Virginia after this.

I wish that thought didn't bum me out. I don't know why I'm still thinking of her at all. She was clear about what she wants—or doesn't want. I've been there, and I don't need another girl in my life who isn't sure she wants me.

*Or you're scared of getting hurt and being rejected again.*

Whatever. I need to at least respond to her.

**Me: Hey, Dani. Thanks for the message and sorry for the late reply, but we're all good. Hope you're having a good Thanksgiving with your family. Take care and be safe when you go back to Virginia.**

I hit send before I can talk myself out of it, but when I read it back, I frown at my phone.

"Why the long face?" my friend Evan asks me from the kitchen. We're at his family's small lake house in Pennsylvania, enjoying a guys' Thanksgiving weekend.

I put my phone on the kitchen table and stand up. I should at least attempt to be helpful in making our Thanksgiving meal.

"Nothing. I'm good."

"You're not. So come on. Out with it. All feelings are accepted here," he says with a grin. "Be open."

I roll my eyes. "When did you become a yogi?"

He shrugs. "What can I say? Falling in love has really opened my eyes."

"And some other things," Garrett rumbles—yeah, fucking rumbles—walking up behind him and kissing his neck.

"Really? Are you two going to be this nauseating the entire time?" I complain.

"Welcome to my life," Evan's cousin, Brooks, says, walking up next to me.

The four of us have been doing a guys' weekend away since senior year of high school when our parents gave us some freedom. Well, *their* parents. Mine wouldn't have been around to know. Usually we do it a couple of weeks before Thanksgiving, but we postponed it this year because Evan and G were busy. *Getting married.* Barely two months after they started dating. Though, it's not much of a surprise. Even as teens, there was something between the two of them they were both terrified to admit to. They went to college together and...*fucked around* a bit. They both considered themselves categorically straight in high school, so they had to take some time and understand themselves before they finally got together back in September. I'm thrilled for them. But yeah, they're disgustingly in love.

"Does this even count as guys' weekend now that you two are married? It changes the whole dynamic," I joke.

"I'm still going to be making the same dumbass jokes. You'll tell me to go suck a dick. Only difference is, now it's pretty much guaranteed I will." Garrett winks at me.

"We're still us, just now G and I aren't denying our feelings. Kissing on dares and pretending it's all in fun. Cornering each other in dark hallways."

Garrett grins at him. "Babe, that's still fun."

Brooks sticks his finger in his mouth and makes a gagging noise.

"At some point, you two will also end up hopelessly in love with the right people," Evan says. "Then you'll get it."

"I already get it." I drain the rest of my beer, then turn toward the hall. "I need another beer."

I don't miss the glance Evan and G exchange, but I continue on my quest to the garage refrigerator. At least I can count on finding a fantastic array of choices in the fridge.

Brooks is a brewmaster at a brewery not far from here. That kind of shit runs in his family. Evan's a chef. Evan's brother Chuck and their other cousin, Ian, work at the family's vineyard in Ida with their grandfather.

In the garage, I pull open the fridge and look through my options. While Brooks's signature pumpkin beer is fantastic, I'm in the mood for something darker, and choose a milk stout. Smooth. Dark. Perfect for a chilly Thanksgiving Day.

"Hey," G says, standing at the doorway to the house.

"Sorry, I'm being an ass."

"You're not. Do you want to talk about what's up with you? Is this still about Carrie? It's fine if it is, I'm just surprised. You seemed to be doing better over the summer."

I was. Then I let Dani get inside my head and fuck me up. It's not just Dani, though.

"It's not Carrie. I met this other girl, and she is... complicated." I swallow hard. "Doesn't matter. Just wish I could find what you guys have. What half the people in my life seem to have."

"A relationship?"

"Love." The word burns my throat as I say it. Usually I'm the upbeat one. I love to give people shit and make them laugh and smile. If I surround myself with happiness, it keeps me from feeling the things I don't have. Love. Family. I know the guys here are my family in some ways. I can always count on them. They pick me up on bad days, just like Jenna does. But it's not the same. Far too often in my life, I've felt like a footnote in someone else's story. Even with my parents. Hell, the only reason I agreed to guys' weekend this weekend was because they were supposed to be back for the entire week. I was going to spend a few days with them and Joel, then come here. Instead, my parents ditched us. So did our brother, Jon. Thankfully, Joel was invited to spend Thanksgiving with the Abbott family. I'm here with people who care, but it doesn't exactly make me feel chosen or wanted.

G puts his hand on my shoulder. "Do you want to talk about it?"

"Yeah, sure, let me stand here and cry about how I just want to be loved."

His brow furrows. "You *are* loved. You're my family, man. You're half the reason I felt safe to come out and admit how I felt about Evan. I wouldn't have started the ice cream shop without your encouragement. I know not all the people in your life have loved you the way you deserve, but you are loved. And you're allowed to feel bummed about the people who have hurt you by not loving you the right way. Holidays aren't easy. But we're here for you." He clears his throat. "Honestly, I'm really glad you said yes to this. Ev's family has done okay with this—his parents are great. But some of his extended family are assholes. My mom's trying, I guess. My brother still won't talk to me. So I get it. I'm grateful to spend this day with people who matter."

"Thanks," I say softly. "I fucking hate feeling this way."

"Well, it's better to acknowledge it and go through it than to push it away and let it fester. Come on, nothing like beer and your favorite ice cream to get you through it."

He opens the door to the house.

"My favorite ice cream?"

"Yeah. The vanilla peanut butter base with the peanut butter swirls, chocolate chunks, and Butterfinger pieces. That's your favorite, right?"

I smile, thinking of the conversation with Dani. "Yeah, it is."

I follow him back inside, feeling the smallest amount better. Dani clearly has her own shit to work through, and I realize part of why I'm so upset is that she took her pain and fears out on me when I only tried to treat her well. After all I've been through, that pisses me off, and it proves that I was probably in the wrong to want something more to happen with her. She's not ready. I'm not sure I am, either.

"Damn. This girl is savage," Brooks says.

Somehow, in my post-Thanksgiving dinner haze, the guys managed to get some information out of me about Dani. And by some, I mean literally every interaction we've had since May.

"Like many of the Abbott women, she knows how to use her words and make them hurt."

"She sounds scared to me," Evan says, looking over at Garrett. They had a pretty big fight shortly before they got together, which pushed them over the edge.

"Yeah, I think her ex hurt her pretty badly. She told me a little about him, and he sounds like a raging douche."

"Oh, adding him to my anti-elevator list," G says.

I squint at him. "Your what now?"

Evan rolls his eyes as Garrett chuckles. "It's the list of people I'm giving myself permission to punch—face or nuts—if I'm ever stuck in an elevator or a room with them. Wickham is on there as well."

"You know the cops probably won't care about your anti-elevator list, but I like your vibe," Brooks says.

"Wickham deserves to be on there. Absolute tool," I say, shaking my head as I mention our old swim coach. He was recently fired after having an affair with a student—he's in his late twenties—and getting her pregnant. Fucking disgusting if you ask me. However, one good thing came out of it, which is that Evan is now coaching Ida's varsity swim team, and starting next week, I'll be joining him as assistant coach. I'm hoping we can turn the team around and get them headed for state, while being positive influences in their lives. I'm also excited to be back in the water again, even if only for a couple of hours each night.

"We're going to whip that team into shape," Evan says. "Plus, since I run a pizza place, I can bribe them with food."

I laugh out loud at that.

"I'm surprised you have time to help him with your fancy job with the Knights," Garrett says.

"I can work from home in the evenings during swim season. Not like I have anything else going on in my life. Better than sitting around an empty house."

"That's the spirit," G says with a laugh.

"Fuck off."

"Ugh, you're supposed to tell me to suck a dick."

I grin at him. "That's why I didn't say it. You'd enjoy it too much now."

He grabs a cardboard coaster off the table and chucks it at me.

"He's just jealous he won't get to ogle Ev in a swimsuit every afternoon," Brooks says with a laugh.

Garrett sighs. "First of all, I get to see him naked every night, so shut up. Second, I'm still busy trying to figure out a good way to turn the ice cream shop into a year-round venture."

"It's indoors. You could do some kind of food," Brooks says.

"I guess. I don't want to have to hire a ton more people, though. Cooking is not my expertise. I could experiment for days with ice cream flavors. It's the same basic idea each time, just adding different things to the base, simmer on the stove, then churn into ice cream."

A thought occurs to me at those words. "You don't do the custard style, right? You just do the milk and cream type of ice cream?"

"I do both. Some are better with a custard base, but simple flavors are usually just milk and cream. Why?"

"What if you did a hot ice cream bar?" He looks at me like I'm insane. Which is fair. That name is trash. "Don't call it that. But think about it... the chocolate ice cream you make is essentially hot cocoa before you make it, right? What if you tweaked your recipes to make them a little less rich, and make a hot cocoa bar type of thing?"

"That's really fucking smart," Brooks says. "To avoid the hot cocoa bar term, you can have a few baked goods and then seasonal ice cream flavors in the winter and seasonal hot beverage flavors in the summer and call it a dessert bar."

G looks at Evan. "What do you think?"

"I think you could be a dessert location year-round with something like that."

"Test it out," I say. "I'm still looking for a few more vendors for the holiday weekend at the stadium. Pick five or six flavors and have a stand. People would love that. It's family friendly, kids would go crazy for it. And you could offer espresso mix-ins for the parents who need some extra caffeine."

He looks at me tentatively, then his face breaks into a smile. "What the hell? Sign me up. Let's give it a shot. Probably wouldn't be worth opening this year, but I can test it at events."

I grab my phone and make a note to send him the forms when I'm back in the office on Monday.

"Any chance you want to bring your brewmaster skills to Ida?" Evan asks Brooks. "Between my pizza place and G's ice cream shop, we could take over the town."

Brooks laughs. "Nah. This is home. But maybe... a satellite location there one day."

"While everyone's inspired, does anyone have any new ice cream flavor ideas or requests for this year? I've already got the Oreo ice cream with an Oreo base for Brooks."

Brooks raises his beer to G. "Hell yes."

"And you're doing the candied brown butter pecan for me," Evan says.

"Yes, you and your bougie taste buds." They share a kiss, and it's less nauseating now. I'm glad they finally opened up to each other.

Before I think better of it, I open my mouth and say, "What about a raspberry cheesecake flavor?"

"Oh, yes. I had a couple of requests for that last summer. Cheesecake bits and raspberry swirl?"

"Yeah, but could you make a cheesecake flavored base, too?"

He grins. "Yeah. That would be great with a custard, I think. Maybe even do a graham cracker ice cream bowl as an option for it." He pulls out his phone and starts typing away.

I don't know why the hell I said it. Dani will probably be back in Virginia after Thanksgiving.

"Fuck, all this talk about ice cream has me starving. Is it dessert time yet?" Brooks says.

I blink at him in disbelief. "How? I've barely digested anything we ate."

Brooks shrugs. "Iron stomach."

"Crazy," Evan coughs as Brooks stands up.

"Whatever. Let's go explode our stomachs together," G says as he and Evan stand up.

I grab my phone as I stand up. My mind still on Dani, I unlock my phone and open the message I sent back to her. Maybe I should send something else. *Maybe I should let it go.*

What's meant to be, right? Ah, fuck. I truly am hopeless.

"J, you coming?" Garrett asks.

"Right. Yeah, I'll be there in a second."

I look back at my phone, uncertain of what else I'd say.

"Jesse! Pie!" Brooks yells.

I roll my eyes at myself. She didn't reply to my last message. Hell, I'm not expecting a reply. I'm not sure I want one. Whatever this thing was with Dani, I need to let it go.

"Jesse!" Brooks yells again, more irritated this time.

And I need to go eat pie. Tossing my phone on the coffee table, I head into the kitchen to see how fast I can make my stomach explode.

# 9

# Insane, Crazy

## Jesse

*"WHO WAS THE 1977 World Series champion?"* Trevor Matteny's voice rings through a microphone as I sit on a small stage in the Binghamton Knights stadium at the winter festival I put together.

Currently, I'm part of a baseball trivia game. Audience members could fill out a card with the questions to play along. They had to drop them in a box near the stage before the start of the trivia game. The people with the highest scores will win a small prize and one person—regardless of their score—will be drawn to win tickets to the Knights season opener.

There's a rotating group of baseball guys here. A handful from the team, including Jamie. Aaron—a walking encyclopedia of baseball—is here as well, along with my brother and their friend Miles. We're facing off one-on-one, and we stay on stage until we get an answer wrong or we've had three questions. Right now, I'm facing off against Aaron, who, by the shit-eating grin on his face, clearly knows the answer. Fine by me because I haven't the slightest clue.

Aaron hits the buzzer he's holding, and Trevor calls on him. "The New York Yankees won the 1977 World Series."

"That's correct," Trevor says with a grin. He has the perfect personality for emceeing.

With that, I make my way off the stage to a tiny amount of applause that I'm pretty sure is coming from Jenna, Brett, Rae, and Sarah. Then there's a whistle—yeah, definitely Rae. But that was for Aaron.

Although, he should keep his cockiness in check, because the next person to face off against him is Marc Demoda, the pitching coach for the New York Metros, who I begged to come up and hang out with us today. He and Aaron have become friends, so it wasn't too hard of a sell.

He and a bunch of the guys from Knights are also doing a signing and taking pictures with people later.

As I step off the stage, I look out across the stadium at all the booths from local businesses and vendors, as well as the many games and the small Santa's village, where families can walk around and take pictures with Santa and Mrs. Claus.

This event took a ton of planning, but I'm incredibly proud of how it turned out, and I'm excited to use it to show the variety of ways we can utilize the stadium during the offseason to generate revenue and support the local community as well.

"J, this is seriously amazing," Rae says, walking over with Sarah, Jenna, and Brett.

"You just like watching your husband own everyone at trivia."

She smirks at me. "That's not bad, but this whole thing is absolutely stunning."

I shrug, shoving my hands in my coat pockets. "I had a lot of help." Jenna laughs out loud as Rae cocks an eyebrow at me. I smile at that. "Yeah, okay. This is pretty fucking awesome. The turnout is already amazing and it should be great for us and for so many local businesses who are here."

"There he is," Rae says. "The cocky boy I've always known."

"What can I say? I rock this job. I did have a lot of help, but the bulk of the ideas were mine, and I'm proud of that. My dad gave me shit when I got this job, telling me it wasn't a long-term career, but to me, this is proof I'm doing the right thing."

"Something that allows you to be active, creative, and a little bit of a troublemaker is perfect for you," Jenna agrees.

"Troublemaker? How am I causing trouble here?" I ask with a laugh.

"You have a pie throwing booth and a hot dunk tank. How the hell did you recruit so many kids from your swim team?" Jenna asks.

Ah yes, the hot dunk booth. Couldn't do a normal one in winter, so the booth is enclosed in a heated tent, and the water is nearly hot tub temperature. It's perfect. And there are plenty of young girls thoroughly enjoying dunking the shirtless guys from my swim team. I'd feel bad about that, but there's something about swimmers. We're a cocky bunch. And they are heckling people until they get dunked.

"Offered them all free tickets to a game this summer," I say with a shrug. "People love the Knights."

"You're only growing that love," my brother says, walking over with Aaron.

"Done already?" I ask Joel, who was in line after Marc.

"Yeah. Marc snowed me three times in a row. Trev's letting him stay up there longer because the crowd loves him."

"Of course they do. He was one of the Metros best pitchers ever," Aaron says.

"Maybe I can get him in the dunk tank later."

"See? Troublemaker," Jenna says.

"You really want to test how much he likes you, huh?" Aaron jokes.

"Eh, why not take a risk?"

"You sound like Dad," Joel says.

I roll my eyes. "Sometimes I wish I knew him better. It's weird that I don't even know how much I'm like him."

"Well, it can't be that much, seeing as he isn't here. You told them about it, right?"

I snort at that. "Of course I did. You know they couldn't change travel plans this close to the holidays."

Joel shakes his head. "Just remember, they're the ones missing out. I know it still sucks."

I shrug. "It is what it is. It's not worth focusing on the people who aren't here when we're surrounded by all this."

"Agreed," my brother says with a smirk, then he nods toward the air hockey tables across the field. "Up for a game?"

As kids, we had an air hockey table in the basement. Joel and I played so much we finally broke the damn thing when I was a senior in high school. I think my parents refused to replace it because we were so cutthroat with each other—though it's not like they were around enough to see it.

"Hell yeah. I'm in. Then we should go grab food. So many good choices."

"Sounds perfect," Rae says. "You two play. I get the winner."

I laugh at that as we walk toward the tables, looking around at the massive event that started as a simple idea in the back of my mind. I'm proud of how this came together and hope it'll become a long-standing tradition.

Out of the corner of my eye, I see a flash of pink and red hair. Spinning around, I search the crowd but see no sign of Dani or her vibrant hair. *I must be going insane.* There's no reason Dani would be here. I don't know why this girl is haunting me so much, but I need to let it go.

Shaking my head, I turn back the other way and head for the air hockey tables to kick my little brother's ass.

## Dani

*I'm a crazy person.*

I have no idea why I came here. Or why I've hidden from one too many people today, like I just did from Jesse.

"Can I get you something?" a deep voice from above me asks. I look up from where I'm crouched between two vendors' tents at a handsome man with a light brown beard. He's wearing a Carhartt jacket, plaid trapper hat, and a warm smile. "Cup of something warm? Or an ass-kicking for the ex you're hiding from?" He smiles, but is clearly fighting back a laugh.

Realizing I'm still crouched and hiding like a moron, I stand up. "Oh, uh, no ex." I clear my throat. "I'm just... an introvert," I lie. "Thanks for the offer, though. I will take you up on the hot beverage, though."

"Okay, crazy girl."

"Ugh. Really? I thought we had a nice rapport here. Now you're going to call me 'crazy girl?'"

He grins as he leans over the counter on his elbows. "I don't know your actual name, so..."

The smile slides off my face. *What a fucking line.* Not that I'm trying to date this random guy, but it was nice having a relaxing moment and some fun banter. Jesus, I can't even have that anymore.

His brow furrows as he takes in my scowl, but before he can say anything, the guy in the tent next to him leans over.

"Don't worry, he's not flirting with you. He just doesn't know how to turn off the charm. That's Garrett."

"My husband, Evan," Garrett says.

His words surprise me. The thought that neither of them seems "gay" occurs to me, but I quickly reprimand myself. That's biased. Then again, I've known way too many guys who would've joked about something like that just to see what reaction they got. Mostly Jason's friends. Thank God they're out of my life. When I look at Garrett and Evan's faces and see the obvious love in their eyes, there's nothing to question.

"Oh…" I breathe out. Olivia's words come roaring back into my mind. Have I become too quick to judge? "Sorry for the death glare. Uh, my name's Dani."

Evan and Garrett exchange a quick glance, but then Garrett smiles.

"Dani. I like that. Now, what flavor of hot chocolate would you like? Salted caramel, raspberry, white chocolate, red velvet, or peppermint?"

"Raspberry would be great."

"Whipped cream?"

"Please."

"You got it," he says, turning to make the hot chocolate as Evan looks at me.

"So, who were you really hiding from?"

Garrett chuckles from across the booth.

"Ah… everyone?"

"You know everyone here?" Evan teases.

"Not *everyone*. I only know a couple of handfuls of people in this area in general. But most of the ones I know are here, and they don't know I'm here, and without getting into it... awkward conversations might ensue." Warmth spreads across my cheeks. Garrett nailed it when he called me crazy.

Garrett returns with my hot cocoa.

"Thanks. How much do I owe you?"

"Four dollars," he says. "I take cards, too."

For once, I actually have cash, and hand him a ten.

As Garrett gets my change, Evan says, "So, you're new to the area?"

"Sort of. I have family in Ida."

"Oh, nice. That what brings you here?"

"That and a job."

"What do you do?" Evan asks.

"I'm an interior designer."

"Oh, cool," Garrett says, handing me my change. "Not to be too forward, but I'm actually looking for some help redesigning my place. When I launched last summer, it was bare bones. I want to create something better. A family friendly place for desserts and relaxation. But I want it to reflect me, too."

"I'd love to help. Here..." I dig a card out of my bag and hand it to him. "Call me after the holidays. I'll be heading back down south for Christmas, but after that, I'll be up and running."

"Cool. I definitely will."

My phone goes off as Evan holds out a slice of pizza. "On the house."

"Oh, you don't have to—"

"If you're going to put up with him, I definitely do."

Garrett shoots him a glare, but Evan flashes a charming smile in return. These two are adorable together.

"Thanks," I say.

"No problem," Evan says.

"I'll be in touch. And if you need to hide out again, you're welcome between our tents," Garrett adds with a smirk.

My cheeks heat, but I laugh it off. "Thanks again."

Checking for anyone I know before I walk away, I step into the crowd and walk toward Santa's village. It's quieter there, mostly families. On the way, I see a bench hidden by a line of people for the spiedie truck. Spiedies are a local favorite. Marinated chicken, pork, or occasionally lamb cooked over a hot grill until charred and served on local Italian bread. They smell amazing, and if I didn't have a slice of fantastic pizza in my hand, I'd definitely get some.

Setting my pizza and raspberry hot cocoa on the bench next to me, I check my phone.

**Amelia: Sorry I never texted you last night. I got caught up working late. Want to come see the apartment today? I'll be home all afternoon.**

Amelia Davis is the paralegal who works on contracts for AB Construction. While going over my paperwork with her, we started chatting, and discovered we're both new to Ida. She moved here in late September and has been looking for a roommate. She's fairly relaxed, and we got along pretty well, so we've been texting the last couple of days to get to know each other and set up a time for me to see the apartment.

I send a quick text back.

**Me: Sounds perfect. I'm just getting ready to leave the Winter Festival at the Knights stadium in Binghamton. 45 minutes good?**

**Amelia: Perfect. See you then.**

She texts me the address, and excitement floods me. I accepted my job offer with AB Construction last week, am working on setting up an LLC for my company—which Amelia has offered to help me with—and now I'm hopefully getting an apartment lined up. My goal is to come back from Virginia after Christmas and fully move into the apartment—and my new life.

I quickly finish my slice of pizza, then stand and throw my plate and napkin away. As I do, I catch a glimpse of Jesse across the stadium. He's talking with Trevor and Jamie. I watch him for a moment, smiling softly when he throws his head back, laughing. Then Trevor squints in my direction. I quickly spin and run through the nearby opening and down the stairs to the inside of the stadium, following the large, open hallway to the exit.

I don't know why I'm hiding from Jesse. Maybe it's the very *succinct* response he sent to my Instagram message. It gave the impression that he's over dealing with me. Either way, it doesn't matter. Sure, we'll see each other again eventually, but I have a new life to focus on building, and that's what I'm going to do.

"This place is absolutely gorgeous," I say as I sit on the couch with Amelia.

Hardwood floors run throughout the space. It's not massive, but more than enough for two people. There's a small entryway adjacent to the kitchen, which is open to the living room. Off the kitchen is the bathroom, and off the living room is my bedroom. Amelia's is off a small hallway on the other side of the living room. There's also a closet in that hallway.

I've just finished filling out some paperwork for the landlord while sipping on coffee.

"You're sure you're up for sharing your space?" I ask her.

Amelia smiles and tosses a hand through her curly blonde hair. "Why? Do I strike you as antisocial? I know I have resting bitch face."

"Hey, I think that's useful for anyone working in law. But yeah, that might be it."

We both laugh.

"I enjoy being social with people I like. I just haven't found that many. Or I haven't been looking. I'm a little guarded sometimes, but I don't know, I have a good feeling about you. Since we're both new kids in town, and you don't seem obnoxious or crazy, I think we'll be a good match."

"I don't know. I was acting pretty crazy earlier today."

Her eyebrows shoot up and she scrunches her nose, which makes her nose ring wiggle. She's got the perfect nose for a nose ring. Tiny and cute.

"How so?"

I drag my teeth over my bottom lip. "You really want to know?"

"Consider this bonding time. Tell me everything."

With a laugh, I start back at the beginning—my breakup in May—and tell her all the major details ending with the carnival today.

When I'm finished, she looks at me, amused. "Wow. Okay, good to know about your crazy side," she says with a laugh. "So, this Jesse guy, do you want him or not?"

"I think I'd like to consider wanting him. But only if he wants me. And I really don't know if he does."

"Well, you're gorgeous, talented, and nice, as far as I can tell. He's crazy if he doesn't want you."

"Maybe he *did*. I don't know if he *does*. And if he does, I don't know if it's for a relationship. I don't want to be a notch in his bedpost." She stares at me for a second, and I laugh. "I totally got that Fall Out Boy song stuck in your head, didn't I?"

She laughs. "Yeah, you definitely did. Well, for whatever my opinion is worth to you, you won't get anything if you don't try. And you won't know anything if you don't talk to him."

"Noted. Okay, you now know a ridiculous amount about me and my life, and I still don't know much about you. Tell me something."

She takes a sip of her tea and tells me her story, how her dad died when she was seventeen, how she dropped out of school and got her GED, then traveled the world with her mom for a couple of years before going to college. She's a paralegal now, taking care of her mom who has some health issues, and has dreams of being a lawyer one day.

She's spunky, sassy, funny, and sweet. We're honestly a perfect match for each other.

"So, you're staying with your grandparents now?" she asks.

"Yep. My plan is to slowly move stuff in here, then come back with a load of stuff after Christmas. Oh, and I'll need a mattress. That's kind of important."

She laughs and looks around. "Everything in the living room came with the place. I hate most of it."

I let out a sigh of relief. "I wasn't going to say anything, but it's all so old and dingy. I mean, old can be fine, but not gross old."

"Well, Ms. Interior Designer, if you don't have any plans for the rest of the day, how about we go shopping for some new stuff?"

My eyes light up. "Yes, please. Shopping with people is my love language."

"Let's go, then. I desperately need some color and less ugliness here."

Laughing, we put on our winter weather gear and head out.

I loved nannying for Mason and Taylor, and staying with Grandma and Grandpa is wonderful, but with the new job, this apartment, and the beginning of a friendship, I finally feel like I'm finding *my* place instead of living in someone else's world.

# 10

## Sweltering

**Jesse**

"Dude, amazing win last night," Brett says, sitting next to me in a circular booth at the club-style second floor of The Rooftop. We're waiting for Jenna to meet us. It's Friday, and after a long week of swim practice, two meets, and my normal work stuff, I'm ready to unwind.

"Thank you. Although, it's all the boys' win. Evan and I have a great group. They're hard workers and they want this."

"Think you'll qualify for sectionals?" he asks.

"As long as they keep working hard, I think so. Honestly, I think we have a shot at state this year if they keep up the way they're going."

"That's awesome, man."

I drum my hands on the table. "So what's the deal? Are we waiting for Jenna to get drinks?"

"I don't know. Let me check my texts." He pulls out his phone and looks at it. "Probably should. They just got here."

"They?" I ask.

"Oh, yeah. She's bringing a friend. Didn't she tell you?" I cock an eyebrow in response. "Right, of course she didn't."

"She just told me to show up here tonight because we haven't seen each other since before Christmas. So who's the friend?"

"I don't know actually. I haven't met her yet. I guess she's new in town."

*New in town?*

"Does she happen to work for Jenna's dad?"

"Yeah. How did you know that?"

"Here they are," Jenna calls and we both look over at them, my eyes locking on Dani's wildcat ones. "Hey, baby." Jenna gives Brett a kiss, but he only half returns it because he's watching Dani and me.

"Hey," he says, not taking his gaze off us.

"Jesse," Dani says in a sultry voice that does not at all make my pants feel tight.

"Dani."

*God damn it. Why does she have to look so heartbreakingly hot?*

When I saw her running away from me at the winter carnival, she still had that red and pink hair. It's a little shorter now, but not as short as it was last May. It's also a shimmery amber color—almost copper. It looks absolutely stunning on her and brings out the golden yellow tone of her eyes. Standing in front of me in a pencil skirt, a loose but perfectly fitted blouse, and ankle boots, she looks fucking gorgeous. If I didn't know how easily she could hand me my balls, I might be turned on.

Fuck it, I'm a little turned on anyway.

"Wait, you two know each other?" Jenna asks, voice all high and squeaky.

"Yes, you traitor." I stare my best friend down. Her brows dip in as she looks at me. Then her eyes go super wide.

"Oh. Wait. Is she the one..." she whispers, though there's no point to the whisper because it's excessively loud.

"Yes, that's her."

"Well, how was I supposed to know that?"

I turn a glare on Jenna while Dani continues smiling like this is the best thing that's happened all week.

"Maybe because I told you I met her through Sarah and Rae and her name is *Dani*?"

Jenna shakes her head and laughs at herself. "Yeah, I probably should've figured that out."

"Probably, babe," Brett whispers.

"You told your friends about me?" she asks.

"Don't be flattered," I say flatly.

Jenna cups a hand around her mouth and dramatically whispers, "He told me you were mean."

Dani's mouth drops and she props a hand on her hips. "I thought we were past that. I apologized twice. You said it was fine both times."

"Well, that's what you do to be polite. To be fair, I thought you were moving back to Virginia until I saw you sneaking around at the carnival at the stadium last month, and my brother told me I wasn't hallucinating. So, you live in Ida now. Thanks for the change of address card."

Her cheeks tint pink, but before she can respond, Brett raises his hand. "I'm sorry, but are you two friends or enemies?"

"Friends," Dani says at the same time I say, "Enemies."

Dani waves a hand. "Don't listen to him. He's just upset because charming playboys aren't my idea of fun, and he doesn't like not getting what he wants."

I'm about to say something not so charming in response when I notice the hint of mischief in her eyes. *Is she playing with me?*

I bite back the smirk trying to form. "Oh, babe. If you haven't been getting the charm or the fun, you've been playing with the wrong boys."

Brett side-eyes Jenna and clears his throat. "Did someone turn up the heat?"

"They must have because I'm sweltering," Jenna replies. "Let's grab a drink, husband."

"Right with you, wifey."

They leave the booth and head for the bar as Dani finally sits down at the edge of the booth, keeping her distance from me.

"Are you still pissed at me?" she asks genuinely, glancing at me.

"No. Not pissed…"

"Oh god, are you going to do the 'I'm not angry, I'm disappointed,' thing like our parents?"

*Don't think I ever got that from my parents, given that they weren't around enough to feel either emotion for me past my childhood years.*

"No. Well, I'm a little disappointed you flat-out hid from me at the carnival. Why did you? If you didn't want to see anyone, why did you come?"

She looks down at the table. "You worked hard. I wanted to see how it came out."

I flex and relax my hands, wishing I had a drink. "You are the most conflicting person I've ever met. One second you act like you hate me, the next you kiss me, then you're annoyed by me, then you act like we're friends. I don't get it. You give me all this shit about how you don't like players, but all you do is play games with me."

She snorts at that. "Then it should be familiar to you."

"Why do you think I'm some asshole who is just trying to play games with you? At what point in my life have I given you that idea? And don't say because you know me or my type, because you clearly don't."

"Well, you go from all charm to acting sincere in two seconds and it makes it feel like everything is an act and I can't trust you."

"And why do you care if you trust me? Why does trusting me matter to you?" I lean in toward her, moving into her space, forcing her to face whatever it is she feels between us. The heat Jenna and Brett could feel watching us for two minutes.

She gulps. "I don't like having people in my life I can't trust," she says, chin raised.

"And you want me in your life?" I glide my hand up her forearm.

She stares at me for a moment, then pulls her arm away. "That depends which version of you we're talking about. This version? Where you move closer and touch me, just trying to get to me... the game player? No, I'm good."

"And you weren't trying to get to me earlier? When you first walked in? Teasing me? Come on, Dani. You can't have it both ways. You either want to have fun with me or you don't, but you can't get mad when I turn things back around on you."

She stares at me for a moment. "I'm tired of feeling like just a game." Her voice is quiet, all the playfulness I saw earlier completely gone.

"You're not a game to me, Dani. You never have been. I like having fun, though, and I won't apologize for being myself." Standing up, I slide out the far side of the booth as she watches me. Before I walk away, I lean down and whisper in her ear,

"Maybe instead of being scared, you need to remember what it's like to have fun. Not everyone's out to hurt you, Dani girl."

Then I walk away, leaving her to think about what she wants from me. I'm tired of feeling like just a game, too, and it's not fair of her to keep turning it into one, especially when she refuses to tell me the rules.

I passed Jenna and Brett on the way to the bar, and since they were going back to the booth to keep Dani company, I stayed at the bar for my first drink, chatting with the bartender, who happens to be Evan's younger brother Chuck. After finishing my drink, I headed to the bathroom. As I walk out of the men's room and into the quiet hallway it's in, someone catches my eye. *Dani.*

She's standing along the wall in a dark corner, looking at her phone and sniffling.

I bite my cheek. There's every chance I'm going to get my ass handed to me if I walk over there, but I hate seeing her cry. There's just something about it that seems wrong.

I walk over and lean against the wall next to her. "You okay?"

She looks up at me, eyebrows pulled in, then she softens and wipes away a tear.

"Fine." She clears her throat.

"You don't seem fine."

"It's really dumb."

"If it makes you cry, it's not dumb."

Shaking her head, she says, "It's Olivia's birthday today. I was just looking through all the pictures of her from her party. I miss her. It's the first time I haven't been there for her birthday. Usually I'd make her pancakes and put candles in them. We'd get coffee, then I'd try in vain to surprise her with dinner or a party I'd planned with our parents, brother, and her friends. We'd spend the night laughing and having an amazing time. This year I'm missing it all." She swipes some tears from her eyes.

"Nothing stupid about that," I say softly. "When I went to college, it was hard to fall asleep the first couple of weeks because I knew Joel was back home alone. I ended up asking him to text me at night that he was safe so I could fall asleep. Eventually we got used to it, but sometimes I still text him late at night if I can't sleep."

She swallows. "I didn't realize you two were so close."

I shrug. "We've grown closer. Not sure we'll ever be like Rae and Sarah—or how you and Olivia seem to be—but I love him. He's my little bro. I'm always going to look out for him. I can't imagine what it would be like to be so far away from him if we were as close as you and your sister are. Did you get to talk to Olivia today?"

She laughs. "Yeah. I called her at midnight so I'd be the first to wish her a happy birthday. Then I called her again at normal waking hours since she cussed me out at midnight. We've texted all day. It's weird when traditions you've always had are just gone."

"It is. Sometimes the holes they leave are filled with new traditions, though, right?"

She nods, then looks up at me. "Why are you being so nice to me?"

"Because contrary to what you believe, I'm not a bad guy. And because it drives me insane seeing you sad. I remember you as this bright, fun person. I want to see that."

"Then why do you give me shit?" she asks flatly.

"Because you were always feisty, too. I like feisty girls."

"Ugh," she says, giving me a shove. "This is exactly what I mean. From sincere to ridiculous lines."

I step forward again, planting my hand on the wall next to her head and leaning toward her. "It's not a line, Dani. I don't enjoy being around people who just give into me. Who take my shit and leave it there. Give it back to me. Have fun with me. It's my love language."

"Funny. I don't recall driving people to the brink of insanity being one of the love languages."

I smile at that, biting my lip, then I wipe a stray tear from her cheek. "See, that's what I'm looking for."

"What do you want from me, Jesse?"

"I want to be friends with you."

"Friends?" she asks in disbelief.

"I want to get to know you better. I want to know your favorite foods, what you like doing on the weekend, what your dreams are for the future... what you look like naked." I get the eye roll I was hoping for with that one. "I meant emotionally."

"Bullshit," she says in a laugh.

I shrug. "Guess you'll have to get to know me to see which one I meant."

"And what about what I want?"

"What do you want, Dani girl? Because if you could at least give me a hint, that would really help."

"I want to live a vibrant life, have fun, play games only if I start them, and"—she smiles, biting her lip—"I want to be naked more."

I inhale sharply at that and get a smoking hot smile in return. Now I remember why I risked everything on the dance floor with this girl. She does something to me. But knowing how guarded she is, I know I've got to take it much slower this time.

"Easy tiger. I didn't say I wanted to be naked with you."

She winks at me as she pushes past me and walks back toward the club.

I smile to myself as I follow her. I got her to stop crying and have fun. Now she's playing games with me too. Win-win-win.

## Dani

"Where have you two been?" Jenna asks as Jesse and I sit back down in the booth. Her eyes bug out and she lowers her voice. Well, as much as Jenna ever seems to. "Wait, were you two—"

"No," I say firmly, flaring my eyes at her.

"I was taking a piss. Dani was waiting outside the bathroom for me like a stalker," he teases.

I shoot him a glare in response. "More like a serial killer, plotting your murder."

He shrugs. "Sometimes the serial killer falls for the person they were going to kill. I've still got a chance."

"Where the hell are you getting that shit?"

"I don't know. Isn't that what that *You* show is about? I mean, all the girls want to bang the serial killer guy for some reason, right?"

"You would die first in a horror movie," I say with a headshake.

"Nah. I'd be with you, and you wouldn't trust a soul, so we'd be fine. We'd escape and be off having—"

I slug him, and he smiles. I do my best not to smile back. Maybe this is a little fun. I was surprised how comforting he was in the hallway. He didn't have to be. Especially after how I've treated him in the past. And I can't deny this sassy, flirtatious vibe we have with each other is hot. I'm still scared I'll end up getting hurt or played, but he might've been right when he told me I needed to remember what it was like to have fun. He might've been right about the other thing he said, too. *Not everyone is out to hurt me.* Sure, my ex was a piece of work, but it is fairly pessimistic to believe anyone I meet is out to harm me in some way.

I'm not a trust-the-serial-killer type, but in a horror movie, you have to know who you can trust, and I've gotten used to hardly trusting anyone to protect myself. I don't know if I can trust Jesse with my heart—not that I'm looking to hand it to him—but I think I can trust him as a person.

"I was going to say ice cream." He shakes his head. "Such a dirty mind." He winks at me and *goddamn.* That troublemaking glint in his eye is the Jesse I remember. "Want anything to drink?" he asks, rising from the table.

I pause for a second. It's been a while. Maybe something simple. "Uh, yeah. Vodka and soda, I guess."

His eyebrows lift. "You guess? You don't have to."

I clear my throat, wanting to be able to just fucking unwind over drinks with my friends. "I want to. Vodka and soda."

He nods. "Coming right up."

As he walks away, Jenna grabs my hand. "So, what *is* going on with you two?"

"It's... complicated. I think we're moving toward friends."

Jenna nearly spits out her drink. "If 'friends' is code for the bedroom, sure."

"Babe..." Brett says. I don't really know him. I've met him in passing a handful of times before tonight, but he seems to have a good read on Jenna, and is thoroughly amused by her frankness and occasional ditziness. It's a hilarious combination. I can see why she and Jesse are so close. She's low drama, finds his shit-giving funny and gives it right back, and he just shakes his head and lets her go when she's on a silly tangent.

"Here you go. Vodka and soda for the lady," Jesse says, sliding back into the booth with a glass for me and a water bottle for himself.

"Water?" I ask, surprised.

"Yeah. I'm done for the night. And parched." He grins and pulls the cap off his water as I reach for my drink and take a sip. A sip I promptly choke on because Jesse's head is tilted back as he drinks his water, and I can't stop staring at the muscles of his neck as he swallows.

Jesse isn't big. No thick muscles. He's lean, but his muscles are perfectly defined.

Jenna hands me a napkin as I sputter and cough. *God, I'm an idiot.*

"You okay there?" Jesse asks.

Finally getting a full breath, I nod. "Yep. Fine. Just got... distracted."

"By watching me swallow?" he asks, amused.

"No." *Yes.*

"Gotta say, babe, you're really giving off stalker vibes. I don't think you want to kill me." He brushes his thumb along the edge of my jaw. "You're *obsessed* with me."

"Says the person touching me right now. I think you want me to be obsessed with you."

"I think you're obsessed with each other," Jenna says. "You two go off on these weird passive aggressive flirtation tangents and we're just over here watching uncomfortably."

Jesse tips his head to the side, looking around me. "You're uncomfortable?"

I turn around, ready to apologize, only to see Jenna grinning at him. "No. It's good entertainment. I wish I had popcorn. Speaking of which, we should order some food. Unless you two are planning to feast on each other."

My eyebrows shoot up as Jenna snickers. She's way more trouble than I thought she was when I met her in passing before. Maybe she's quieter in groups, but here, she gives her share of shit.

"I guess that depends if you're the type of serial killer who kills *and* eats their victims." I spin around at Jesse's hot breath against my ear. My wide eyes make him smile. "I'll grab some menus," he says, winking at me as he rises from the table.

I decided to give him a tiny bit of trust and play this game of cat and mouse, but I didn't realize how hot it would make me. My blood feels like lava as I watch him walk away. Grabbing my drink, I down the rest of it. I'm in trouble. I had no intention of crossing any lines with Jesse tonight—or maybe ever—but the more we banter, the more I see that troublesome smile or the mischief dancing in his eyes, the more I want to explore the electricity sparking between us.

I sip on my drink as we all chat after dinner. Though the banter between Jesse and me died down while we ate, the tension did not. He kept moving closer until his thigh was brushing mine. Then he had the audacity to drape his arm over my shoulder. I don't know what's happening to my body—I don't feel in control anymore. My head spinning might have something to do with that.

"But why would you do that?" Jenna asks loudly.

I focus back on the conversation as Brett says, "Inside voice, babe."

She smacks his chest.

"Do what?" I ask.

"Get distracted again?" Jesse purrs in my ear. "I wasn't even drinking this time."

No, but his fingers were grazing my arm. How can a simple touch cause such a stir in my body?

"Just lost in thought. What did I miss?"

"My sister said she and her husband snuck out of here and had sex in a storeroom a couple of weeks ago," Jenna says. "Then this one says they should've done it right here in the booth." She points at Jesse. "I don't understand why you'd risk that, though."

My gaze swings to Jesse, whose smile has morphed into a deep smolder, telling me something I wasn't expecting to find out about him—at least not tonight. Then again, since I've let my guard down with him, plenty of things have happened that I wasn't expecting—namely inside my body.

"It's less about the sex then," I say, looking back at Jenna. "And more about the risk. The risk of getting caught or the challenge of doing it without getting caught."

Jenna squints at Jesse. "Things I didn't need to know about my best friend." She sticks her tongue out at him, but he keeps that smile blazing. Hot like fucking fire. But not as hot as his body so close to mine.

"What is it for you? The challenge or the risk?" he asks me.

Jenna is waiting on the edge of her seat for my answer, but I'm not giving one. At least not what they want.

Instead of answering, I stand up and damn near climb over Jesse to get out of the booth. As I half-straddle him, I lean in close and whisper, "Guess you'll have to get me *naked* and find out." Finally free of the booth, I take a deep breath and steady myself, trying to ignore the throbbing in my head. "I need to use the bathroom. I'll be back."

Then I walk away, the heat of his gaze on me until I'm out of sight.

I let out a breath as I get to the hallway the bathrooms are in. My head feels buzzy and my cheeks are hot—and not because of Jesse's proximity to me tonight.

After using the bathroom, I splash some water on my face, trying to quell the heat spreading in my cheeks. Whatever. At least the flush on my cheeks makes me look more vibrant. I stare at my reflection, a pinch of dizziness making me grip the sink tighter. I close my eyes and try to push it all away. I'm shocked by how intensely I want Jesse. How much I want to carry the fun we've had tonight into a release that I think we both desperately need.

For how long I spent denying him and pushing him away, this feels a little crazy, but I made myself a promise that I'm going to live my life, and going after a guy I want, who turns me on and pulls me in and makes me want more is living life to the fullest.

I give my hair a little tousle, then walk out of the bathroom, surprised to find Jesse waiting in the hallway.

"Now who's stalking whom?" I ask with a smirk, walking over to him and running my hands down his chest.

His brow furrows slightly at my seductive voice.

"You'd been gone for a while. I wanted to make sure you were okay."

"I'm fine. I could be better, though..."

His eyes flare. Maybe I had the player thing all wrong, because he seems surprised by my suggestiveness. "Better how?"

"If we were at my apartment with fewer clothes on."

The brow furrow deepens, and he steps back.

*Seriously? This is his response?*

Hello, rejection, my old friend.

Tears prickle in my eyes, though I try to blink them back.

"Dani—"

"Don't. You want to know why I thought this was all game? It's this, right here. You've been flirting with me all night. I finally make a move and now you don't want me. It's all a game," I mutter.

He gently grabs my upper arms and tilts his head down to look into my eyes. "I told you before, this is not a game to me. *You* are not a game to me. But you had four drinks tonight, your cheeks are flushed, and you stumbled when you walked out of the bathroom. You're drunk, Dani. I'm not. And I will never be the guy who takes advantage of someone." More tears burn in my eyes. "Believe me, Dani, I want you, but not this way."

I look up at him, taking in the sincerity in his eyes. The way he's looking at me doesn't seem like rejection. But he has it wrong, and I'm feeling like an idiot right about now.

"I'm not..." I trail off, sighing. He won't believe me, anyway. "It's fine. I'll just go home."

He slips one of his hands into my hair and I hate that my stupid, traitorous body leans into it.

"I didn't say no to being around you, Dani. I'd love to spend more time with you tonight. And I definitely am not letting you leave here alone. Let me take you home. Or we can go back to my place. Whatever you want."

"Your place? You mean your parents' house?" I sass.

His lips pull flat. "Not like they're ever there."

There's a hint of sadness in his eyes that cuts at my heart. The last thing I wanted was to be alone tonight, but now what matters more to me is making sure he isn't alone. "Okay. Your place."

The smile I get at those words makes everything else worth it.

"Brett and Jenna were getting ready to leave. We can all walk out together."

"Sounds perfect."

He takes my hand and I'm shocked at how perfectly it wraps around mine, how our fingers twine together like they were meant to be that way.

*Calm down*, I tell my rapidly beating heart.

But I can't calm down because the more time I spend with Jesse, the closer I get to the edge of the cliff. If we keep going like this, it's only a matter of time until I fly over the edge and get lost in the freefall.

# 11
# *Stranger Things Have Happened*

## Dani

BY THE TIME WE make the short drive back to Jesse's parents' house, my cheeks are more flushed, and even the heat of Jesse's hand on my thigh can't cut through the nausea I'm feeling.

Once he's parked, I open my door and step out, pausing to take a deep breath of the cold January air, praying it will help, but it doesn't do much. I close my eyes, trying to stop the light-headedness, but I know it's all futile.

"Dani?" Jesse asks, wrapping a hand around my waist.

I flash my eyes open and look at him as my stomach gurgles. *Shit.*

"I need the bathroom," I groan.

Jesse, who still thinks I'm drunk, wraps his arm tighter around me and guides me to the front porch and up the stairs. Once he's unlocked the door, he leads me inside. "Can you walk up the stairs?" he asks softly. "There's a bathroom down here, but that one is bigger."

"I can walk," I answer.

"There are pain meds in the cabinet. I'll bring you some water."

"Thank you." I start up the stairs, then turn back to him. "Jesse?"

"Yeah?"

"Uh, any chance you have something more comfortable I could put on?"

The tight black pencil skirt and flowy blouse I wore to work now feel constricting and uncomfortable.

"Of course. Be right there."

My stomach gurgles again, and I don't wait another second to run upstairs.

What happens next is the after effects. What I like to refer to as the Cinderella at midnight moment. The carriage turns back into a pumpkin. Or in my case, my body feels like it's going to explode. That's what happens when I drink alcohol, though I like to wish it away and pretend that's not true. Which is why I allowed myself to have two actual drinks tonight before having the bartender switch me over to seltzer.

It always feels nice and warm going down. Then anywhere from thirty minutes to two hours later, I'm a disaster.

I say a quick prayer of thanks that they have that essential oil spray stuff that helps take care of smells, because puking is not what's about to happen. I almost wish it were. That would be easier. But, no. I sit down on the toilet and curse my genetics for the next six minutes until I've finally shit everything out of my body.

This is *not* how I wanted the night to go. Surprisingly, I wanted to be in Jesse's arms tonight, but if that didn't happen, I definitely did not want to be locked in his bathroom praying he'll drop a bottle of water and the clothes off at the door and run away, not ask to come in.

After fully cleaning myself up, I scrub my hands, and again splash cold water on my face. I feel better now, but still a little run down.

"Dani?" Jesse knocks at the door. "I've got water and clothes."

"Okay, thanks. Just leave them at the door."

"Okay. I'll be downstairs. Yell if you need me."

"Will do. Thank you."

After he's gone, I let out a sigh, then pull the door open, grabbing the clothes and the water bottle. I find some ibuprofen in the medicine cabinet and take it, then look at the clothes Jesse gave me. An Ida High baseball tee and a pair of sweats. After slipping them on and drinking more water, I feel a little better.

Making my way downstairs, I find Jesse on the couch, legs tossed up as he leans against a pile of pillows in the corner.

"Hey," I say, softly.

He lifts his legs and shifts so I can join him.

"Hey. I made some lemon ginger tea with honey. It should help soothe your stomach. I can get a bucket if you need one, though."

"Thank you, but I'm not drunk. I wasn't drunk."

He looks at me like he doesn't believe me. "But you had—"

"Two drinks, then two sparkling waters."

"Wait, what?"

"I had the bartender switch me after two. I shouldn't have had the second. Hell, I probably shouldn't have had the first."

"Why?"

"I have an alcohol intolerance. My doctor said I probably lack one of the enzymes needed to fully digest it. If I only have a little, I might get queasy, my cheeks will flush, and I won't feel well. When I drink more than that—like I did tonight—I get all those things plus a few bonus symptoms like low blood pressure which leads to light-headedness, rapid heartbeat, bad headache, and... stomach distress."

"Oh. Wow." He runs a hand through his hair. "Well, I'm glad I insisted on taking you home then."

"I'm glad you did too." I move closer to him. "I didn't want to be alone. Even though I feel a little crappy right now, I'm glad I'm here."

He grabs a blanket and pulls it over us.

"Has the alcohol thing always been an issue?"

I chuckle at that. "Oh yeah. I learned that the hard way my freshman year of college. I mean, I'd had alcohol before that, but never much. My mom loves wine and she'd let me have a taste here or there, and at parties in high school, I never usually drank because either my older brother was there to make sure I didn't, or I was watching out for Olivia. She's like my mom and will go hard and polish off a bottle of wine alone. I went to college near my hometown but still lived on campus. I went to a party my first week, and it was the first time I didn't have Weston hovering over me, so I decided to have some fun. I only had a few drinks, but the alcohol intolerance made me so sick I ended up in the hospital with dehydration. Everyone thought I'd gotten alcohol poisoning. It was embarrassing, but thankfully, most of the people at the party didn't remember it. The ER doctor didn't believe me at first, but after talking with my parents, it turns out, Gram has something similar. My uncle Darren can't drink either, and I think Rae is sensitive to it as well."

He nods. "Yeah, that sounds right. Wow. Talk about a shitty way to find that all out. Why didn't you just tell us that?"

My cheeks heat and not because of the alcohol this time. "Because most people are weird about it."

He frowns. "Did you think we'd try to pressure you?"

"It's what most people do. Or they act like I'm the weirdest person in existence or no fun. Most people think they need alcohol to survive, so if you tell them you can't have any, they act like it's the most devastating thing they've ever heard." I grab my tea and swirl the spoon in my mug. "My ex... used to complain that I made all his business dinners harder. I couldn't drink with people without getting sick, which was 'unhelpful' to him."

"Your ex sounds like a fucking douche who needs a punch in the nuts."

I chuckle at that. "Yeah. That's about right."

"Well, just know I'll never push you about drinking. And if you ever want me not to drink when I'm around you, I won't."

"I appreciate that. I don't care if you drink, though. I just don't like it when activities are focused solely on drinking. I was actually surprised you didn't drink more tonight."

"Oh." He clears his throat. "Well, you seemed anxious about drinking, and I wasn't sure why, so I figured I'd stay sober."

My eyes widen in shock, but just as quickly I soften, looking at him in awe. "You stopped drinking because of me?"

His cheeks are a little red as he shrugs and looks at me. "I wanted you to feel safe."

And just like that another one of the locks guarding my heart cracks open.

Leaning up, I press my lips against his cheek, an overwhelming amount of gratitude flowing through me.

"Thank you," I breathe.

He looks at me for a moment, then softly kisses my forehead. "Anytime, Dani girl."

# Jesse

I think I've finally popped Dani's bubble. She's letting me in and not just to play games. She's talking to me. Snuggling with me. In fact, her arm is wrapped around my stomach and her head is resting on my shoulder. It's quiet and more intimate than anything I was expecting tonight. Or at all. With the walls Dani has had up, there were times I thought I'd never see what was behind them.

I imagined doing a lot of things with Dani—some of them not so appropriate—but I didn't imagine this. When she agreed to come over here tonight, I didn't think we'd be doing anything like this. Then again, I thought she was drunk. Her explanation makes more sense, though, because she seemed poised and wasn't slurring.

"Why are your parents never around?" she asks, twisting the fabric of my shirt between her fingers.

I let out a sigh. "They retired early and started traveling. They always liked to travel. We went a bunch of places in the US and a handful in Europe when I was a kid."

"But... why did they start traveling when you and Joel were still in school?" she asks, genuinely confused. I'm not surprised. Knowing her family as long as I have, I can pretty safely say none of them would ever do what my parents did. Rae's parents never commented on it, and they're friends with my parents, but I always got the sense they didn't agree with my parents' choices.

I shrug one shoulder. "Honestly? I think they were burned out, and..."

"What?"

"Joel and I weren't exactly chosen kids. We were *surprises.* And though our parents never outwardly said anything to make us feel that way, their actions said they were ready to be done with hands-on parenting. I get it. My oldest brother is a pain in the ass on a good day. My other older brother is so easy he practically raised himself. Joel and I were both pretty easy, but once we could take care of ourselves, our parents were slowly around less and less. Even before we were teens, they started taking more solo trips. Joel would stay with Aaron or Miles, and I'd stay with one of my friends—Jenna, usually. Leo was great about letting me stay there. He'd put me in the guest room and watch baseball with me."

"Wow. It sucks that your parents weren't around, though."

"It does, but it is what it is. And don't get me wrong, my parents aren't mean. They aren't bad people. If anyone in their life needs something, they'll help however they can. But being around every day and cultivating relationships isn't their strong suit."

She wraps her arm tighter around me. "That must be hard."

"It can be. Especially when I see how other families support each other. I'd love to have that." I clear my throat. "That's part of why I was so bummed at Rae's wedding. Seeing your family is beautiful, but also a reminder of what I don't have."

"I'm sorry, Jesse. For what I said that night—for pushing you away."

I turn to her and see her looking up at me earnestly.

"Why did you?" I whisper, grazing my thumb down her arm, trying to put her at ease. It's hard to ask her that question and it feels like a risk given how our communication has gone, but I need to know. I want to understand.

"Because I was scared. My last relationship really messed me up. Trusting is hard. When I looked into your eyes on that dance floor..." She trails off and shakes her head.

"What? You can tell me. You can always tell me anything."

"It sounds crazy now, but all I could see was the potential for heartbreak. And I panicked. I don't ever want to go through the lies and betrayal I went through before—and at that point, I didn't know you well enough to know if you'd do that to me."

"And now?"

She sighs and shifts on the couch, tucking her legs under her as she moves back but turns her body toward me. "Now I'm trying to trust the way you treat me. You respect me. You're kind. You listen. I'm not handing you a key to my apartment—or my heart—but I feel like I can trust you as a person. Especially after tonight."

*That's progress and I will fucking take it.*

"I promise you, Dani, I will always do my best to protect you, take care of you. You deserve that."

"So do you. I haven't exactly returned the favor, but I want to. It's why I came over here tonight." She brushes her hand over my cheek. "You looked so sad when you said your parents are never here. The last thing I wanted was for you to be alone."

My body heats with desire at her words. How badly I want to grab her and finally kiss her again, but we aren't there yet.

"I'm glad you're here. It makes the house less lonely. I should be used to it by now, but I'm not sure I ever will be."

"When was the last time you saw them?"

"Briefly at Christmas before they went to my older brother's house."

"When will they be back again?"

I laugh at that. "That's the million-dollar question. I was on the phone with my dad the other day, and I was telling him about this benefit we're doing at the stadium in May. It's going to be a huge deal, and for the first time, he seemed to understand this is the right career for me. And that it is a viable career, not just a short-term job. I was excited that he was excited about it and asked if they'd be around. He told me he wasn't sure where they would be, but to let them know how they could donate. I get it. In his mind, those two things are equatable. Spend time or spend money. But the thing is, I don't care about the money. I'd much rather feel worth his time."

To my surprise, she lurches forward and wraps her arms around me in a tight hug. "Everyone deserves to feel that from their parents. I'm so sorry you don't."

I give her a quick squeeze, then she sits back.

"It's okay. I mean…" I laugh at myself. "Yeah, it's okay."

"It's not. And it doesn't have to be, but I know what you mean." She takes a drink of her tea. "Will you tell me more about the benefit?"

My heart lights at those words and the genuine interest on her face.

"It's a benefit to help fund the building of the new neonatal intensive care unit at the hospital. They have a small one that can handle small things and stabilize enough to transfer to a bigger hospital. The general manager of the Knights has a granddaughter who was in the NICU for months and his daughter and her husband had to stay out of town for most of that. He really wants to help with this so fewer families will be displaced during difficult times."

"Wow. That's amazing. I'd say the benefit is in good hands based on what you did with the winter carnival."

I smile at that, thinking of how she hid from me. She's ridiculous. Maybe we both are.

"Thank you. It's already sold out, so I'm a little nervous. I mean, I'm confident in myself, but there was less pressure for the carnival. I want to nail this."

She smiles softly, running her hand up my arm. "You will. Let me know if I can help at all."

"Thanks, Dani." I clear my throat. "So, what about you? What are you working on? Are you enjoying working at AB?"

"I am. Everyone there is great. Leo and Noah are both really nice and they're funny, too. Maia, Vince, and Nick have been awesome as well. Nick is great to bounce ideas off of," she says, mentioning Leo's daughter and his business partner Noah's two sons. "Right now I'm helping with a kitchen and living room redesign. Eventually they're going to do their whole house, so I'm keeping that in mind. They're taking it from a nineties interior design with horrible wallpaper and bright carpets to something more modern but also timeless. The kitchen is the most fun because they want to bring in pops of color in small places which gives me room to play. Outside of AB, I just finished a really small project helping a single mom design a bedroom for her daughter, and I'll be working on redesigning this awesome ice cream place, too."

*Wait.*

"Ice cream?"

"Yeah. I met this guy at the carnival, actually, I was hiding between his tent and his husband's tent. His husband does—"

"Pizza."

Her eyes widen. "Oh. You know them?" She shakes her head. "Of course, you do. You planned the carnival."

I chuckle at that. "Well, yes. I did. But they're also two of my best friends. I didn't realize *you* were the crazy girl who hid between their tents. He didn't mention interior design, though, which makes me think Garrett knew who you were."

"Damn them. That's cool, though. And now I know he makes great vanilla ice cream." She shakes her head. "It's a small world."

"Or maybe it's fate, pushing us together."

"Maybe," she whispers, a soft smile on her face. The tension between us thickens as we stare at each other, and I internally war with myself about whether now is the right time to kiss her.

Given what happened last time, I don't want to rush or make her uncomfortable. I don't want to push her, but the pressure of her fingertips against my arm has increased and her eyes are on my lips. Now's the right time.

She moves closer, running her hand up through my hair. Slowly, I drag my hand across her navel, dipping my head toward hers, when her stomach growls loudly. It's such a rumbling growl I can feel it.

She pulls back and looks at her stomach, then starts laughing. Big, beautiful laughter spilling out of her and making her eyes crinkle at the edges. The kind of laughter that is instantly contagious, and a second later, I'm laughing, too.

"I guess I'm hungry." She pauses, still laughing. "Actually, I know I am. I'm so freaking hungry."

I'd be sad that I missed the opportunity to kiss her again but the way she's laughing makes it all worth it.

"I can make something. What are you in the mood for?"

"Nothing too intense. My gut still feels a little off."

"I have instant mashed potatoes. If you're up for it, I can add some garlic and cheddar cheese. It's my specialty."

She nods vigorously. "That sounds so good."

"Sweet. I'll make it, then we can watch something while we eat?"

Her eyes light up. "Can we watch *Stranger Things?* It probably sounds weird, but it's my comfort show. Something about the '80s vibes."

I chuckle at that. "Sure. I love that show, but I've never gone back and watched it from the beginning, so that's perfect. I like the feel, too. In fact, it's why I went back and watched a bunch of classic '80s movies."

She claps her hands. "Yes, I love it!"

I can't help but smile watching her. "Up for helping me in the kitchen?" I ask as I stand up.

"Of course." She stands up, a vibrant smile on her face. It's damn near magical, and it reminds me of the way she used to smile when we were kids. The warm sunshiney Dani smile I've been wanting since we first saw each other again back in May.

Now that I've gotten to see it, it's my mission to bring out that smile as often as I can.

I wake up to a mostly numb arm. I almost question the tingling in my fingertips until I recognize the warmth pressed into me. I flash my eyes open and am rewarded with the image of Dani nestled between me and the back of the couch and her head on my chest. It doesn't hurt that she's wearing a shirt with my last name on the back.

Damn Aaron for that shit. He told me how even before he was with Rae, he loved seeing her in his shirts because he loved having his last name on her back. Probably should've been a sign they were meant to be, but whatever. Can't say I don't get it now. She's not my girl, but when she wears my clothes, it makes me feel like she is, and I can't deny how good that makes me feel.

I pull some hair off her face and she slowly stirs, then looks up at me.

"Morning, Dani girl."

"Morning. When did we fall asleep last night?"

"Sometime during season two."

"We made a good dent." She sits up and stretches, and I'm instantly bummed at the loss of contact. I love having her in my arms.

"Hopefully you don't have any plans this morning. I don't even know what time it is."

She grabs her phone off the table. "Just before ten."

"Not a record," I say with a shrug.

"Last night was fun. Thank you. And thanks for taking care of me."

I sit up and scooch over to her, tucking a strand of hair behind her ear. "No need to thank me. I like spending time with you." Her eyes meet mine. *Grow some balls and do it.* I clear my throat. "Dani, I'd really like to take you out on a date."

She bites her lip. "I thought you said you wanted to be friends."

I shake my head. *This girl.* "I do want to be your friend. I want to get to know you, spend time with you, and build a strong foundation so that we can grow into something more. We started that last night. I'd like to continue it."

She inhales sharply. "Damn it, Jesse. You better fucking mean it."

"I know your ex hurt you and it's hard for you to trust, but I promise I'll do my best to heal what he broke and to always be someone worthy of your trust."

She stares into my eyes for a moment, begging for my words to be the truth. I brush my hand over hers, but otherwise don't move. I want her to see the certainty and sincerity in my eyes. It's hard to trust after you've been hurt—I know it all too well. Though her hesitance has been frustrating at times, I respect her desire to protect her heart. What she doesn't realize is I've been trying to protect it, too. As much as she'll let me.

She swallows hard and takes my hand. "I..." I brace myself for another rejection, but she continues. "I'd really like that."

*Fuck, yes.*

I blow out a breath. "You had me nervous there for a minute."

She laughs. "Sorry."

"Hey, you said yes. That's what matters. How does next Friday sound? Between work and swim practice, that's the easiest time for me. Plus, I need to come up with a perfect first date for you."

She blushes, and it's a massive ego boost. I love that I can affect her with just my words.

"Friday's perfect. I, um, just... could we not tell *everyone* yet? I mean, I'll tell my roommate and you can tell Garrett and Evan, Jenna, just not—"

I laugh lightly, knowing who she doesn't want to tell. Rae, Joel, and all of their friends, who have big opinions and love giving people shit. That's fine. I can live with that. As long as I get her.

"I know *who* you mean, and I can agree to that."

"Okay, then. Friday."

"Good. Now, what are you doing the rest of the day? I figure if you don't have any plans, we can continue our friendship building activities." She squints at me, and I roll my eyes. "That was not a sexual innuendo. You have such a dirty mind," I say dramatically.

She shoves my arm. "I have plans with my roommate this afternoon, but if you can make bacon, I'll make pancakes, and we can continue our *Stranger Things* binge."

"I can make bacon."

"Good," she says with a smile, rising from the couch.

"Dani?"

"Hm?"

"Are you more excited to spend time with me or watch *Stranger Things*?"

She doesn't answer, she just smiles that radiant smile at me and heads for the kitchen.

Day two of getting that perfect smile out of her. *I could get used to this.*

# 12

# A Good Boy

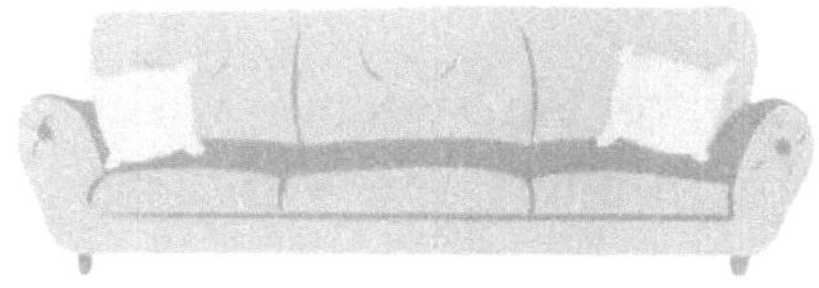

## Dani

NINETY-SEVEN MINUTES. THAT'S HOW long before my date with Jesse. I hurry out of my car and over to the bakery. It's just down the block from my aunt Kara and uncle Charlie's house, and it's owned by one of Rae's best friend's family. Instead of going inside, I head for the door leading up to the apartments above it, one of which Rae and Aaron live in.

I wasn't intending to stop here today, but things got a little crazy, and I wanted to check in with her and maybe catch Sarah, too, before my date.

When I get upstairs, I give a quick knock on the apartment door, then swing it open. Rae and Aaron have an open-door policy—if the door is unlocked, you're welcome to walk right in. If it's locked, run away, and probably cover your ears as you go. But when I swing the door open, I wish I would have ignored their policy and waited for it to open. Because what I see is Rae in the middle of the living room with Jesse. He's holding her tightly and whispering something to her.

My stomach drops. The fear that he's just playing me, and another that I haven't admitted to—that he has feelings for Rae and only wants me because I remind him of her—roll through my mind.

"Uh, sorry—" I stutter out, suddenly wishing I were invisible.

They quickly pull apart and while Rae doesn't act like anything is abnormal, Jesse's brow is deeply furrowed as he looks at me.

"I should head out," Jesse says to Rae.

*Don't cry, Dani. No one needs that. Keep it together.*

"Thanks for stopping by, J," Rae says softly, squeezing his hand before he turns toward me.

Where is Aaron? Why is Jesse here? And why is Aaron okay with him being here when he's not home? *Why am I freaking out about this?*

Jesse's gaze is hot on me as he walks across the room. I have no idea what's about to happen. Is he going to be playful? Pretend we're still frenemies? Show her how he feels about me?

None of that happens, though.

He stops when he gets to me and squeezes my arm. His eyes are intense as he looks into mine. "Hey, Dani girl. I'll see you later." It would sound innocuous to anyone else, but to me it's a promise. He's not letting me get away. He's going to see me later.

I nod, even though I'm so shaken, our date is the last thing I want to think about right now.

One more tiny squeeze to my arm, and he's out the door.

Rae looks at me. "Everything okay there?"

My eyes snap to her—they involuntarily followed Jesse as he walked out the door. As soon as I get a good look at her, I push everything else aside, remembering why I'm here. One of Rae's close friends, who I've gotten to know a bit and is very sweet, is in the hospital right now after some severe mental health stuff happened last night and this morning.

After a beat, I walk across the room and pull her into my arms. "It's fine. How are you doing? How's Hyla?"

Rae hugs me back tightly. The Abbott men know how to call you on your shit and the Abbott women know how to give the best hugs. "I'm okay. Nothing quite like thinking one of your friends is going to die, though. Thankfully, Hyla is doing better, and she's in the right place to get help."

"That's good. How's Trevor?" Hyla is Trevor's best friend and essentially his sister.

"Rough," she says with a sigh as we pull away. "Aaron and Joel took food up to everyone still at the hospital for dinner."

"Of course," I say, more to myself than her. I open my mouth to say something else when Sarah walks in. She looks rougher than Rae, but that's not surprising. Sarah has had her share of mental health stuff over the years, too. "Hey," I say softly.

She walks into my open arms and we hug tightly.

I stay for a little while, talking with the girls and making sure they don't need anything before heading back to my apartment. It's only a few blocks away, so the drive is short, but that doesn't stop my brain from hyperfocusing on what I saw when I first walked into Rae's apartment. I don't know why the hell my brain can't settle down. It's not like Rae would ever cheat on Aaron. Right? I mean, I know with certainty she'd never hurt me like that, but she doesn't know I'm dating Jesse—or whatever the hell we're doing. Maybe we shouldn't be doing it if I'm so worried about this. I'm thinking about canceling as I turn onto my block, but when I pull into my driveway, I see that's not an option because Jesse is sitting on the front porch waiting for me.

I park my car in the back of the driveway, then take a few deep breaths, wishing I could somehow get out of this, but there isn't an exit. If I don't get to the front porch soon, he'll probably show up at my car door. One more big breath, and I force myself out of the car. *Let's get this over with.*

As I walk up the driveway, I square my shoulders, trying to look strong but also unfazed. Even though I'm so freaking *fazed*, it hurts. That same nagging voice bounces around in the back of my mind. *Don't trust him. It's not worth the risk.*

When I come around the corner of the front porch, Jesse stands up, looking me over, trying to gauge my emotional state. *Good luck, buddy. I don't even know.*

"Hi," he says softly.

"Hi." I try to keep my voice even, but it comes out terse.

I walk up the stairs, not stopping when he extends his arm toward me. I unlock the front door of the building and open the door slightly, when he steps up next to me.

"Dani..."

"What?"

"Nothing happened with Rae."

"Then why do you look upset and guilty?"

"I don't feel guilty. And I'm not upset. I'm worried about us. I promised you I would always try to be trustworthy and protect your heart. That hasn't changed, and I haven't stopped. But I know how seeing Rae and me hugging looked to you, and I think we need to talk about it."

"Talk about what?"

"About Rae and me. What happened between us."

"I have no desire to talk about your one-night stand with my cousin," I say, gripping the edge of the door tightly.

"I'm not suggesting we get into the minutiae of that. We need to talk about my friendship and *flirtationship*, I guess, with Rae. We've all dealt with it and moved on, but for you, it's all new, and I'm assuming you don't know many of the details, because it's not something Rae or I were dying to talk about. If we're going to do this, you deserve to know. Because I don't ever want you to worry about my friendship with her, or think you're a consolation prize. Because you're not. And even though you haven't said it with words, you've said it with your tone of voice, your demeanor, and the hurt in your eyes whenever this comes up. So, let's talk about it."

I stare at him for a moment, lifting my chin as I say, "I know I'm not a consolation prize."

"You know you shouldn't be, but you don't trust that you aren't. I'm guessing your shitty ex is to thank for that. And I get it. Because I was treated the same way. I could say that's why I strive not to treat anyone like that, but I'm not a guy who has to learn by example. No one should ever feel like they're second best. *I* don't ever want you to feel that way."

I shake my head. "I appreciate that, but honestly, it doesn't matter. This—whatever this is—it's not going to work. It's too much. It's too—"

"No," he says forcefully.

My eyes dart up to his, the hurt in them unmistakable.

"No?"

"Stop trying to derail this every time you get scared. I know you care about me. I know you want this. Stop pushing me away because you got hurt before. I get it. I've been there, but I'm not your ex, Dani. And it's not fair for you to make me into a villain and run from me every time something triggers you. God damn it, I shouldn't have to keep proving myself to you. If you're upset or hurt or scared or triggered, talk to me. I'm right here. I'm always right here." He blows out a breath as he finishes talking and shoves a hand through his hair.

Tears fill my eyes because he's absolutely right. I do want to do this with him, but I am so fucking scared I can't think straight. And among the many positive traits that come from my genetics, the desire to run and hide when I'm overwhelmed or scared is in there too.

I turn away from him, a sob lodging in my chest. He's not having that, though. He spins me around and into his arms, holding me as I cry.

"I'm sorry," I whisper. "You're right. I'm scared. Looking back, I was too naive. I fell in love with someone who lied to me and used me. I swore I'd never do it again. Then you came into my life. My brain is constantly telling me you're going to hurt me. My heart—can't be trusted."

"What about your gut? Shut everything else up and listen to that instinctual feeling. What does it tell you about me?"

"That I'm safe with you."

"Damn right you are. I will always take care of you. You just have to let me. I mean, I'll still do it if you don't, but it makes it a lot easier when you do."

I laugh lightly, and he steps back and wipes away my tears.

"Thank you for being patient with me. For pushing me. No one's ever done that for me before... honored my fears while still encouraging me to work through them."

"I will always be here to talk through these things with you, but you have to stop pushing me away. Lean in. I'll be here to catch you."

I nod. "Okay."

"Does that mean you'll talk this through with me so we can work it out and go on our date? Because I have a pretty great night planned."

He smiles at me, and I can't help but return it.
"Yeah. Let's go inside."

# Jesse

Dani's ex did a number on her, and as much as I understand that pain, I want her to trust me. I want to be her safe place, for her to know she can run to me whenever she needs me. Thankfully, we made it through this bump, but we still need to talk about my friendship with Rae. That's probably overdue, but I honestly try to forget about the bad parts. We've both moved on, and I want everyone else to as well.

Dani swings open the door to her apartment, and I follow her inside. It's a gorgeous old Victorian house converted into apartments, and this one has the high ceilings and hardwood floors expected of the style. Throughout the kitchen and living room I notice pops of color I'm sure are from Dani.

"This is it. Not huge, but cozy. I love the Victorian vibes mixed with some brighter more modern things. It's cozy-timeless, and that's my vibe. Amelia likes things more modern, but she's cool with me taking over and designing things."

"I can see the sprinkles of you throughout the place. I love the Victorian style, too. It's what I'm looking for. I'd like to stay in Ida, though, so it might take me some time to find it."

She smiles. "Well, if you ever want me to go house hunting with you, I will. I'm a nerd about that stuff and could sit in bed all day watching *House Hunters*."

"*House Hunters* and *Stranger Things*. Mental note."

She takes a deep breath. "Come here." She kicks her shoes off, sits down on the couch, and tucks her legs under her, much like she was sitting the other night at my place.

I sit down next to her and slide my shoes off before settling in the corner of the couch.

She looks at me tentatively, so I hold my hands out. "Ask me anything."

She bites her lip, then asks the question I've been waiting for. "Were you in love with her?"

"No," I answer immediately. "Not for a second."

"Then what? I don't understand."

I blow out a breath, not looking forward to reliving a lot of this. "Rae and I have chemistry. We always have. It was easy to flirt with each other, to—"

"Hook up with each other?"

"To some degree, yeah. Look, the best way I can explain it is... you love *Stranger Things*. Joyce and Hopper are the couple everyone wants together, right? Because they have amazing chemistry."

"Right."

"But Winona Ryder and David Harbour aren't together in real life. They're close friends. They respect each other. They have chemistry, but they clearly are not in love."

"Okay... chemistry, but you have been with her. Did you have even a crush on her? I just... I need to know the truth."

Reaching out, I squeeze her leg. "I don't know. I never thought of anything between us as a crush. We never wanted to date each other. We're both flirts and we were a safe space for each other. We could kiss or whatever without strings and feel completely safe. And that same feeling of safety is part of what made us feel like sleeping together was a good idea. Plus a hefty dose of alcohol."

Dani is still chewing on her lip, but she nods. "Will you tell me what you've done with her? Like, was it an ongoing thing?"

"How much do you actually know? So I know where to start."

She looks at me, uncertain, then shrugs. "Not much, I guess. In conversation, Sarah poked fun at you two hooking up before Rae and Aaron dated, but then the conversation always turned to Aaron. And as for you two sleeping together... Rae, Sarah, Olivia, and I were up late one night talking. She and Aaron had recently gotten back together, and somehow, Olivia ended up asking if Rae had been with anyone else when they were apart. Rae got quiet and said she'd been with you, but she seemed upset about it, and Sarah changed the subject." She lets out a rough sigh. "You're right. I'm assuming things when I don't know much."

I reach over and squeeze her thigh. "It's okay. It's all complicated. But, no. It was never ongoing. There were three times. Once during her junior year of high school—that was just making out, but we considered taking it further. We might have if Joel hadn't caught us. It wasn't long after that when things really started with her and Aaron, and I backed off. I didn't ever want to prevent them from being together. In fact, the second time something happened, part of me was trying to push Aaron to react and figure his shit out—which he did by punching me, among other things. That night, Rae was hurting. She wanted to get Aaron off her mind, and I was the perfect person. Comfort, safety, and chemistry. It started out with us dancing and flirting, but later that night, she wanted to take things further, and I was happy to oblige. I didn't do more than take her shirt off and *kiss* that part of her." I sigh and run my hand through my hair.

Dani reaches over and squeezes my hand. "Thank you for telling me this. I know it's awkward, but if I don't know the truth, I'll always wonder, and then I'll build it up in my head and let it eat away at me. I don't want that."

"I don't want that either, so thank you for talking this through. Listening. Not running. I know this is... complicated." I fidget with the hem of my shirt, wishing there wasn't more. You never hook up with a girl thinking, *uh oh, what if I fall for her cousin one day?* "Anyway, uh, she gave me a hand job that night. And that was the last thing that happened until..."

"You slept together. How did that happen?"

"She and Aaron were broken up, and she was hurting. I was in the same boat. Sober, we wouldn't have done it, but we'd been spending a lot of time together commiserating—and drinking. One night, I walked her and Sarah home, and one thing led to another and we slept together." I look down, not proud of this. "The next morning we woke up and immediately regretted it, but that wasn't quite enough, because then Aaron climbed through her window."

Dani's eyes get huge. "Shit. Really?"

"Yeah. I was trying to get out of there. Rae was still naked in bed, and Aaron walked in. I got the hell out of there before anything was said, but the hurt was written all over his face." I clear my throat, feeling like I'm back in that moment. "Then I went home, poured myself a whiskey, sat down in the living room, and started bawling."

Her expression changes, eyes softening as she runs her hand over my arm. "What? Why?"

I pinch the bridge of my nose, not liking the swell of emotions in my stomach. "Because I'd hurt Aaron, thought I'd ruined my friendship with Rae, and was more heartbroken than ever. Joel found me and let me cry it out. Obviously, Rae and I got through it, and Aaron... he's a good guy. Incredibly forgiving. Doesn't fully stop the guilt, though. After all that... it changed things between Rae and me. That flirty chemistry we always leaned into slipped away, and we became more like family to each other—the way she is with her other friends. Which is why I went over there today to check in." I shrug. "Now you know."

She crawls over and wraps her arms around me. "I'm sorry for what I said to you at the wedding. I know I apologized before, but I didn't know..." She shakes her head, sniffing back tears. "I'm sorry. Sorry I judged you and jumped to conclusions. I was so afraid to be your second choice. That you wanted me because you couldn't have her."

"Never. You're who I want, Dani. The only one I want. It kills me you don't see that, because I've spent months trying to show you, and sometimes it feels like I'm begging you to want me back."

She stares at me for a moment, eyes rolling over my face, then she does the last thing I'm expecting and slams her lips into mine.

*God, I forgot how good her lips on mine feel. Like heaven on earth.*

I wrap my arms around her back and pull her tighter to me. Our tongues haven't even gotten involved yet, but this kiss is still deep and unhinged. She rakes her fingers through my hair, then suddenly pulls her lips off mine.

"I want you, Jesse." She grabs one of my hands and holds it against her chest, letting me feel her rapidly beating heart. "No one else has ever made me feel like you do. No one else has ever made my heart race like this. That's why I get scared. I want this, but I don't want to get hurt again."

"I promise I will always protect your heart, Dani."

She cups my face in her hands and kisses me softly again. "I'm trying to trust that... and do the same for you."

"That's all I want, Dani girl."

Her eyes drop to my lips again, and this time when we crash together, our tongues are instantly tangled as we pour ourselves into this kiss. It's hot and passionate, and it makes me want to rip her clothes off and fuck her right here on the couch, but that's the thing with her. I'm always ahead of myself. She pulls me in so deep, I lose sight of where I am.

Of course, the way she's rolling her hips over mine is not helping.

I'm losing any shred of control I was holding onto. Probably shouldn't have sex with her on the couch, but I need more. I want to feel her. Something, anything.

Gliding my hands up her thighs, I push her skirt up and slide my hands over her ass. She groans and kisses me harder, riding me over my khakis.

Haven't even had a first date with this girl yet and we're dry humping on her couch.

"Jesse," she breathes as I harden more. Her name on my lips is enough to make me come in my pants.

She runs her hands under my shirt, and her fingers against my skin are high voltage. Electric shocks bringing my heart and my body to life.

"Oh, shit."

Dani rips her lips off mine and leans back, staring at her roommate, Amelia.

"Hi," Dani squeaks.

"Damn, put a sock on the door next time, girl. Or send a text."

Dani wipes her mouth as she stares at Amelia.

"Sorry, Ames."

"It's fine." She nods at me. "Nice to meet you, Jesse."

"You too, Amelia," I say awkwardly.

"Okay, well, I'm just going to go to my room and put my headphones on."

"You don't—we're going on a date," Dani calls after her.

"Whatever you say," Amelia calls back, shutting her bedroom door.

Dani looks at me and we burst out laughing.

"I guess that was a good reminder that we have a date to get to." I slide my hand into her hair and look into her eyes. "Assuming we're okay."

She smiles brightly, and it undoes me. Every fucking time. That smile could kill me.

"Did the kissing not make that clear?"

"I just wanted to be sure. I know we both have histories and all of this is complicated, but I meant it when I said I wanted us to have a strong foundation."

She runs her hands up my chest. "Your honesty means so much to me. Sometimes I feel like I'm damaged goods. It's not worth trying to fall again because my heart is too messed up."

"You're not damaged." I put my hand over her heart again. "Your heart needs to heal. If you'll let me, I want to be the one to help do that." I lean in and give her a quick but firm kiss. "Now, go get ready for our date. I will be back in a half hour to pick you up."

She smacks a kiss on my cheek, then hops off the couch. "See you soon, Wilkinson." She winks at me, then disappears into her bedroom as I climb off the couch.

"Hey," I call.

She sticks her head out of the doorway of her room. "Hm?"

"I expect a continuation of those kisses later."

Her eyes dance and she cocks an eyebrow. "You better be a *good boy*, then."

I inhale sharply at that. She smirks at me as she slowly closes her bedroom door.

She surprises me more every day, and I love it.

# 13

## That Flex

## Dani

I shouldn't be surprised that Jesse knows how to plan a date, but of course he does. We're in a quiet room at the River Row Steakhouse at a small table by a wall of windows that looks out over the river. The entire meal has been delicious so far, and our date has been the perfect balance of tension and comfortable conversation. We're waiting on our desserts and talking. Jesse came prepared with a game to ask each other ten questions—whatever we wanted—but the rules were that we had to ask more than small talk questions.

We've talked about our favorite foods and colors, our jobs, and I've told him more about my family.

"Okay, my next question... what's something you've done before that you'd love to do again or something new you want to try?" Jesse asks.

My cheeks heat. *Am I going to tell him about my list?* Why not?

"Don't tease me, but when I visited Ida in May, I was staying with Grandma and Grandpa, and they insisted I make a list of all the things I wanted to do or wanted for my future."

He rubs his hands together. "Yes. I need to see this list."

"You promise no teasing?"

"No. I'll never promise that. But I promise it will only be playful teasing. And only if you have something like square-dancing on there."

I pretend to be offended. "You're against square-dancing? I can't believe you."

He leans forward, a troublemaking smile on his face. "Show me the list."

I dig it out of my purse and unfold it, waiting a beat before handing it to him. "They're not all funny, okay?"

"Hey, I'm not going to pick on you. I want to see it so I get to know you better. Hell, maybe I should make my own list."

"Maybe you should."

"For now... let's have a look at this."

He reads through them, mentioning a few out loud. "So you've tried oysters. Still hate them?"

I make a gagging face. "Let's not ruin our meal by talking about them."

"Yes, wishing on the stars is too Aaron and Rae, but I could get behind dancing in the rain." He looks over at me. "Dancing in the wet grass in pouring rain as our clothes stick to us. Your hair sticking to the sides of your face. You'd be laughing and spinning in circles. I wouldn't be able to take my eyes off you. Eventually, I'd grab you and kiss you as we'd try to breathe through the rain pouring over us. I could definitely get behind that."

Our eyes lock, and I want to crawl over the table, curl my fingers into his shirt, and pull his lips to mine.

"You've got me excited for the spring rain," I whisper.

The smile on his face grows, and he looks back at the list. "Driving across country would be fun. So would Paris. Mental notes made." He chuckles. "Be naked more? Isn't that what you told me last week at the club?"

"Yep."

"So... you never told me what you meant by that. Physically or emotionally?"

"Both," I answer honestly. "My cousin Taylor is the kind of person who finds clothes suffocating and prefers to be naked as much as possible. She's my inspiration for that. But as I wrote it, I meant it emotionally, too."

He rolls his bottom lip between his teeth. "I'm happy to help with both. *Eat more ice cream.* Was that because of our ice cream night?" He looks at me with surprise in his eyes.

"Yes. I didn't handle things well at the end, but I enjoyed myself that night. And it was fun having an ice cream partner in crime."

"Babe, I am happy to eat ice cream with you every single night. We'll try a thousand concoctions. Get an ice cream maker and make our own."

"I like the sound of that. Life's too short not to fill it with ice cream."

"Dani, what's the last thing on this list?"

I squint at him, trying to remember, then it hits me. *Stop being a scaredy cat (or a bitter hag).*

"Oh, uh..." I look down at the table. "It's based off something Olivia and Trevor said to me at Rae and Aaron's wedding."

Jesse looks at me. "Trev called you a bitter hag?"

"No. Not Trevor. Olivia was teasing me, and she said that about how I'd been talking about you." I clear my throat. "That was before I understood... who you really are."

"It's okay," he says softly, squeezing my hand.

"Before the wedding, Olivia said I was acting out of fear. Trev said something similar after he saw what happened with us on the dance floor. I felt awful after what I said and then our conversation outside the barn. Anyway, um, I was sitting in bed that night, replaying everything, and I wrote that down."

He tilts his head to the side, looking at me. "Is that why you came to the carnival?"

"Part of it. I didn't like how we left things, but I didn't know what to say, either. I thought I'd go and talk to you, but by the time I got there, I decided that was crazy and I was probably reading way too much into everything. Basically, I was a mess."

He chuckles. "Having everything figured out is overrated. And I loved seeing you at the carnival. It helped me believe *maybe* you wanted this, too."

Before I can say anything else, he squeezes my hand and pulls it away, then a waitress sets our desserts down.

As I stare happily at my dessert, Jesse folds up the list and slides it back to me.

"So, there's something on that list I can help you with—besides being naked."

"Oh?" I ask, enjoying the heavenly raspberry chocolate torte I ordered.

"Snowboarding. It's one of my favorite winter activities. We used to go to the mountains a couple of times each winter when I was a kid. As I got older, I continued the tradition and went with my friends. We were thinking about planning something for my birthday, actually."

I put my fork down. "I can't believe I don't know this, but when is your birthday?"

"January thirtieth."

"Jesse! That's in two weeks. Why didn't you tell me?"

"Because until a week ago, I thought you hated me."

"I've never hated you. I just thought I knew your type and wanted nothing to do with that. You can go ahead and put a huge neon sign on me that says 'I was wrong.'"

He laughs at that. "I'll keep that in mind. So, Dani girl, when is your birthday?"

"June fourth."

"Gemini. That tracks."

"You know about astrology?"

He shrugs. "I've read up on occasion. It fascinates me how it can be incredibly accurate for some people and also mirror their enneagram numbers. For some people, it's not accurate at all, though. I don't know. It's fun learning about that stuff. Marketing utilizes psychology and the understanding of people, and zodiac signs, personality types, and enneagram numbers can sometimes help you with that."

"Hm. Now I want to look up how Gemini and Aquarius pair together."

He leans forward and takes my hand. "I don't need to look it up. I already know."

"Oh, yeah? How do they go together?"

"Perfectly." Then he flashes that panty-melting grin that both irritates me and makes me want to jump him. I narrow my eyes at him, but he matches my gaze, holding it with his olive-green eyes before reaching across the table and stealing a bite of my dessert.

My mouth drops open, but he looks at me innocently and pushes his salted caramel crème brûlée toward me so I can take a bite. Damn it, I can't help but smile at the adorable look on his face.

As I take a bite, a snippet from *Pride and Prejudice* hits me. Lizzy and Jane are talking about Mr. Bingley and Mr. Darcy returning and visiting them. Lizzy warns Jane to be careful, and Jane is shocked that Lizzy would think she's 'in danger' of falling for Bingley again. Lizzy smiles at her sister and says she's very much in danger of making Bingley even more in love with her. The implication, of course, is that Jane is in love with Bingley, too, and will only fall more for him.

And while I don't know about love, I'm definitely in danger of falling *hard* for Jesse Wilkinson.

## Jesse

So far, I think we're crushing this first date thing. Dani and I have had a hell of a twisted path to get here, but the more we open up to each other, the more our walls come down. Even though I don't show them, I have walls, too. After what I went through, it's hard for me to feel certain of someone's love or care for me. The more time I spend with Dani, the more I believe she truly wants this—me. It's lame as hell and high school me would probably laugh out loud, but I want to be wanted. As I fall for Dani, that means I want *her* to want me. I want to be her first choice. I hope after our conversation earlier today and then everything we talked about at dinner, we're getting closer to that.

I squeeze Dani's hand as we approach our destination.

"Our next stop is right up here, m'lady." I lead her down the sidewalk to the corner where a huge antiques emporium sits.

"Oh my god..." she breathes, eyes lighting up. She whips her head to look at me. "Are you sure you want to take me in there? I might get distracted and forget about our date. And you." She gives me a wily smile.

I lean in close and whisper. "No way will you forget about *me*." A chill rolls over her as my lips brush her ear. *Damn right, babe.* "Besides, I want to see you in your element, so bring me along into your world. Point things out, show me stuff, get excited. And then choose one thing. Something you love that speaks to you and I'm getting it for you."

Her eyebrows shoot up. "Really? You know antiques can still be expensive, right?"

"Yep. Don't care. And you're going to help me pick something out, too."

She squints at me. "You figured out my love language."

I shrug. "Your passion, at least."

She leans up and presses a soft kiss to my lips. "Let's get lost."

Dani is like a machine as we go through the antiques store. She's organized and focused, going quickly through things, pausing at things one of us is interested in, and making sure we see *everything.* No wonder her clients love her. She's amazing at this. I had no idea what I was looking for when I walked in here, other than the enjoyment of watching her, but as we walked through, she asked me questions that were less for her and more for me.

Now we're at the last few aisles of items before the checkout, and I have my choice. Dani, I can tell, has a mental list of her favorite items so she can go back and choose something. I don't have my item with me because it's too big to carry, but I chose a 1970s record player cabinet. I got into collecting vinyl albums a couple of years ago when one of my favorite artists released a colored vinyl set of their entire discography. Since then, I started going through my grandfather's old record collection, which had been sitting in the basement at my parents' house. While I have a modern record player, this cabinet is so much cooler and it'll be a unique piece of furniture whenever I have my own house one day.

Dani stopped at a few different things, but she lingered the longest at a set of vintage band T-shirts, including Queen and Journey—both of which she told me she loves.

The last two aisles we go down are stocked with books. Many are nothing to write home about, but halfway through the last aisle, she stops in her tracks and picks up an old version of *Pride and Prejudice.*

"This is my favorite book," she breathes, running her hand over the cover. She flips it open and smiles. A perfect Dani smile. Every time I see it, I commit it to memory. That's what I want, to keep thousands—millions—of her smiles. They light up the dark moments and fill my needy, hurting heart. One smile from her heals me more than she could understand.

I step closer, wrapping my arms around her waist and looking over her shoulder at it.

"There's writing in it."

"Yeah, someone annotated it." She runs her finger over a line of writing in the margin above the paragraph, then she closes the book. "This is it. This is what I want."

I step back and spin her around. "Then it's yours." She leans up and kisses my cheek, then makes a beeline for the checkout. "Hey, Dani."

"Hm?"

"Go get the T-shirts, too."

She stares at me, then she scampers over to the T-shirts, smiling the whole way. I tuck it away. Something to hold on to on lonely nights. Maybe it's stupid, but I hope there will be fewer of those in the future.

We walk up the stairs toward Dani's apartment hand in hand. She's got her shopping bag full of goodies, and my record player cabinet is being delivered tomorrow afternoon.

When we get to Dani's apartment, I press her against the door and give her a hard kiss. She moans against my lips and I instantly harden. She pulls her lips from mine, laughing. "Really? That's all it takes? Are you going to be a one-minute man in bed?"

"Do you want to find out?" I tease, softly kissing her neck, but her hand comes to my chest. I stand up straight and take a step back. "I'm not trying to push you."

"I know. And I do want to find out." Her cheeks go red, and I can't stop my smile. "Just not tonight. But…"

"What?"

"You wanted a continuation of our kisses, right?"

"Definitely."

"Then would you like to stay the night? Nothing more than kissing. And snuggling."

"Dani girl, did you like falling asleep in my arms last weekend?"

"Maybe," she says with a coy smile.

I trace my finger along the edge of her jaw, looking into her wildcat eyes. "Tell me why you liked it." She lets out a shuddery breath as my hand slides down to her neck and I let my lips trace the line of her jaw to that spot just below her ear. "Tell me how

I make you feel." I kiss across her cheek to her lips and press a soft kiss to them. "Tell me."

"You make me feel safe. When your arms were around me, I stopped questioning everything, and I felt. I closed my heart off, yet with your arms around me, I felt what we could be."

"And?" I mutter.

"I liked it," she chokes out. "I wanted it. Wanted you. Us."

I lift her up and lean into her, capturing her mouth in a powerful kiss as she wraps her legs around my waist. I'm forceful and demanding with my kisses, owning her mouth. She's fucking mine. The world might not know it yet, but she does. There are no more questions. She knows I belong to her, and she belongs to me.

"Jesse," she groans, raking her fingers through my hair as I rock my hard-on against her.

"Sorry," I breathe, stepping back and letting her down. "You make me forget where I am and what I'm doing. And... you make it hard to calm down."

A tiny smirk crosses her lips and she steps forward, grabbing my shirt as she presses onto her toes and whispers in my ear. "Don't apologize. I like it." The smirk grows as she drops back to flat feet, spins around, and unlocks her door. Then she picks up her bag and walks inside. "You coming, Wilkinson?"

I quickly step into the apartment and follow her to her bedroom.

When we walk through the door, I stop and take it in. It's filled with vintage furniture, all rehabbed and stained the same. There are pops of color throughout with pillows and wall-hangings. A royal blue and yellow dreamcatcher hangs over her bed. At the far side of the room is a bookcase overflowing with books, both old and new.

She sets her bag down by the old Singer sewing machine she's using as a desk.

Everything about this room screams Dani. I love it. I want to create something like that as well. Other than vaguely with clothes, I've never known my own style. I'm hoping Dani can help me find it, since she's a magician like that.

"I love this room."

She beams at me. "Thank you. It's my space. One day, I want to expand into an entire house because I have so many books that need shelf space, but I didn't have room here. And I have more restored furniture, too. Most of it is being stored in Grandma and Grandpa's barn right now."

She walks over to her closet and pulls a shirt and pair of pajama pants off a rack on the inside of the door, then turns to me.

I look down at my date clothes. "I should've brought sweats with me."

She smiles and turns to her dresser, handing me the clothes I let her borrow last week.

"I washed them for you."

She turns away from me and starts changing. As I unfold my clothes, I realize they smell like her. Not just her detergent. No, they smell like her fucking perfume. *Did she put her perfume on my clothes?*

Damn, that's a flex. I thought guys had it all figured out. We give our clothes to our girls because it's possessive in a sexy way. *See that girl with my last name on her back?* Now she's cranking it up a notch by giving those clothes back to me with her perfume on them, so I'll think about her every time I wear them—hell, touch them. I'd just hold them and sniff them. *Damn, she's good.*

"You gonna put those on, or...?"

I spin to face her and see her smiling innocently at me. *She's gonna kill me.*

"Yep." I quickly pull off my sweater and khakis and slip on the sweats and shirt, then I climb onto the bed next to her.

She's lying down, amber hair splayed over her pillows. I love that color on her. The way it plays off her eyes is absolutely stunning. While I love her hair in any color, I secretly hope she'll keep it like this for a while.

I lie down next to her and wrap my arm around her back as she snuggles closer to me.

"Mm, you smell good," she whispers.

Threading my fingers through her hair, I crush my mouth against hers and kiss her deeply, beginning an hour-long make-out session that's more intimate than some of the sex I've had in my life. I understand what she was saying earlier, about how my arms make her feel. Being with her does things to me too. It makes me feel alive. It makes me feel seen. When she pushes all those fears and insecurities away, she looks into my eyes and just sees me.

We break our kiss when she yawns. Then I yawn, and we both laugh.

"Maybe that's a sign we should get some sleep," she says.

"What are you doing tomorrow?" I ask.

She laughs. "Hanging out with you."

"Such a good answer." I kiss her again. "Then yeah, we can go to sleep. As long as I get to kiss you more tomorrow."

"You better." She kisses my cheek. "Night, Wilkinson."

She flips off her lamp and I pull her close, then press my lips to her temple. "Night, Dani girl."

Then, for the second Friday in a row, I fall asleep with Dani in my arms.

# 14

# Pain Reliever

## Dani

"I'm glad we were able to sneak in some roommate bonding time this morning," Amelia says. I'm genuinely surprised by how well we hit it off, especially since she seemed a little closed off initially.

"Me too. It's nice feeling like I have a friend here in Ida who is just mine and didn't come from my cousins," I say with a laugh.

She reaches over and squeezes my leg. "You definitely do. Glad I took a chance on you." She sips on her tea, smiling over the rim at me.

"I think I'm relatively easy to live with. Just let me decorate things and I'm happy."

"It's true. And our bedrooms are far enough apart that I haven't heard you getting freaky with Jesse."

I roll my eyes. "We have not *gotten freaky* yet."

"Could've fooled me based on how I found you two on the couch the other night."

"We'd had an emotional conversation, and it led to some... intense kissing."

"Uh huh."

"Shut up. Are you saying you never lose yourself when you're kissing a sexy guy?"

She looks down at her mug of tea. "I don't usually focus on the kissing. We get down to the orgasms pretty quickly."

"Who broke your heart?"

"What?" she asks, surprised.

"Look, I get the hookup and never see them again thing. I didn't act on it after my breakup with my ex, but I had no desire to even consider letting myself fall for someone else. I never felt that way until I had my heart broken and my trust taken advantage of. So, who hurt you? And do you have his address so I can punch him in the nads?"

She laughs at that. "I probably still have his parents' address, but that's the best I could do. If you must know, he was my high school boyfriend. He strung me along, then broke up with me when I needed him the most. It sucked. I spent the next few years traveling and in college. Hookups were better, and frankly, I started to enjoy them more. As long as you're safe, they're low risk with a solid reward—if you're selective. No damage to the heart."

I nod in understanding. "I didn't want to risk damage to my heart, either. Somehow, though, it stopped being my choice. So, just be aware that there is *some* danger in hooking up. You never know if your soulmate is looking for a hookup, too."

"If he's my soulmate, that's all he'll want."

"If you say so." I smile at her, letting her know I'm on to her bullshit. No one is impervious to love, and given how Amelia has opened up to me, I think she wants that more than she'd admit.

"Speaking of soulmates, where's yours?"

"It's too early for a soulmate conversation, okay?" I check the time. "He is late, though."

"Text him."

"I did. A couple of times. He hasn't responded."

She looks at the clock. "Whoa, he's almost an hour late."

"Yeah, at first I wasn't worried because I didn't know if he was one of those chronically late people. Now..." I clear my throat, trying to tamp down my anxiety. *Why didn't he text me back? Why isn't he here?* It's unlike him. Especially given he spent the night Friday night and then we spent all day together yesterday. He went home last night after another long make-out session. My insecurities are raging, but I'm trying not to give into them. He keeps asking me to trust him. It's hard to trust him over the nagging voices in my head right now. "Anyway, I was thinking I'd go check on him." I rise from the couch and take my mug to the kitchen, then pause before walking to the door. "Do you think it's stupid for me to go check on him? I mean, I doubt he'd ghost me when we haven't even had sex yet," I attempt to joke.

"Or maybe he ghosted you because you didn't sleep with him." My eyes widen as her joking comment hits my very real insecurities. Seeing my expression, she stands and walks over to me. "Hey, I was kidding. For what it's worth, he doesn't seem like that kind of guy. He seems to adore you, and I have a pretty good read on people." She rubs my arm. "Go check on him."

I nod, grab my bag, and head out of the apartment. Since he only lives a couple of blocks away, I walk, fighting against my negative thoughts on the way.

*He cares about me.* After the last two days, there's no way he would be leading me on. In turn, that makes me sick to my stomach. Because if he's not leading me on... what's going on? Am I going to walk into his house and find his dead body?

My blood runs cold at the thought, tears pricking in my eyes. Now I'm worried. I don't know when I started cutting off pieces of my heart and handing it to him, but I did. He matters to me, and though it's hard to trust, I believe I matter to him, too.

When I get to the house, his car is in the driveway, but I don't see any lights on inside. The nausea I'm feeling grows, so I hurry around to the back of the house and find the hidden key, my mind racing with worst-case scenarios.

It's dark in the kitchen when I walk in. Locking the door behind me, I slip off my shoes, then walk through the living room to the stairwell, my legs shaking. When I get to the top of the stairs, I see the light in the bathroom is on, but I see no sign of Jesse. Maybe the light is a good thing. Swallowing my fears, I walk down the hall to his room. The door is ajar, so I push it open and step inside. It's nearly pitch black other than the light from the hallway streaming in. I grab my phone from my bag and turn on the flashlight. Looking around the room, I see Jesse in bed, asleep, but not comfortable from the looks of it. He groans in his sleep, and I notice a small bucket on the floor next to him. I let out a sigh of relief. He's okay, but he's clearly sick.

I set my bag down, close the door again, then climb onto the bed next to him. Once I'm settled, I switch off my flashlight and open the ebook I've been reading, settling in to read until he wakes up.

I've been reading for nearly an hour when Jesse groans, then moves suddenly. A second later, he leans over the bed and feels around for the bucket, grabbing it and pulling it up. He dry heaves for a second, then throws up twice.

I set my phone down and lean over, rubbing his back as he whimpers. "Shh, you're okay," I whisper, running my hand up and into his hair.

"Dani?" he mumbles, still leaning over the side of the bed. He moves slightly, looking up. "What time is—shit. Oh, fuck." He sets the bucket down and rolls over. "I'm sorry. I'm so sorry. I—"

"Shh," I say again. "It's fine. You're obviously sick. Stomach bug?"

He shakes his head. "Migraine. I get them every so often—not usually this bad, though. I haven't had one like this in a couple of years. I thought if I laid down, maybe it would settle and I could still see you. I must have fallen asleep."

He flips his lamp on the lowest setting, then grunts and rolls back over, looking at me, but keeping his face shielded from the light as much as possible.

"That sounds awful," I whisper, still playing with his hair. "Is there anything I can do? Get you? Does anything help?"

He rubs his forehead. "I took ibuprofen, but it didn't help. Caffeine helps, but the thought of drinking coffee..." He groans again. "They make acetaminophen with caffeine in it, but we don't have any. Sometimes hydrating helps." The tiniest smirk creeps onto his face—as much of one as he can muster. "An orgasm."

I raise my eyebrows. "Are you fucking with me?"

"No. It honestly does help. There's even science behind it. I looked it up once. As much as I wish I could be *fucking* with you, I can barely move, so I think an orgasm is out of the question."

"Yes, you need to rest," I say, though there's a warmth blooming in my stomach. *Not right now, Dani.* Ignoring me, he tries to sit up, only to collapse back on the bed. "What are you doing?"

"I've gotta take care of that." He gestures to the side of the bed. He tries to sit up again, but I push him back down.

"Lay down." I climb over the top of him. "I'll take care of it. And see what I can find that might help your migraine."

He looks up at me in awe. "You don't have to."

"I know." I lean down and kiss his cheek. "Rest. I'll be back." I pick up the bucket of barf and move the garbage can over. "Just in case." Then I head for the bathroom and clean the bucket out. I leave it in the bathroom and go downstairs, rummaging through the kitchen to see if there are any of the pain meds Jesse mentioned since there weren't any in the bathroom. I don't find any, but another idea occurs to me, and I quickly text Amelia, asking her to bring something over.

While I wait, I make some lemon ginger tea, not letting the bag steep too long, but enough to add some flavor. Once that's done, I find myself wondering how serious Jesse was about the orgasm thing, so I Google it. I'm shocked to find a bunch of scientific articles about it. There are a few different reasons why, depending on the type of headache, but apparently the increase in dopamine is one thing that can help.

Knocking on the back door jolts me out of my research, and I run over and open it. Amelia hands me a few bottles of the caffeine water she keeps in the fridge.

"Thank you. You're the best."

"No problem. I hope it helps. Caffeine usually helps with my headaches, so it's worth a shot. Let me know if you need anything else."

"Will do. Thanks, Ames."

"Of course. See you later." She grins at me. "Or maybe not."

With a laugh, she's gone, and I shut and lock the door again, then I dig around the kitchen until I find a wooden tray I can carry everything upstairs on. I stop at the bathroom and grab the bucket and the towel, barely managing to hold them with the tray in my hands.

Jesse looks up when I return to the room.

"I've got a few things for you," I say softly, setting the bucket and towel on the floor and the tray on the bedside table. "Lemon ginger tea to help with nausea. I steeped it lightly, and put some cool water in it so it's room temp and you can sip it through a straw. Then I've got the strongest Tylenol I could find—no caffeine in it, but Amelia brought over this caffeine water she drinks. Coffee doesn't settle well with her, but the caffeine water is fine. No weird taste, so you can try that. I brought a straw for that, too."

"You did all this for me?" he asks, genuinely surprised.

I squat down next to the bed and run my hand through his hair. "Of course I did. You deserve to be taken care of. I want to be the one to do that for you."

He looks at me with glassy eyes. "Thank you. That means a lot to me."

"Has no one ever taken care of you when you feel like this?"

"Not really. My mom did when I was young. I started getting migraines like this in late elementary school. She'd bring water and Tylenol and rub my back. Once they weren't around as much, Joel would make sure I had pain meds and water and tell me to text him if I needed him, but I usually took care of myself."

"What about your ex?" I ask. I know it ended badly, but I can't imagine seeing the person I was dating suffer and not want to take care of them.

He laughs bitterly. "She'd get me pain meds and sit with me for a bit, then she'd start complaining about how boring it was and everything she was missing out on if we had to cancel plans with friends. It got to the point where I'd tell her to just go without me when I was sick or had a migraine, so I didn't have to listen to her complain about how my pain was inconveniencing her."

Leaning over, I press my lips against his cheek. "I'm so sorry she treated you like that. You deserve so much better."

He takes my hand and looks into my eyes. "I have someone so much better."

My heart flies out of my chest at his words. This learning to trust again thing is so damn hard, but he makes it worth it.

Our gaze on each other lingers for another moment before I grab the caffeine water and hold it out to him. He drinks a bit, then takes a couple Tylenol and drinks some more. He also sips on the tea before rolling onto his back and letting out a long breath.

"How are you feeling?" I ask as I grab the towel and climb into bed with him, pulling the sheets up over me.

"Still a lot of pain, but the nausea has stopped for the moment at least."

"Good."

"What's the towel for?" he asks, squinting to avoid the light seeping in from the hallway.

I bite my cheek, feeling nervous.

*Maybe this was a dumb idea.*

I hesitate for a moment. "It's... you said an orgasm would help. I looked it up and... you're in too much pain to do anything, but maybe I could do something for you."

His eyes go wide. "Oh."

"If you want me to."

He smiles softly. "If you want to, I'm yours."

I exhale a sigh of relief. Leaning forward, I kiss his neck. "I want to help you," I breathe. "Relax you. Make you feel better. Do you have lube?"

He nods. "Bedside drawer." His voice is thick and raspy.

This is a completely crazy way to have our first sexual interaction, but I truly do want to make him feel better.

I grab the lube from the drawer and settle in next to him.

"If it's too much or you need me to stop, just tell me."

"I will."

He runs his hand through my hair, looking at me reverently.

"Relax," I whisper, kissing his cheek as I push down his sweats and boxers. I squirt some lube into my hand then reach for his semi.

The moment my fingers wrap around his length, he hardens fully, gasping with pleasure.

I am so damn horny just from this, I might have a mini orgasm when I see him come.

Slowly, I stroke him, applying slight pressure. With my other hand, I play with his hair.

He lets out a long groan as my fingers brush his tip, and though in any other instance I would tease him, this is about relief.

Keeping my pace steady, I increase the pressure and work him as he moans.

He's still squinting, trying to block out the light.

"Close your eyes," I whisper. "Breathe deep. Let go."

He does, letting his eyes close and his body go limp.

I stroke him harder and faster, relishing his moans and groans as the throbbing between my legs intensifies.

His moans get breathier and higher-pitched until he's whimpering. I grab the towel and position it between us, then finish him with a few hard strokes.

I watch raptly as he comes, relief and pleasure mixing on his face. He's still breathing hard, but hasn't opened his eyes. I wipe my hand with the towel, then clean him up before pulling his boxers and sweats back up. He looks more contented now, but still hasn't opened his eyes. I run my clean hand through his hair, then kiss his forehead and climb out of bed, tucking him in before I put the towel in the laundry and wash up.

When I get back to the room, he's snoring softly, sleeping much better than he was when I first got here.

My heart lights knowing I helped him be more comfortable. I crawl under the covers, wrap my arm around him, and close my eyes.

# Jesse

I wake slowly, disoriented. *Where am I? Who am I? How long have I been asleep? Is it night or day?*

A glance at the clock tells me it's just past two in the afternoon. Afternoon. As my brain processes, it all comes back to me. Waking up early this morning to a migraine, trying to deal with it, falling asleep, Dani showing up. *Dani.* I look around, but don't see her, though her bag is still on the floor by the end of the bed.

I'm glad she didn't leave, and I'm grateful for how she took care of me. The caffeine water was a brilliant idea and definitely helped. So did that orgasm. It was fucking hot watching her take control, wanting to make me feel better—and she did. I was so relaxed I was half-asleep by the time I came, which made the orgasm stronger, but also more peaceful than I've ever experienced. It also knocked me the hell out. I slept hard for the last hour and a half, and I feel a lot better now. My nausea is completely gone, as is most of my migraine. I still have some vague pain, but otherwise, I'm almost back to normal. Except that I'm starving.

Slowly, I push myself up to sitting, expecting my head to throb when I do, but it doesn't. I take a drink of the caffeine water, letting it soothe my dry throat. I stand up and take my time walking downstairs, feeling grateful when the light doesn't hurt. I'm halfway down the stairs when I smell food cooking. My stomach rumbles and warmth spreads through me.

*She's still taking care of me.*

I've been with Dani all of two days, and in that short time, I've realized how crappy my relationship with Carrie actually was—or rather how one-sided it was. She cared about me, but she didn't care *for* me. Yet I always took care of her.

I missed meeting up with Dani, didn't text her, then she showed up here and took care of me in every way. Though I hate how her ex treated her, I'm glad it got her out of that relationship. He didn't deserve the way she loves. Sometimes I'm not sure I do, either, but I'm sure as hell grateful for it.

"Hey," I say softly, walking into the kitchen.

She spins around from where she's standing at the stove, a giant smile on her face. "Hey, how are you feeling?"

"A lot better. I've got a bit of a sickness hangover and my head still hurts a little, but those are both normal when I'm coming down from a migraine." I walk over and wrap my arms around her, pulling her close. "Thank you for taking care of me."

"Stop thanking me," she whispers, squeezing me tightly. "You deserve to be taken care of."

"Just know I'll always do the same for you, Dani girl. You deserve it too."

She looks up at me like she might kiss me, but then she sniffs a couple of times and flips the burner off. Grabbing two plates, she puts a grilled cheese sandwich on each, smiling happily at the perfectly browned exterior. "Hungry?"

"Mm. Yes. That smells amazing."

"Perfect. I figured grilled cheese was a good option. Easy to eat, not super flavorful, and one of the ultimate comfort foods."

"These look perfect."

"I love grilled cheese."

"Come on, you goof. Let's eat in the living room."

We're snuggled in the corner of the couch, talking after devouring two grilled cheese sandwiches each. I might have to beg this girl to make me a grilled cheese at least once a week because damn, they were perfect.

"So, tell me the truth. Were you mad when I didn't show up this morning?"

She shakes her head. "No. Not really."

"Were you worried I was ditching you?"

She lifts her head off my shoulder and looks up at me. "That kind of thought was rolling around in the back of my mind, but I chose not to listen. I chose to believe what you've told me and trust what I've seen."

Wrapping my hand around her neck, I lower my lips to hers and kiss her deeply. She slides onto my lap and drapes her arms around my neck, kissing me back as ferociously as I'm kissing her. I'm falling harder for this girl than I ever could've imagined. After everything Carrie put me through, it was hard to keep believing in a better future—a new forever with someone else—but Dani has made me believe in it again and want it in a way I never have before. I'll be so screwed if she breaks my heart, but like her, I'm trying to trust. It's not always easy, but in moments like this, nothing could be more natural. When her body feels like an extension of me and her heart holds pieces of mine, it's impossible not to believe in a future with her. It also makes me want her more than I've ever wanted another person.

"Dani," I whisper, pulling back. "How are you feeling?" She looks at me, confused, so I continue. "I was thinking if you have a headache or anything, I know a way to fix it."

She stares at me for a moment, then her eyes flare when she realizes what I'm saying.

"Come to think of it," she breathes, "my head does hurt a little." Her cheeks flush and her breathing quickens, but she doesn't drop my gaze.

"I guess I better take care of that, then." I shift on the couch, laying her down next to me. Then I pull off her shirt and am rewarded with the sight of her hardened nipples poking through a thin cotton bralette. I run the pads of my thumbs over them, roughly stroking them through the fabric. Her back arches, and I want more. I pull her upright again and pull her bra off, tangling my hand in her hair to hold her in place as I play with her nipples, sucking them and biting them.

"Ahh..." she rolls her hips toward me.

*Easy, babe, I'm going to savor this.*

Leaning her back against the couch, I let my mouth roam lower, kissing down her stomach until I hit the waistband of her leggings. Heat radiates off her, making me harder by the second. I *need* to taste her.

I love sex, always have. When I lost my virginity, I laid there thinking it was the best thing that ever happened to me. For the price of a condom, I could experience the power of pleasing someone else and then having the same release. Before I ever had sex, though, I was obsessed with something else—and I still am—oral sex. I love tasting a girl, teasing her, feeling her wet pussy against my tongue. It's intoxicating. Carrie and I hadn't done foreplay like that nearly as often in the last few months of our relationship. Now I finally have the chance again with this goddess of a woman splayed on the couch in front of me.

I pull her leggings and underwear off at the same time, revealing her glistening pussy. *And it's all mine.*

I don't waste another second. Pushing her legs up, I dive between them.

Her moan is loud and instantaneous. She wraps her hands around her thighs, digging her fingers in. I lick up her center, then swirl my tongue over her clit. Her butt shoots off the couch, so I wrap my arms around her thighs and hold her tight to my face as I eat her pussy. She tastes sweet and salty—perfectly Dani.

The strokes of my tongue are gentle but powerful. She moans again and rakes her fingers through my hair.

"Jesse... ahh... that feels so good."

I continue the pattern of flicking her clit a couple of times, then swirling my tongue around it, but absolutely none of this is enough for me. I need her falling apart. Screaming my name. I need her to forget where she is—forget about anything but us.

Releasing one thigh, I slip my hand down and circle her opening with one finger and then two, before slowly pushing them inside. I give her a second to adjust, then I curve my fingertips forward and pump in and out of her hard and fast.

"Oh my god," she cries out. "Fuck, Jesse..."

*That's right, baby. Say my fucking name.* I can't wait until I get to talk her through an orgasm.

"Holy shit, don't stop. Please don't—ah! Oh..."

She whimpers and moans, rocking her body against my face as I own her clit and her pussy.

Her walls tighten and so do her legs, urging me on.

She pulls on my hair, then tries to wriggle away.

"Oh my god. I need to—I'm going to—" She screams as she squirts, shaking and gasping, trying to break free, but I don't let her. We're almost there. After a second, she settles, and her thighs tighten around my head. "Shit. Jesse. Jesse!" *Oh yeah.* She comes apart, filling my mouth with her decadent flavor. I suck it down like it's my last meal. I'll never get enough of her. I wait until she's stopped spasming before pulling my fingers out. I take one long lick of her pussy before sitting back on my heels.

She reaches for me, grabbing my wrist and pulling me over the top of her. I kiss her softly, but she kicks it up a notch, absolutely voracious.

"You need more?" I mutter against her lips.

She nods. "It's crazy. That orgasm was an incredible release, but it made me want even more," she says breathlessly. She brushes her hand over the crotch of my sweats. "Seems like you need something, too."

I shift off her, so I'm standing, bent over her. As she pushes down my sweats and boxers and wraps her hand around my shaft for the second time today, I almost come like some prepubescent kid who can't control himself. I'm convinced she could make me come without ever touching me.

*Keep it together. She needs more, too.*

Grazing my fingers down her abdomen, I slide them between her legs, pushing two fingers inside her like I did before. This time, instead of my tongue, I use my thumb on her clit, coating it in her wetness first, then flicking it and swirling around it. That combo seems to be the perfect thing for her.

Her breath shudders and she whimpers.

"Yes, babe. Take what you want. Ride my hand."

She continues stroking me, but it's erratic. She's too focused on her own pleasure, and that's what I want. I'm painfully hard, but I'll get my chance after she's had hers.

"You like my fingers inside you? You like how I play with your clit?"

"Y—yes. Oh, please don't stop."

"I don't stop till you come, babe. Let go, let me see how beautiful you are when you come for me."

"I'm so close."

"What do you need?"

"Faster, on my clit."

I do what she wants, and her hand drops off my cock as she rocks her hips into me.

"Yes. Right there. Oh..."

She grabs the edge of the couch, crying out as her eyes slip closed and she comes hard.

"Yes, babe. You're perfect. So fucking beautiful when you come on my hand. Good girl."

Her eyes flash open and she smirks at me, wrapping her hand around my cock again and making me groan.

I pull my hand from between her legs and lick my fingers.

"You like how I taste?" she asks.

*Oh shit. Is she going to talk me through an orgasm?* I shudder at the thought. It's possible I enjoy a bit of praise. And when a girl takes control.

"Yes, babe. You taste delectable."

"Mm, I bet you taste even better." She grabs my hips and pulls me forward, and the next thing I know, her lips are around my cock, sucking, licking, taking me deep.

*Ah, fuck.*

I grab her hair and thrust into her mouth, trying not to choke her—that's for after our first time, once we've discussed it.

She moans around my cock, and I am not going to fucking last. I don't think she wants me to. She guides my hips, alternating her pattern of long sucks to bobbing her head up and down on my dick.

"Fuck, Dani." I groan again, rolling my hips toward her. "I'm so fucking close." She sucks hard, then pulls back before taking me so deep I hit the back of her throat. That does it. I see stars as I come in her mouth.

When I'm finished, she holds me there for a second, then releases me, licking her lips. "Good boy," she whispers.

*Dead. I'm fucking dead.*

Panting, I climb onto the couch and wrap my arm around her.

"Best you've ever had?" I ask teasingly.

She rolls her eyes. "Eh, it was okay..."

I run my hand down her thigh. "Well, I don't need to do any of that again, if it was just okay..."

She glares at me, then snuggles closer. After a moment, she whispers, "You made me squirt. No one's ever done that before. It was amazing."

*Ego boost of the century.*

"Well, as much as that makes me want to jump on the table and beat my chest, I'm a little exhausted, because that *was* amazing. And you calling me a good boy..."

Her eyes light up. "Hm?"

"It was a big turn on," I rasp.

"I'll remember that." She kisses my neck. "I know I didn't handle things right the night we kissed in October, but I'm glad we didn't go further. It wouldn't have meant as much as this did."

"Dani, I never would've let you go further than you were comfortable with. And I never wanted just one night with you. I always wanted more. I wanted this."

She smiles a little, biting her lip. "We ended up where we were supposed to be. I don't think I would've been ready then."

"But you are now?"

She laughs lightly, looking at our mostly naked bodies. "I think that's obvious."

I softly kiss her and look into her eyes. "Does that mean you're my girlfriend?"

"Is that what you want me to be?"

"Nah. I thought it would be more fun to call you the-girl-down-the-street-who-I'm-kinda-dating. Has a nice ring to it, right?"

"A little wordy."

I sit up, pulling her upright, too. "Dani girl, will you be my girlfriend or do I have to get on my knees and beg?"

"Ooh, I like the sound of you on your knees. Don't give me ideas."

"Dani..."

"Yes, Jesse. I will be your girlfriend."

"Good, because I don't ever want you questioning my feelings for you. I want you to know I'm in this."

She pushes my shaggy hair off my forehead. "I know you are. So am I." She bites her lip.

"You still want to wait to tell people?"

"Is that okay? It just seems like everything will be more complicated once *everyone* knows."

I swallow my fears, reminding myself she's not Carrie. She's not trying to hide this. She's trying to protect it.

"Yeah, that's fine. As long as I still get to kiss you like this," I kiss her neck. "As long as you're mine."

"I'm yours, Wilkinson. Especially if you keep kissing me like that."

"I could keep doing that." I kiss her neck again, and then her lips. "I could kiss you like this all damn day." I grab a blanket and pull it over us, content to spend the rest of the day on this couch with her, kissing her until neither of us can think straight anymore.

# 15
# Ruthlessly Sexy

## Jesse

I CROSS ANOTHER BUSINESS off my list now that they're positioned on the layout for the NICU fundraiser. Like at the winter carnival, I'm keeping the food trucks separated, so people will walk around more and discover more things. This is the relatively easy part.

Finding the right mix of entertainment and family fun has been trickier. We're going to have a kids' corner where there will be a local musician singing songs, puppet shows, and all kinds of other fun things. I've made sure there will be plenty of seating there so parents can use it as a place to rest with their kids. We also have a feeding and changing tent for quiet feedings and changing. There will even be a few booths for pumping. I can't take credit for that. Our secretary is a new mom and gave me a whole list of things to include. Seeing as this is a NICU fundraiser, that's exactly what it should be.

I pinch the bridge of my nose, my eyes glazing over. I close them and immediately an image of Dani flashes through my mind. I didn't get to see her last night because we had an away swim meet. After what we did on Sunday, we couldn't keep our hands off each other. We took a nap on the couch, then took things up to my bedroom for another round. We haven't moved on to sex, but as someone who has a tendency to rush, I like taking things slower with her. We spent the night together on Monday and I made her squirt again. It's crazy to me that she's shocked when it happens, because it's not hard to get her there.

Do I take pride in knowing I'm the only one who has ever made her do that?

Yes.

But do I feel like a cocky son of a bitch because I can work her body so perfectly?

One hundred percent, yes.

There's a knock on my office door, so I reluctantly open my eyes, pushing the thoughts of Dani away.

"Come in."

The door swings open and, to my surprise, Garrett walks in.

"Hey, man."

"Hey. What are you doing here?"

He plops down in the chair in front of my desk. "Ev's nagging me about what we're doing for your birthday. I'm here to find out what you want to eat for your birthday dinner."

"Why doesn't he just ask me at swim practice tonight?"

"Uh, yeah. He doesn't know I'm asking you. The dinner is a 'surprise.' So, shh."

"Wow. Thanks."

"Like you didn't know we'd do something. Obviously, we've got to celebrate you. Did you want us to invite Dani? I don't know where you two are on the officially dating meter."

"We're official. Just not officially telling everyone in our lives yet."

"Why not?"

I shrug. "She's not ready. And I get that. My brother, Rae, all of them will ask a billion questions. Give us shit. It's nice that it's quiet while we settle into this."

"As long as you're cool with it. She seems like a chill girl, even if she is a little crazy."

"I'll be sure to tell her you said that."

"I'll tell her myself. I've gotta invite her to your birthday dinner, anyway. But remember, it's a surprise." He taps his nose twice.

He's ridiculous. I swear, he and Evan are like Merry and Pippin—if Merry and Pippin had secretly been in love and gotten married. That would've made *Lord of the Rings* more diverse. Maybe more interesting, too.

"Whatever you say." He drums his thumbs on the arms of the chair. "Did you need something else?"

"Yes, your attention. Entertain me."

I throw a balled-up piece of paper at him. "I'm working. Don't you have something better to do?"

He groans. "Yeah. I'm on assignment from your girl to go pick paint colors." He makes a face.

"So really, I'm your distraction."

"Precisely." He winks and does a finger-gun point.

"Why am I friends with you?"

He puts his hands under his chin like he's an angel. "Because you love me, obviously."

"Eh."

He holds his chest in mock offense, but I ignore him. Mostly because Dani just sent me an email, and she's far more entertaining than G. I click on her email and read through it.

*Mr. Wilkinson,*

*Attached, please find design options for the signs for the NICU fundraiser. Since purple is for prematurity awareness month, I went with variations of that color. Please let me know if you have any questions.*

*Sincerely,*

*Dani Malone*

I blink a couple of times, then grab my phone and text her.

**Me: Are we roleplaying?**

**Dani: Uh, no? If you're suggesting you want to, you have my interest.**

**Me: Mental note. I was referring to your very formal email.**

My phone rings, and I smile like a dumbass when I see her name.

"Hey, Dani girl."

"Sorry. I wasn't sure if your bosses could view your emails. Or HR. I was trying to keep things businesslike."

"Oh, you don't have to apologize. I like the sound of *Mr. Wilkinson.*" Across the desk, G makes a loud retching noise. "Payback," I tell him.

"Who are you talking to?" Dani asks.

"Who am I talking to?" Garrett waves his hands in front of his face in an attempt to stop me from telling Dani he's here. Fat chance. "That would be Garrett. He's hiding out here so he doesn't have to pick out paint colors."

"Traitor," he grumbles, dragging his hands down his face.

"Put him on speaker," Dani says authoritatively, and I immediately start thinking of ways to get her to call me *Mr. Wilkinson* in that tone later.

With absolutely zero loyalty, I put the phone on speaker.

"Okay, you're on with G."

"Garrett," she hisses. "Why are you hiding from paint?"

He groans. "I hate picking colors for shit, Dani. That's why I hired you."

"Look, I'm designing *your* business. I can't pick the colors for you. It's not that hard. Get your ass out of Jesse's office and go to the hardware store. Pick a bunch of colors you even kind of like, then I'll tell you which ones are trash." When he doesn't say anything, she continues, "Now. Or I'll find you and drag you by the ear."

He shoots me a death glare and I smile brightly in return. "Fine, crazy girl, I'm going."

"Ugh. Can that nickname die already?"

"Never." He pushes out of his chair. "Thanks for the help, asshole."

"No problem," I say as he walks out of the office. I grab my phone and take it off speaker. "He's gone."

"Good. Now I'm going to text Evan and make sure he does as he's told."

"You're ruthless."

"It's fun."

"It's sexy."

"Yeah?"

"Definitely."

"That mean we're still on for our date tonight? I missed you last night."

"I'll be there a little after five. And did you miss me? Or my tongue?"

For a second, all I hear is the sound of her breathing. "Maybe both."

"Good, something to keep you hanging on until tonight."

"Whatever you say, *Mr. Wilkinson*."

Damn it, why is she so good at that?

"I need to get back to work before I get a hard-on."

"Aw, but what fun is that?"

"I'll see you later."

"Yes, you will. Bye."

She hangs up and I lean back in my chair, willing the blood to flow away from my dick.

Focusing back on my computer, I look through the ideas she sent for the signs. She's so damn talented.

Sexy, talented, smart, caring, and knows exactly how to push my buttons.

Five out of five ain't bad.

# Dani

"Hello," Amelia calls from the kitchen as I walk into our apartment.

"Hey," I yell back, slipping off my shoes and hanging up my bag. "I had the best day." I walk into the kitchen and over to the counter.

"Best day, huh?"

"I get to design a *Stranger Things* themed bedroom. *And* a romance themed one. The kids of the people I'm designing for are awesome. I mean, the whole house has been fun, but this is the ultimate. It's the combination of my two loves. I also managed to get Garrett to go paint shopping. Oh, and I got a bunch of sign ideas over to Jesse for the NICU fundraiser, plus we're going on a date tonight."

Amelia leans over the kitchen counter on her elbows, smiling at me. "You're living your best life."

I smile at that—actually I can't stop smiling. "I really am." Suddenly, I feel emotional. My mind goes to the list I made. *Live my passion. Find the sunshine again.* It took some time but I really do feel like I'm finally living the life I wanted—the life I deserve.

"What's that face?" Amelia asks.

"You're going to pick on me."

"Probably, but tell me anyway."

"Okay, when I first came up here in late May, I made a list of things I wanted out of life. I didn't write *live my best life* on there, but it was the overall implication. Given where I was then, it feels good to be here now."

"That is sappy and adorable. Perfectly you."

"Thanks for being a part of it. I didn't know where I'd end up, so I didn't have anything about making new friends on my list, but I'm really glad I did." I laugh. "In fact, I referred to you as my best friend to Olivia today. She was unamused."

Amelia laughs. "For someone I've only talked to on video calls with you, I can tell she's possessive. Definitely tell her I'm encroaching on her territory and she should be worried."

"Believe me, she's already there."

My phone rings, and I wonder if it's Olivia sensing that we're talking about her. When I look, though, I see Garrett's name.

"Oh, it's Garrett. You're coming next weekend, right?"

"I can't get the day off Friday, but depending on the weather, I'll come up either Friday night or Saturday morning."

"Given that you're a workaholic, I'll take that compromise." I wink at her and walk into the living room as I answer my phone. "Hey, G."

"Dani."

"Are you calling about next weekend or to cuss me out about paint colors?"

"That was mean..."

"But?"

"I found some I liked," he huffs.

"Ha!"

"Anyway, about next weekend."

"Everything set up?"

"Yep. I have the day off lined up with Jesse's boss. Day passes at the ski resort for Saturday are booked and Evan is picking which restaurants we should eat at. Brooks is handling food and drinks for the cabin—with a list provided by Evan. Jesse told me what he wants for his birthday dinner and I successfully convinced him we're all having dinner at my place. What time do you want to leave on Friday?"

"It takes two-and-a-half hours to get there, right?"

"Yep."

"Around ten? That'll give us plenty of time there on Friday to hang out, explore the area, maybe go tubing."

"Oh yeah. Let me see if that place needs passes as well."

"You're the best. Thank you for helping plan all this."

"Of course." He pauses. "Thanks for wanting to do this for him. You two are good together."

"Thanks," I say, blushing.

There's a quick knock on the front door, then it opens. "Hello," Jesse calls.

"Jesse's here. I gotta go," I whisper.

"See you next week."

"Can't wait. See you then. Bye." I quickly hang up.

"Who was that?" Jesse asks.

"No one," I say, turning around and flashing him a little smile, but he's not smiling. He's standing between the kitchen and living room, body rigid.

From the kitchen, Amelia meets my gaze, then quickly goes to her room.

I rise from the couch and look at him.

"No one?" he asks, anger and hurt in his voice. "No one like a client or no one like some other person you're talking to?"

My mouth drops open. *Did he seriously just say that?*

When I look in his eyes, though, there's very little anger. He mostly looks scared and hurt. The initial surge of anger I felt fades and I think of all he's told me—especially about his ex. How she talked to that guy behind his back. Of course what I just said would trigger him. I don't want to give away the surprise, but I will if I have to. Nothing is worth him feeling worried about this.

"Come here," I say softly.

He looks up but doesn't move. "Why?"

"Wilkinson, get over here." I hold out my hand to him, and he takes it, though he still looks uncertain. I lead him into my room and push him onto the bed, then I climb on next to him and take his hand. "That was Garrett. I really don't want to tell you what we were talking about because it's... something special. But if you need to know for your own peace of mind, I'll tell you."

He looks down and rubs his hands over his face. "I'm sorry. I shouldn't have said that."

"It's okay," I whisper, rubbing his back. "I understand why you did."

"No. It's not okay. I've been asking you to trust me, and then I didn't trust you."

"Because this is the first time you've really felt triggered. I felt triggered a lot when we first reconnected. It was your patience and support that helped me move past that. And I still feel that way sometimes, but this sweet, charming guy I know told me that when I feel triggered, I need to talk about it. Talk to me." I thread my fingers through his and squeeze his hand.

"The charming guy sounds smart," he says with a soft smile.

"He can be. At least when he's not being annoying," I tease.

He leans forward and kisses my cheek. "Thank you for being understanding."

"I owe you that much, but I get it, too. We both have baggage. We just have to keep talking through it."

He nods. "I hate feeling unwanted," he admits. "Between Carrie and how my parents can be sometimes... that's what hits the hardest. More than once, Carrie made me feel like second best—if that. She didn't know what she wanted, but she clearly didn't want me and that fucking hurt."

My eyes drift closed. "I didn't really help with that when we were getting to know each other again."

He tucks some hair behind my ear. "No, but I understand why. You were afraid of being played—of not truly being wanted either." My eyes flash open. "We have a lot of the same baggage. It just hits us in different ways because of the people we were with."

I brush my thumb over his cheek. "So, what you're saying is we're a good match."

That half-smile appears. "It seems that way."

"If you ever have a moment where you wonder who I'm talking to or even want to check my phone—"

"Dani, no."

"I'm serious. I might ask you to avoid a conversation or two so I don't reveal any surprises..."

"Like a certain surprise birthday dinner at G and Evan's next weekend?"

I dramatically roll my eyes. "Damn it. How'd you find out?"

He shrugs. "G didn't feel like keeping up the lie."

I bite back my smile, knowing we have something so much better planned.

"Pain in the ass."

Jesse shrugs. "Doesn't matter to me. As long as you're there, I'll be happy."

"I'll be wherever you want me to be," I whisper.

His fingertips brush across my collarbone and up my neck, leaving a trail of sparks behind them. He wraps his hand around the side of my neck. "Right here." Then he kisses me. It's slow and intense, the simple pressure drawing me in and wrapping me up in him.

He pulls me backward onto my bed, kicking his shoes off as he does, but never breaking our kiss. Holding me, he rolls me onto my back and rests his weight over me, deepening our kiss by twisting his tongue around mine.

I throw my arms around his neck, enjoying the feel of his body over mine. I pull him tighter, losing myself in our kiss—how much I want him. It took so long for me to feel safe with someone again. I never thought it would be him, but he broke down my walls and found the keys to all my locks. His unwavering support and patience proved again and again that we were worth the risk. Worth everything.

Pulling back, I look up at him, smiling as I do. The freckles, the gorgeous green eyes, swollen lips, and messy hair.

I bite my lip as I breathe, "Let's stay in tonight."

## Jesse

*Let's stay in tonight.*

My eyes flare at the implication of her words. Not that I want to rush, but I've been letting her set the pace. I'm not against taking things further, but I'm a little surprised she wants to. But when I look into her eyes, what I see is desire with a hint of that bright Dani joy.

*No, I'm not against this at all.* She tilts her pelvis up so she brushes my hard-on. *I'm very much for this.* But we've got to have a little fun, right?

I brush my lips down her neck. "And what would we do if we stay in?"

She turns her neck to the side, giving me more access. "Order food, eat in bed." She pauses and takes a breath, trying to steady herself. "Then fuck each other until we can't breathe," she says nonchalantly.

I rip my lips from her neck and stare down at her, a slight smile on my face. "You have the order wrong. If you think I'm letting you eat before I bury myself inside of you, you're sorely mistaken. The only thing you'll be eating is my cock, but not until I've devoured your perfect pussy." She moans in response. "Protection."

"I'm on birth control, but I have condoms as well. No STIs here." She cocks an eyebrow, asking me the same.

"I got tested after Carrie and thankfully everything came back clear. I haven't been with anyone else since."

Her mouth slides open. Brushing my thumb over her chin, I close her mouth, then kiss her nose. "I wish you'd stop being surprised by things like that. Although it surprised me a bit when I didn't want to hook up with anyone. I've realized since then I want more." I graze my lips over hers. "So much more."

"So, no condoms?"

"If you're comfortable with that."

She looks into my eyes and nods. "I am. I trust you."

I crush my mouth into hers again, and then we're frantically tearing off clothes.

Once we're naked, she wraps her hand around my neck and whispers, "What do you like?"

*No one's ever asked me that before.*

Sweeping my hand into her hair, I look into her eyes. "I don't think I fully know the answer to that yet, but I know I like being teased. In case that's not obvious. It's a turn on. And then..."

"What? You can tell me anything. I'm up for trying pretty much anything."

Her confidence is incredibly sexy. It also relaxes me and makes me feel safer. "I like being choked—when it's done right."

She nods. "You need to feel safe doing anything like that."

"My ex would sometimes do it randomly when I was least expecting it. Then it made things less enjoyable for me."

"Okay. Do you want me to try?"

My throat feels dry at the thought. "Yes," I rasp.

"Good. I'll go slow, and you can tell me to stop any time. For the record, I'm familiar with that because I like it sometimes, too."

"What else do you like?"

"I like a mix of things. Sometimes I like being a little dominant and taking control. Other times I like to be helpless and submit. I haven't explored any Dom/sub stuff, but it might be fun in the future. Sometimes I like really classic vanilla love making. Really, I just like sex, and I like exploring with the right person."

"I volunteer as tribute."

"Good. Now I believe there was a promise of you devouring my pussy. Where are we on that?"

I kiss her jaw. "Be a good girl, and you'll find out."

I know what she wants now, but I have every intention of taking my time. Pushing onto my knees, I lean down and kiss her, then grab her hips and flip her over. Slowly, I rub my hands down her back, massaging her. I take my time, working out knots in her back as she groans.

People underestimate the power of foreplay. I'm lucky that a girl I hooked up with my freshman year of college was older and taught me a lot. Really, there should be some kind of sex ed class that teaches us about foreplay, pleasure, kinks, and where the clit is—something too many people don't know.

After massaging every inch of her back, I glide my hands down to her ass and slap both butt cheeks at once.

She grabs her pillow and moans into it. We definitely have some kinks to explore.

I tease my hand over her supple skin, then spank her until she's moaning and rubbing against the mattress, begging for some friction on her clit.

I flip her over, then tease her some more, gently rolling my fingers over her pussy and around her clit as she writhes with desire. When I finally slide one finger inside her, she's unbelievably slick and ready to go off like a rocket.

"Please," she whimpers.

"Please what, baby?"

"I need to come."

"Be patient. I'll take care of you," I whisper as I bend down, changing my position so my face is between her legs. Then I gently kiss her clit.

"Oh…" she whines and whimpers, fisting my hair as I slowly lick her, then push another finger inside her.

I increase my pace a little at a time, keeping her orgasm building. Now that I know what she can do, I want it all.

I suck her clit into my mouth and pump my fingers faster.

"Oh fuck," she shrieks, ass flying off the bed as she squirts everywhere, then her abs tighten and she cries out again as she comes hard, squeezing my fingers tightly. I groan, thinking of feeling that around my cock.

She whimpers as she finishes, going limp against the bed.

"Did I give you what you needed?" I whisper, kissing her cheek.

"Yes. But I want more. I want you inside me."

Gliding my hand between her legs, I use her wetness to coat my cock. Just that makes me shudder. I have to take this slow or else I'll come in seconds. Not the first time I had in mind with this girl.

With my hands gripping her thighs, I pull her to me, guiding her pussy to my cock. I groan as I push into her wet heat.

"Fuck, Dani. You feel incredible."

"Deeper, Jesse. I want all of you."

"Patience, babe. You feel too good for me to go fast."

It takes a minute before I'm seated all the way inside her. The slightest wiggle makes her squirm. She drags her fingers through my hair and our eyes meet as I thrust into her, slowly at first, then harder and faster with each stroke. I've been painfully hard for the better part of the last hour, so I'm not wasting time.

Gliding my fingers between her legs, I find her sweet spot again, teasing and flicking it over and over while trying to keep myself from coming. I want to feel her pulse around me.

"Jesse," she groans, head falling back as her walls tighten.

"That's it, baby," I whisper, sliding my hand up the side of her neck and gently pressing my thumb against her throat. "Come for me. Show me what a good girl you are. Let me see how gorgeous you look coming on my cock."

She whimpers again, hands fisting the sheets and toes curling against my legs.

So close. So tight. So—

"Oh my god, Jesse," she screams my name as she pulses around me.

"Fuck," I growl, emptying myself deep inside her as her pussy milks me dry.

When we're both finished, I lie down next to her and kiss her deeply. It takes a moment for the haze of lust to fade and for me to realize that it's never felt as intensely good with anyone else before. It's not only the physical sensations, but the emotional connection and the safety I feel with her.

"Wow," she breathes. "I like your dirty talk. Most guys I've met aren't particularly good at it. My ex mostly told me to fuck him or asked me if I wanted to be fucked. And I did, but... this was more."

Twirling my fingers through her hair, I rumble, "So I gave you everything you need? Because I'm open to suggestions and feedback."

"No current suggestions," she says with a laugh. "Feedback is ten out of ten would definitely recommend—though I have no one to recommend you to because I am definitely not sharing."

I chuckle at that, then let out a breath. I'm starving now. "Should we order food?"

She props herself up on her elbow and looks at me seductively.

"I believe you told me there's something else I need to eat first." She kisses my neck as she massages my balls then brushes her fingers over my half-hard dick.

*She's going to kill me.*

Then I'm going to die a very happy man.

## Dani

There's something about the way Jesse groans that sets me off. Some guys are more growly, which is sexy in its own way, but I can hear the pleasure dripping from Jesse's moans, and that sets me off every damn time.

I give his shoulder a push so he's lying flat on my bed, then I climb on top of him, shimmying my body down his as I lean forward and pepper kisses across his cheeks and jaw, then I move down, going slower over his neck, sucking the skin into my mouth.

With one hand, he fists my hair, with the other, he mindlessly rolls his fingers down my back.

I slide slowly down his body, kissing as I go. I want to sear every inch of his skin with my lips. Brand him as mine. Because he is.

Sex was good with Jason. I never really went unsatisfied, but it wasn't *this.* It wasn't the all-consuming, powerful connection that excites me, takes my breath away, and leaves me begging for more.

I'm halfway down his body when he fully hardens again, but I continue taking my time. When I get to his hips, he tugs my hair, but he's not in control. Avoiding that hardened muscle, I work my way down one leg and up the other. I consider making him flip over so I can continue kissing him, but his groans and gasps tell me how desperate he is.

Pushing up onto my knees, I reposition, settling between his legs. I rest my hands on his thighs, then slowly lower my mouth, swirling my tongue over his crown. His deep moan lights a fire in my stomach. I don't know how much longer I can hold on. I'm desperate to see him fall apart for me.

His hands tangle in my hair again as his body tenses. He's hanging on by a thread. A thread I'm about to pull as slowly as possible until he finally unravels.

I lick up his shaft, then swirl my tongue over his crown again before taking him deep and sucking.

"Yes, babe. Suck my cock."

*Oh, does he think he's in control?*

I pop my mouth off him and stare at him. "Say my name." He inhales deeply and stares at me, so I sit straight up. "You want my mouth on you? Be a good boy and say my name. Tell me who owns you." He pants a couple of times. "Tell me."

"You. Dani. Fuck... please. Just—"

"What, baby?"

"I need your mouth on me, Dani. Please."

"Who do you belong to?"

"You, Dani. Just you. Always you."

"Good boy," I purr, then lean down and take him deep again.

"Fuck yes," he whines.

What is it about a guy whimpering and whining that is so damn sexy?

Holding his thigh with one hand, I gently massage his balls with the other, then slip my middle finger behind them, giving him an external prostate massage.

He pulls hard on my hair, his body tightening as his breathing quickens.

"Dani... oh. I'm going to..." He lets out another whiny noise and then... "Fuck yes. Dani. Fuck!"

He comes hard, filling my mouth as he shudders, crying out my name.

When he's finished, I lift my mouth off him. I'm lost in a haze of lust as I lean forward and kiss him. "You're mine. All mine." I glide up his body, lifting my hips as I get to his chest. "Open." His eyes light up, then he grabs my hips as his lips part.

*Have I ever ridden a guy's face before?* No. But Jesse makes me feel out of control. I want to try everything with him.

He guides me so I'm in the perfect spot with his tongue caressing my clit.

I squeeze my boobs as I ride his face, pinching my nipples. I close my eyes tight, doing my best to hang on, but I need him hard again. I let out a shaky moan and keep going as he laps at my clit with his tongue.

When he moans against my pussy, I reach back and feel that he's hard again.

Lifting my hips, I move backward until I'm centered over him, and slide down his cock.

"Yes, Dani," he hisses, grabbing my hips again.

He's already on the edge, and I'm ready to push him over. I ride him a few times, then run my hand up his chest to his neck and brush my thumb over his throat. He looks at me and gives a tiny smirk, so I apply a little pressure as I lift my hips and drop them down again.

He moans loudly, then gives a tiny nod, so I press harder.

He whimpers in response, and I ride him.

"More," he groans, nodding to my arm.

I add a little more pressure and he moans loudly again. Squeezing my hand around his throat, I ride him hard, slipping my other hand between my legs and furiously rubbing my clit.

"Dani," he chokes out.

"Come for me, baby. I want to watch you fall apart. You're so sexy, Jesse. You fill me up perfectly."

He gasps and groans. "Ah, Dani. Fuck..."

Still working my clit, I watch as pleasure washes over him and he falls apart. The look of ecstasy on his face and the way he fills me up sends me over the edge and for the first time with my fingers on my clit, I squirt everywhere, then immediately come so hard I can barely stay upright.

Jesse steadies me, holding me through my orgasm, then pulling me against his chest.

"Good boy," I whisper, kissing his neck.

"You're incredible," he breathes before giving me a tongue-filled kiss.

"I can barely move now. I need to pee. And I'm really hungry."

"Me too, but we definitely needed to do that first."

I look down at my bed. It was all extremely hot, but now we have to clean up, and given I squirted multiple times, it's messy.

"Hey," Jesse says, running his fingers through my hair, "it's fine. You go to the bathroom and order food—I need some kind of steak. I'll clean up the bed."

"Thank you."

He kisses my neck. "If you squirt and scream like that for me, I'll clean up every time."

I kiss his cheek. "You're sweet. There are towels and sheets in totes under the bed."

"Got it."

I hop off the bed and walk toward the door, but then run back and throw my arms around him, giving him another intense kiss. "I'm all yours. Don't ever doubt that, okay?"

He kisses me softly. "Promise." He swats my butt. "Go clean up and order food. I'm famished."

I grab my robe and head for the bathroom, heart beating wildly in my chest.

I've never felt like this about anyone before, and while it's utterly terrifying, it's also the most exhilarating thing I've ever experienced. We're just getting started, but I can't wait to see what comes next.

# 16
# Proverbially Speaking

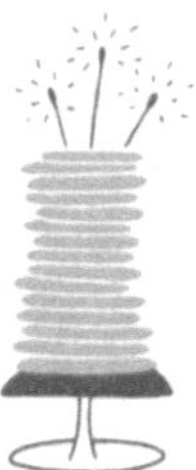

## Dani

I SNEAK A GLANCE at the clock. I'm vibrating with excitement, but Jesse is snoring softly next to me, unaware that I turned off his alarm so he could get a little extra sleep. He doesn't seem to be an early riser unless he has to be. I'm not a crack of dawn person, but I usually wake up naturally by eight. I've been up for almost an hour, mostly texting with Olivia and not-so-patiently waiting for Jesse to wake up so I can reveal the surprise.

My phone vibrates in my hand, and I flick the screen on.

**Olivia: Any fun plans with the boyfriend this weekend?**

Though I'm reluctant to announce my relationship with Jesse to the world, I made a sibling secret pact with Wes and Olivia and told them. I'm not against my parents knowing, but I don't want them to have to keep it from the rest of the family.

It's probably stupid that I want to keep it to myself. I love my cousins, but their entire friend group is meddling. Given Rae's history with Jesse... it feels like everything will get more complicated when they know, and I don't want complexity. It makes it harder for me to feel settled, and right now, I'm in a cozy little bubble that I don't want to wreck.

**Me: As a matter of fact, his birthday is tomorrow and we're going on a ski trip with his friends and Amelia.**

**Olivia: Sure, you invited her but not me.**

**Me: Livvie, she lives with me. You live in Virginia.**

**Olivia: [picture message]**

**Olivia: See that? That is me pouting because you don't love me anymore.**

I stifle a laugh. I love my sister, but she's such a little drama queen sometimes.

**Me: I will always love you, Livvie, but don't I deserve to have a best friend? You have Kelsea. Wes has Nora. I was a loner for most of my life and stole your friends by proxy.**

**Olivia: *sigh* Well, when you put it like that...**

**Olivia: NO. I'm the only one you need. Ever.**

**Me: Yeah, if the last few weeks with Jesse have taught me anything, that is definitely not true.**

**Olivia: Fine. Enjoy your fancy life in New York, but if it matters, I miss you.**

**Me: It more than matters. I miss you too. Maybe you should come visit. Spring break?**

**Olivia: I could be convinced. Okay, I have to pay attention in class now. Have fun with the snow (gross). Byeeee.**

**Me: Bye, freak.**

Shaking my head, I flick my phone screen off, then check the time again. Nine. I think it's time. Leaning over, I kiss Jesse's cheek while running my hand up his stomach.

He groans, grabbing my hand. "It's too early for a booty call."

"Sure about that?" I whisper, kissing his neck.

His eyes fly open and he looks at the clock. "Oh shit. How is it so late? Did I forget my alarm? I have to get to work." He throws the covers off as I laugh. He whips his head around to look at me. "Why are you laughing?"

I climb off the bed and wrap my arms around his neck. "You're so cute when you're stressed. You don't need to go to work." I press a kiss to his lips.

"I actually do," he says against my lips, then pulls away. "And I definitely have to call them—" He grabs for his phone, but I snatch it before he can, holding it up. His eyes narrow. "You know, I don't mind you playing the brat, but I'd rather it not affect my job."

I laugh again, throwing my head back so my neck is on full display for him. He groans again and I smile.

Meeting his gaze again, I say, "You don't have to call work or go in because you have the day off. Garrett already talked to your boss. It's a done deal."

His eyes roll back and forth a couple of times, then he looks at me. "That's why Garrett really came to work last week. And the dinner—"

"Will be held in the mountains for our ski trip. I made sure all your snow and ski gear was packed and did the basics of your regular clothes after you fell asleep last night, but you should go through and grab anything you specifically want."

He stares at me for a moment, then his face breaks into a smile and he steps over to me, wrapping his arms around my waist and dropping his lips to my neck. "What time are we leaving?"

"An hour."

He picks me up and carries me back to the bed, setting me down and laying over the top of me. "Perfect. I'll deal with the suitcase after I deal with you."

The menacing smile on his face goes right to my core. I've never felt as free as I do with him. I can take control or submit, give or take, it doesn't matter. In the end, we both end up sated and happy in each other's arms. The vulnerability of the quiet moments after surprises me the most. Good sex isn't that hard to find, but finding someone who makes you feel safe and cared for after is much more difficult. These last two weeks with Jesse have shown me what it means to have someone who truly cares—and how much I overlooked that for sweet words and a decent orgasm. I know I'm safe with him, and that's the ultimate freedom.

## Jesse

"We have to get out of bed," Dani says, dragging her fingers across my naked stomach.

"Do we though?" I ask, running my fingers through her hair.

"I didn't plan a ski weekend for our friends to go without us."

Warmth creeps into my chest. "You planned this whole thing?"

"With help from Garrett and Evan. Jenna and Brett are coming too. So is Amelia, but not until tomorrow morning."

For someone who was so damn guarded, it surprises me how easily she's let me into her world. It took so long to get her to open up, but now that she has, it's like she hands me another piece of her heart every day and steals some of mine in return. It also makes me realize for the hundredth time what an absolute douche her ex was. I'm so thankful she's here with me, but how he let someone like her go is beyond me. It shouldn't surprise me she's a caretaker. It's probably built into her genetics. I will never take that or her for granted. I'm acutely aware of how fucking lucky I am to have her in my arms.

I roll on top of her, not caring at all that we're supposed to leave soon. So we'll be a little late. It's my birthday weekend, after all.

"It means so much to me that you planned this. When I mentioned wanting to go sometime around my birthday, I didn't expect you to file that away and plan all this, but it means everything to me you did. You make me feel like the most important person in the world." I drop my lips to hers. "And I like making you feel the same. I hope I do." I kiss down her neck.

"Jesse..." She runs her hands through my hair. "Mm. You always make me feel that way. Special. Wanted." She gasps as I pull one of her nipples between my teeth and slide my fingers up her center. "Needed."

"Oh, I need you, Dani girl. I always need you."

I'm buried inside her a second later. I can't get enough. We've done it every day—usually multiple times—and I always want more. She drags her feet down my legs, wrapping herself around me.

"How does it feel this good every time? You're barely moving, and—"

The front door opens and slams shut. "Yo, Jesse, crazy girl. Where are you?" Garrett's voice rings out.

"You didn't tell me they were meeting us here."

"You didn't tell me he had a key." My cock twitches inside her. "Really?" she hisses.

I pump into her a couple of times and she moans.

*"Really?"* I ask, lips on her neck.

"How fast do you think we can—"

"I'm coming up the stairs and will be in your room in T-minus ten seconds. Rip yourselves apart."

Dani smacks my chest, but I stare down at her, slowly pull almost all the way out, then go deep as hard as I can before quickly pulling out and rolling over, making sure we're both covered by the blanket. Dani is glaring at me like she might murder me. I give her my most charming grin in return and she rolls her eyes at me.

"Like I said, babe. Not a turnoff." I wink at her right as G swings the door open.

He stops and sighs. "Dani, you're the one who picked the time to leave. I expect this from him." He nods at me. "You're the one who's supposed to keep our shit in line."

She glances at me, then shrugs. "What can I say? The birthday boy disagreed with my schedule of events."

"More like he needed to add a couple." Garrett shakes his head. "Be downstairs in ten minutes or Ev and I will haul you two out to the car, naked or not."

"Aye aye, Captain." I salute him. He sticks his middle finger up at me and walks out of the room.

The second the door is closed, I throw my covers off. "C'mon, G isn't kidding. He once dragged me out of the house without socks or shoes because I wasn't going fast enough for him."

But Dani doesn't move. No, she looks up at me, bats her lashes, then whispers. "Maybe the eye roll isn't a turnoff for me, either." Then she shrugs and *rolls her eyes.*

I stare at her, then look over at the door. Her. The door. *Fuck it.*

I lock it, then pounce on her again, finishing what we started.

"Holy shit. This place is incredible," I say, looking around in awe at the massive luxury cabin Dani rented for us. Even Dani is gaping as she looks around.

"The pictures didn't do it justice."

I eye her suspiciously. "How much did this cost?"

She gives me a little glare, then pokes my ribs. "Doesn't matter. You're not paying for any of it. It's your birthday." She kisses my cheek. "You deserve to be spoiled."

Those words shouldn't make my heart swell as much as they do, but I can't remember the last time I felt like this. My friends are wonderful and they always do something special for me—like we all do for each other—but that Dani took this all on, found the beautiful place, planned this out *for me* means everything. My friends and I would've planned this together, but she planned it without me to make it special.

I'm not typically much of a crier. If I'm really upset, it all spills out, but it takes a lot to get me to that point. I'm known for celebratory drinks and bear hugs when I'm happy—not tears—but I find myself fighting them back, anyway.

"Thank you," I whisper, sliding a hand into her hair and giving her a not-so-PG kiss.

"Yeah, we're actually all standing right here," Brooks says. "You're getting to be as nauseating as those two."

Out of the corner of my eye, I see him nod at Evan and Garrett. After another second, I pull back, meeting Dani's gaze before looking at my friends. "I appreciate you all coming together to help Dani and surprise me. This is awesome."

"Hell yes, it is," Jenna says. "This mountain view is fudging incredible."

"Wait till you see the views from the bedrooms. Choose whichever you want, but we get the master." Dani grins at me and grabs my hand, leading me up the stairs and down the hall to the farthest room. "Wait for it." She swings the door open and *damn.* The far wall has French doors leading out onto a balcony, but that's not the most stunning thing. It's the view beyond those doors. A sweeping view of the mountains in the distance.

Mindlessly, I walk over to the doors, drawn to the stunning beauty beyond them. I pull one open and step onto a moderate-sized deck complete with hot tub.

"Gorgeous, right?" Dani asks, walking onto the balcony.

I spin to face her, still in shock over all this. "It's stunning. And I can't wait to use that hot tub." She's rubbing her arms since it's frigid outside and we left our jackets downstairs. I pull her close, wrapping her up in my arms and kiss her head. "Thank you for this. This must have cost a fortune. Are you sure you don't want me to—"

"Shut up. You're not paying a cent. Split between all of us, it was completely doable, not even a splurge." She looks up at me. "But for the record, even if it was, you're worth splurging for, so let me celebrate you."

I shake my head, my heart on fire as I look at her. Normally, I'm the one splurging on other people. But what means more is the thoughtfulness behind it. We could've been in a shack and it would've meant the same to me. "Two weeks," I whisper.

"What?"

"We've been together for two weeks, and in that time, you've taken care of me, shown me so much more affection than my ex ever did. You make me feel less alone and like I'm truly wanted. Not for what I do for you or can give you, but for who I am."

She turns and grabs my face, looking into my eyes. "I never want you to feel alone or unwanted. I know I messed up initially, but God, Jesse, I want you. In every single way. No one makes me feel like you. I want you to have the best birthday weekend possible. Hopefully, I can make it extra special for you."

"You already have." I lean down and give her a hard kiss, then look back at the view for a moment more, holding her tightly as I do.

"What do you think? Ready to go explore some mountain fun?" she asks.

I look down at her, incapable of doing anything else but smiling like an idiot. "I'd love that. Let's go."

"Let's see how much air we can catch this time!" Evan yells, as he, Brooks, Garrett, and I all climb onto a large snow tube and take off down the hill.

Brett is at the bottom, recording it all on his phone. He's a bit of a tech nerd and has been playing with some fancy video settings on his new phone.

We careen down the hill hitting bumps here and there that give us some air time, but we're almost to the biggest one.

"Hold on, men," G yells.

We hit it and hang in the air for a few seconds, landing with a cushioned thud that has us whooping and cheering. We come to a swirling stop not far from Brett.

"That was fucking sweet, guys. I'll show you the video later, but seriously, that was awesome."

"Uh oh, look out," Evan says as he and Brooks quickly pull the tube out of the way.

Jenna and Dani are coming down the hill fast, catching even more air than we did and laughing hysterically. This is one of the best birthday weekends I've had in a long time, and it's barely even started. Dani and Jenna's sled comes in with a bit of a crash landing and both girls go tumbling out, still laughing.

I walk over to Dani, who is lying on her back with her eyes closed. "Okay?" She flashes her eyes open and smiles. I extend my hand to her.

"I'm perfect," she says, grabbing my hand and jumping to her feet. "In fact, I really want to do that again." She fists my jacket and pulls me closer, bringing our lips so they almost touch. "With you." We stare at each other for a moment, and just when I think she's about to kiss me, she gives me a shove backward and says, "Race you to the top, Wilkinson." Then she takes off running. I watch her for a second, utterly enamored with this beautiful, vibrant girl—and unbelievably happy to see that side of her come out again.

Realizing how much ground she's gotten, I take off running after her. I might need to tackle her in the snow and kiss her for a minute to slow her down.

After a killer day snow tubing, followed by dinner at a cool local brewpub, we're back at the cabin and have been hanging out, talking, and drinking for the last few hours.

Well, not everyone has been drinking—at least not a ton. I had a beer with dinner and another dark, high-alcohol content one of Brooks's when we got back to the cabin. I only finished it a little while ago because it's a big beer. The rest of the guys are at various stages of tipsy or drunk, with Brooks being the drunkest. He's hard to predict because sometimes he's a one-and-done guy and others he will drink until he blacks out.

Dani returns from the kitchen and places a glass of water in my hand, then sits down next to me, kissing my cheek. She sips on a glass of lemon water as she cuddles next to me on one of the oversized couches.

Brooks pouts and holds his glass out toward Dani, saying in a British accent, "Beer wench, another."

"Dude, what the fuck?" Garrett, who is sitting next to him, asks.

"What? She got him more to drink." He tips his glass back, trying to get another couple of drops from his beer.

I pull my arm out from behind Dani, looking at her out of the corner of my eye as I approach Brooks. Dani's cheeks are pink and she's looking down. *Fuck no. Not my girl.* I take the beer glass from Brooks's hand and shove it at G, then yank Brooks off the couch. "Do not ever fucking talk to her like that again. She's not a waitress and it sure as fuck is not her job to bring your drunk ass beer."

"Okay, Jesus. I'm sorry." He wriggles out of my grasp, holding his hands up.

Brooks is my friend, but he's also a bit of a tool. Always has been. If it wasn't for my close friendship with Evan, Brooks probably isn't someone I'd stay close to.

"Apologize to her, not me," I growl.

He steps toward Dani. "I'm sorry," he says. It's genuine, but I doubt he'd have said it if I hadn't made him. He's not a bad guy, but I like him a lot less when he's drunk.

"It's fine," she says, cheeks still pink.

He grabs his glass and stalks into the kitchen. I sit down next to Dani and pull her close again, squeezing her thigh. "I'm sorry."

"It's okay," she whispers, leaning against me, but I can tell she's uncomfortable.

When Brooks returns with another full glass of beer, G sighs, then whispers something to Evan, who nods. Probably agreeing to cut him off after this. Frankly, I wish we would've done it sooner. Dani shouldn't have to deal with his dumb drunk ass. It's an extra slap in the face since she can't drink—which he gave her a little shit for earlier, and I also put him in his place for that.

After a moment, Dani squeezes my arm, then gets up, saying she has to go to the bathroom. She disappears from the room and the guys start in on some topic about Evan's and Brooks's family. I'm only half listening, because I don't really care. Jenna and Brett went to bed an hour ago, and I'm hitting my tipping point as well. Plus, I'd really like to be alone with Dani, who has been gone longer than it should've taken for her to go to the bathroom. She couldn't have gone upstairs because she would've had to walk through the room to get to the staircase.

"I'll be back," I say, and set off toward the kitchen, which the bathroom is off of.

I find her in the kitchen, rinsing out beer bottles and putting them in the recycling.

I walk over and wrap my arms around her waist from behind. "You don't have to do that."

She shrugs, not turning around. "It needs to be done." I lift the beer bottles from her hand and turn off the water, then spin her to face me.

"*You* don't need to do it. My friends can clean up their own mess. It's not your responsibility." She doesn't say anything, but she wraps her arms around my waist, so I take that as a good sign. "I'm sorry for what Brooks said. I should've cut him off sooner."

"And *that* is not your responsibility. But I get it. It's fine."

"It's not. How he spoke to you was not okay."

"He's drunk, and while I don't enjoy sloppy drunkenness, my sister can be the same way. I love her, but when she has a bad day or gets in a funk, she gets sloppy drunk. She's a drama queen normally, so it turns into crying and screaming and eventually puking. As someone who hardly ever drinks, it's extra frustrating. There's nothing like being sober when someone else is super drunk."

"Were you the one who usually took care of her?"

She nods. "Weston would lecture the hell out of her the next day, so she'd take a cab to my place instead of her apartment. Then my ex would…"

"What?"

She sighs and looks away. "Usually he was at least a little drunk, too. Getting wasted was his favorite pastime. He'd laugh that she was drunk too and make a joke that he got with the wrong sister because I was boring. He'd try to flirt with Olivia—"

"Did she flirt back?"

"No. Never. She'd never do that to me. Usually she told him to fuck off, then went to throw up. Somewhere in there my ex would also say we should have a threesome."

"Your ex is a piece of fucking trash. If I ever meet him, I'm going to make sure he knows that. He's also the biggest idiot on the planet."

She smiles. "True. But why do you say that?"

"Because he let you go. Your beautiful heart. Your kind soul. Your caring nature. Your sexy body." I flash my signature smile and she laughs. "Stop cleaning up after stupid guys." I glance at the beer bottles.

She nods. "No offense, but I don't really feel like dealing with any more of the guys tonight."

"Good. Because I wasn't planning on going back out there." I pull my phone from my pocket, and connect it to the Bluetooth speaker in the kitchen, then put on a playlist I've been making for longer than I probably should have been.

"What are you doing? Don't you want to hang out with your friends?"

"I do, but remember what I told you last week? I want to spend my birthday with you. I know it doesn't officially start for another couple of hours, but I'd still much rather spend the rest of the night with you. Now, if I ask you to dance, are you going to proverbially hand me my balls again?"

"Did you seriously just say 'proverbially?'"

"What? Do you think I'm just some dumb jock?"

"Not for a second." She looks up into my eyes. "And I would love to dance with you."

"Good." Taking her hand, I lead her to a more open part of the kitchen, then pull her close, my hand sliding up her back, my fingers twisting with the strands of hair that have fallen from her messy bun. My heart beats faster having her so close. She rests her head on my shoulder, arms wrapped tightly around my back as we move to the music.

We're quiet through several songs, just enjoying holding each other and swaying to the music.

When Brantley Gilbert's *She's the One* comes on, Dani looks up at me. "I love this song."

I kiss her forehead. "It makes me think of you. That's why I put it on this playlist."

Her eyes widen and fill with emotion. "This is why I pushed you away the first time we danced. I saw the same look in your eyes then that I see now, and I thought..."

"What?"

"You could destroy my heart."

Pulling my hand from her hair, I cup her face, brushing my thumb over her cheek. "Could? Maybe. But I never would. *Never.* I'm acutely aware of how lucky I am to be with you. I will never take that—or you—for granted. I promised to protect your heart, and I meant it. With everything inside me, I always will." I swallow down the words that bubble in my chest. It's too soon, but they're there, regardless.

"When did you make this playlist?" she breathes.

"Uh... I started it in September. Mostly just adding romantic-ish songs when I heard them. It didn't start as a playlist for us, but then..."

"Hm?"

"I heard this song, thought of you, and added it to the playlist. Then I realized that damn near every song made me think of you."

She tilts her head. "When was that?" I look away, feeling like an idiot. "Tell me," she whispers, tipping my head back toward her.

"November."

She inhales sharply, then presses onto her toes and kisses me. "You aren't the only one who's lucky. I'm lucky you were so patient, gave me so many chances even when I didn't choose you." She swallows hard. "I'm sorry I didn't choose you. I saw what I thought you were, not who you are."

"And who am I?"

"The man who makes me feel safe and cared for." Her eyes meet mine like she's stuck on the same words I thought earlier. There's no rush to say them. After all we've both been through, they're scary. We can both quietly feel them until we're ready.

Dipping my head down, I softly kiss her, still moving to the music. She fists my shirt, pulling me closer and deepening the kiss until we're making out as we dance, her hands twisted in my shirt and mine tangled in her hair.

"Hey, everything okay in here..." Garrett trails off when he sees us.

Reluctantly, I break our kiss, then look at him over my shoulder. "We're good."

"Right. Sorry. I'll leave you to it."

"Hey, G?"

"Yeah?"

"Dim the lights."

He smiles and nods, then hits the dimmer switch as he walks out of the room.

With Garrett gone, I pull Dani close again and get back to kissing my girl.

# Dani

I slept amazing last night. The room was just the right temperature. There's a sound machine, so I set it to crackling fire. And, of course, I was cuddled up with Jesse all night. He's a much more snuggly sleeper than I would've guessed. I assumed he'd be a sprawler—maybe he is when he's alone in bed—but he's an excellent cuddler. It's not so much that it leaves me feeling smothered, but it's the perfect amount so I feel cozy.

I'm awake right now, but my eyes are still closed. I'm still lying in his arms, just freaking happy. After what I went through, I was terrified to fall again, but with Jesse, it gets easier every day. I still have those nagging fears in the back of my mind, but I do my best not to listen and put my proverbial ear plugs in.

*Proverbial.* Hm. Jesse must be rubbing off on me.

Speaking of which, last night he was so damn swoony it nearly knocked me off my feet. I'm officially a Victorian woman in need of a fainting couch. Elizabeth Bennet would probably be disappointed in me for falling over myself for a man, but even she swooned over Mr. Darcy, even if she didn't want to admit it.

Dancing in Jesse's arms last night lit a fire inside me, but it wasn't the type that leads to sex. Not a tear-off-our-clothes-and-do-it kind of fire. No, it was subtle, warming me slowly and consistently as I melted in his arms—and into our kisses. We didn't do anything more than dance and kiss last night, but it's all emblazoned in my memory. How perfect it felt to be in his arms. The rush of excitement and the calm of safety balancing each other. I remember complaining to my ex at his stupid corporate parties that he'd only ever dance with me to one song, just to make an appearance on the dance floor. Dancing was boring and a waste of time to him. I always loved it. Going to dances in high school was one of my favorite things. Slow dancing in some cute guy's arms. I loved it. Doing it with Jesse was next level.

I'm still kicking myself for how I lashed out at the wedding. If I'd given in then, maybe I could've been experiencing this the whole time. Then again, I probably wasn't ready. I'm still fighting off my fears and insecurities, but damn it, this man is so worth it.

On the bedside table, his phone rings and he groans. My man does not like waking up until he's good and ready. Unless he's lured with food or sex. Surprisingly, food works better. Since I'm a decent cook, I'll try not to take offense to that.

He leans away from me, grabbing his phone, then groans again.

"Who is it?" I ask.

He looks down at me, surprised, then smiles. It's quickly replaced by a grimace, and he says, "My parents. Guess it's the birthday call. I better answer."

"I'll hide," I say, shimmying down in the bed.

He drapes his arm around me, then sexily says, "Stay right there." Like my arm isn't resting dangerously close to his crotch, he answers the call. "Morning." His voice is still a little raspy from sleep as he rubs his face.

"Morning?" his mother chirps. "Oh gosh, it is morning there, isn't it? I'm all out of sorts. We crossed two time zones today, and I wanted to make sure we called before the end of the day. I forgot it's the beginning of your day, isn't it?"

"It is, but that's all right."

"Happy birthday, honey."

"Thanks, Mom."

"What are you doing today? Anything fun?"

"Yeah. I'm actually on a trip with my friends. We're in the mountains and going snowboarding today."

"Oh, that's wonderful. Who all is there with you?"

"Garrett, Evan, Brooks, Jenna, Brett, and Dani."

"Dani. That's Rae's cousin, right?"

I immediately frown at that. Is it my fault his parents don't know I'm his girlfriend? Yes. But being reduced to "Rae's cousin" feels a little like a slap in the face. Maybe I'm still sensitive about that. It's not like his parents know they've been together.

As if he senses my frustration, he slides his hand down and twirls it through my hair.

"Yep, that's her." He's got a hint of mischief in his voice.

"Well, I'm glad you're having a good birthday so far."

"I am. So when will you guys be back next?"

"Oh, I'm not sure. You know we like to keep things open."

I glance up at him, watching as he nods, the mischief I heard in his voice before not evident on his face.

"Uh, did Dad mention the fundraiser I'm doing in May? I was hoping maybe you two could come—"

"He did! We're so proud of you. Depending on where we are, we'll try to make it back. And of course we'll donate whatever you need."

"Right. Thanks."

"Hey, bud," Jesse's dad says. "Happy birthday."

Jesse flashes a smile, but it's not his real one. It makes me sad his parents don't get to see his real smile, and even sadder that they don't realize it.

"Thanks, Dad."

"So you're in the mountains? That's great. Enjoy a few trips down the mountain for me. Been too long since I've been on a snowboard."

"Maybe we should plan a family trip," Jesse says.

"That would be fun. We could try somewhere new. Maybe Tahoe. So many fun options. I'll start researching," Mom says.

"Sounds great," Jesse says, but his voice has a flatness to it.

"Well, enjoy your weekend, son. We've got to get to our dinner reservations. We'll talk soon. Love you."

"Love you too. Bye."

"Bye, honey."

Jesse ends the call and tosses his phone to the side. I slink out from under the covers and rest my head on his shoulder. "I'm sorry," I whisper.

He shrugs. "It's fine. That's how it always is."

I lift my head from his shoulder, then climb onto his lap. "No. Maybe it's normal for you, but it's not fine. Do you remember how I cried because I missed my sister on her birthday? Obviously I couldn't go home because I'd just started my job, but I wanted to be there. They should want to be with you. I'm sorry you don't have that."

He runs his hands down my back and looks at me tenderly. "I guess you'll just have to make me feel extra special, then. To cheer me up." A cheeky half-smile pulls at his lips, and I can't help but smile too. It's funny how my feelings about his smiles have changed as I've gotten to know him. I understand the feeling beneath each of them.

Raking my fingers through his hair, I give him a deep kiss.

"I suppose I could do that. Starting with pancakes!"

I hop off his lap, throw on some sweats and a sweater, and head for the door, leaving him smiling as he watches me go.

I open the oven a crack and slide another pancake onto the sheet tray, then pour more batter onto the built-in griddle on the stovetop.

Jesse came downstairs for a few minutes, but since I wouldn't let him help me make anything, he went back upstairs to shower. No one else is awake yet, or at least not downstairs.

I get a couple more pancakes done, then Brooks wanders into the kitchen, stopping short when he sees me.

"Dani. Hi."

"Morning. There's coffee." I point toward the pot, focusing on the pancakes.

Brooks hoists himself onto the counter and rubs his face. "I'm sorry about last night."

"It's fine."

"You say that, but you don't sound like it's fine."

Sighing, I flip both pancakes, then turn to look at him. "It is *fine*. It's not bad. It's not good, either, though. No, I didn't appreciate what you said or how you were acting, but it's nothing worse than what my ex used to do to me. I know Jesse told you I'm the one who needed your apology, but he does, too. This is his birthday weekend. He deserves a hell of a lot more than having to worry about when to cut his friend off or how his friend is treating his girlfriend. That's not his responsibility. Jesse has had enough people in his life not treat him the way he deserves to be treated. If you want to be his friend, be his friend. Otherwise, step back."

"Damn, girl. You know how to pack a verbal punch."

"I'm not trying to be mean. I just..." I pull the pancakes off the griddle and slide them in the oven, then pour more batter on, turning to Brooks again once it's sizzling. "I'm protective of him."

"Funny. Wasn't that long ago that you didn't seem to feel that way."

I stare at him for a second. "You're right. I didn't. But that was because I didn't know the kind of guy he was. Now that I do, I'd do anything to protect him. The difference is you *do* know who he is. He should have your respect if you're truly his friend."

He nods and hops off the counter as I flip the pancakes. "Yeah. You're right. For the record, I'm glad you're protective of him. Carrie... she sure as hell never was. In fact, if the same thing had happened last night, she'd probably have been drinking just as much as me. Jesse would've gone to bed, and she would've let him... then thrown herself at me."

My eyes flare. "Did you ever—"

"No. I mean, I might've flirted, but I never acted on it."

"Does Jesse know that?"

He shakes his head. "No. I never wanted to tell him. He seemed so into her. I know I probably—"

"You still should. Not this weekend. But he deserves to know."

"Yeah." He runs a hand through his scruffy hair. Brooks is the kind of guy I thought Jesse was. He's not as bad as my ex, but he's immature and selfish at times. Funny, since he's the oldest of us. "Anyway. Like I said, I'm glad he has you."

"Thanks," I say softly.

He nods, then walks away, nearly bumping into Jesse as he goes.

Brooks stops and grabs Jesse's arm, pulling him closer and saying something to him I can't hear. Jesse says something back, then they share a bro-hug.

I look back at the pancakes as Jesse swaggers over to me. He throws his thumb back in the direction he came from. "What did you say to him?"

I look at him with an innocent smile. "Who me? I'm just cooking pancakes."

"Mhm."

He wraps his arms around my waist and pulls me close. Tangling one hand in my hair, he dips me back and gives me a long kiss. "You're fucking amazing," he mutters against my lips. "I—" He stops short and my heart pounds. *Was he just going to say...* "I'm so glad you're here with me." It's a good recovery, but I think we both know what those words were going to be.

Part of me thinks it's too soon. But another part knows I've felt the same words trickling through me, too.

"So am I." We stare at each other for a moment more, then I remember I'm holding a spatula for a reason. I put the last two pancakes in the oven, then flip off the griddle. A moment later, Amelia walks through the door.

"Damn, how early did you get up?"

Amelia shrugs. "Eh, I'm an early riser most days. Happy birthday," she says to Jesse.

"Thanks. Glad you could make it."

"Who?" G asks, walking into the room hand in hand with Evan. "Oh, crazy girl's roommate. Hey."

"Hi," Amelia says with a laugh.

"Well, everyone is just in time. Breakfast is ready."

Brooks, Jenna, and Brett join us as I pile pancakes on a plate for Jesse, then stick a candle in it. We sit down at the dining room table and sing him *Happy Birthday.* As soon as he blows out the candle, everyone claps, then goes to fill their plates. Before I can move, though, Jesse pulls me onto his lap and feeds me a bite of pancakes.

"Happy birthday," I whisper in his ear.

"Thanks, baby," he whispers back, kissing my neck.

I'm not sure my heart has ever felt this full.

# Jesse

This may be my best birthday on record.

After our pancake breakfast this morning, we headed to the ski resort where I spent the morning teaching Dani some snowboarding basics. She fell plenty of times, but by the end of the morning she could confidently go down the bunny hill. I don't think she's quite ready to cross *learn to snowboard* off her list, but she's got the basics down so we can keep building on it. After lunch, Garrett, Evan, Brooks, Amelia, and I went up to one of the bigger slopes to snowboard. Amelia was surprisingly good, though a little rusty to start. Apparently it was something she used to do with her father before he passed away when she was in high school. It was cool getting to know her a little better, seeing as she's Dani's best friend.

Brett, Jenna, and Dani hung out at a chalet restaurant that overlooks the slope we were snowboarding on, and eventually Brett came up to ski, which he's great at.

Ev cooked an incredible dinner for us at the house. Steak, chicken, potatoes, roasted vegetables, pizza, and salad. We spent two hours around the table, eating slowly, talking, and laughing. It was insanely fun. Then G spoiled me with a double-decker pineapple upside down cake.

I'm stuffed now, but the hot tub is the perfect way to relax. Did I ditch my friends by nine at night?

Yep.

Am I sorry about that?

Hell no. Because right now I'm in the hot tub with my girl in my arms, staring at the mountains in the distance as snow gently falls. Talk about a killer fucking day.

This is the moment when I realize I want to do something just as spectacular for Dani for her birthday in June. I think back to her list and remember there being something on there about Paris, but I'm worried she'd see that as too extravagant. Maybe we could take a trip down to see her family, or I could have them come up. I know she loves living in Ida, but she misses her family a lot.

"What are you thinking about?" Dani asks, grazing her fingers over my thigh as she sits with her back pressed into my chest.

I lean down and kiss her neck. "How amazing you are. How happy I am. How much I need to do something special for you tonight." I suck on the skin of her neck, then softly roll it between my teeth. She lets out a little moan, then quickly spins around, straddling me and nestling her barely covered crotch over my boner.

She kisses my cheek, then moves her lips lower, brushing them over my jawline, then the spot just below my ear. "You've got it wrong. It's your birthday. You'll be the one getting special treatment tonight." She grinds her hips over me, and I don't give a fuck about the mountain views or the perfectly snowy night. All I care about is Dani.

"Okay." I wrap my hands around her ass, then stand up and climb out of the hot tub. She gasps, but holds on tight as I carry her inside.

The second the door is closed, she shimmies out of my arms and strips off her wet swimsuit, then reaches for the ties of mine, undoing them and sliding the suit down my legs. She tosses our wet suits into the bathroom, then shoves me against the door and drops to her knees.

She swirls her tongue over my crown as I groan.

"Mm, is this what you want, Mr. Wilkinson?" she blinks up at me innocently, but there's a troublemaking glint in her eyes that tells me she noticed my reaction when she called me that the other day.

I run my finger over her pouty pink lips. "I want these wrapped around my cock."

"Yes, Mr. Wilkinson."

*Oh fuck.*

She wraps her lips loosely around me, teasing me first, before suctioning them around me and sucking me as hard as she can.

She pulls off and looks up at me. "Like that, Mr. Wilkinson?"

"More," I growl, grabbing a fistful of her hair. "Suck me harder. Take me deep until you choke."

"Show me," she says innocently, but her eyes meet mine with a serious look. She's giving me permission.

A second later, she wraps her lips around my crown again, then slowly goes deeper. She moves lightly, but not much, then looks up at me again.

"Like this." I use her hair to hold her in place as I pull my hips back, then thrust deep into her mouth. I've learned from the past couple of weeks that she can take me pretty far without gagging, so I hold her steady and fuck her mouth. At some point, she stops playing innocent and starts massaging my balls, sending a shiver up my spine.

"Just like that, baby girl. You want me to come in your mouth?"

She moans something that sound like yes, so I keep going.

With her other hand, she reaches up and pinches my butt, then slaps it a couple of times.

*Shit.*

"I'm about to come down your pretty throat. Are you ready? You want this?"

I groan, barely able to finish the sentence.

She massages my balls more firmly and adjusts the position of her tongue slightly, letting me get a touch deeper and then...

"Oh, fuck. Oh, yeah. Take it all." I groan again as I empty myself in her mouth.

As blood thunders in my ears, I let her hair go, and she slowly sits back on her heels, wiping her mouth with the back of her hand as she smiles up at me.

She stands up and kisses me, and as she does, I yank her closer, dipping my hand between her legs and roughly fingering her wet pussy. I brush my thumb over her clit and her weight sinks against me. That's what I want. Her limp and trembling against my body as I make her come.

She moans, her body moving with the thrust of my fingers.

With my other hand, I sweep some hair off her neck, holding it gently in my hand.

"That's right, baby girl. Let me take care of you. Let me give you what you need."

She whimpers into my shoulder, her breaths growing ragged. I'm not sure if I have a tell or something, but Dani always seems to know what I want. Knowing her, she could easily stand back, ride my hand, kiss me, or sass me, but she's giving me exactly what I want.

She says nothing. The only sounds that come out are moans and whines. *God, I didn't know I needed that noise, but I do.*

She inhales sharply, then whimpers as her legs tremble.

I go faster, and a second later, she cries out, whining and moaning against my chest as she shatters for me.

"That's it. Good girl, Dani. Fucking perfect."

After she catches her breath, she leans up and kisses me. When she pulls back, she sucks in a breath, then takes my hand. "Come on."

She grabs some pillows and blankets from the bed, then puts them on the floor next to the fireplace.

*Seriously, how does she know?*

"How do you know exactly what I want?"

I get her beaming smile at that. She kisses my cheek. "It's in your eyes. But it's also what feels right. Plus, it's giving me what I want, too."

Threading my hand through her hair, I whisper, "What do you want?"

"You, Jesse. Just you."

I quickly kiss her, then grab her hand and pull her to the floor with me. "Good, because this is what I want. Your sweaty body writhing beneath mine right here."

I lie over the top of her, hand fisted in her hair again as I line myself up and look into her eyes. She grabs my hips, guiding me in. Once I'm seated inside her, I stay still for a moment, enjoying the feeling of her surrounding me. Then I slowly pull out and thrust in again, taking my time.

I kiss her cheek. "You're amazing." Her other cheek. "You're phenomenal." Her lips. "My perfect girl. So fucking perfect for me, Dani."

She runs her fingers through my hair and smiles up at me. "My perfect match," she whispers.

"Exactly."

We kiss again, tongues tangled, absolutely lost in each other, enjoying every tantalizing moment as we make love by the fire.

It wasn't on her list, but since the moment I walked into the room with her last night, it's been on mine.

It's just before midnight when we settle in bed, her in my T-shirt and me in boxers. I pull her to my chest, holding her tightly as I kiss her temple. "This was the best birthday I've ever had. That's because of you. You bring me joy, you tease me and play with me, you make me laugh, you support me and encourage me, you know me." I look down and brush my thumb over her lips. "And that smile. That smile does dangerous things to my heart." *Like making me fall a little more in love with her every single day.*

She leans up and kisses me. "Funny, that's how I feel about you. I'm glad I stopped running from who I thought you were and opened up to the thoughtful, caring man you are. Happy birthday, Wilkinson."

"Night, Dani girl."

"Night," she breathes, tossing her leg over mine.

As we drift off to sleep, I'm not sure how any other birthday will ever top this.

# 17

## Tangled Together

## Dani

THE INTERCOM ON MY office phone buzzes as I hit send on an email.

"Hey, Dani. Are you available right now?" Leo Barone's voice comes through the speaker.

"Yep. What do you need?"

"Can you come to my office for a second?"

"Sure thing. Be right there." I lock my laptop, then head down the hall to Leo's office. The door is open, so I walk in and drop into the chair in front of his desk. "What's up?"

"So, this morning we found out we're in the top three contenders for the small development project we bid on. I'd like you to take the floor plan mockups that Vince has made and use them to create sample interiors."

"How many houses and when do you need it by?" I ask, grabbing a scrap of paper off his desk and a pen.

"It'll be four full houses to give a few different design options encompassing the different style homes they'd like to see in the development. This is where you're going to hate me. I need it by next Monday."

My heart beats faster, and I'm suddenly grateful the only freelance design project I'm working on is Garrett's ice cream shop and the man makes decisions about as fast as ice cream melts in the winter.

I scribble the information down on the paper, then look at Leo with a confident smile. "No problem. I can handle that."

What am I if not a design aficionado? This is my job. I can do this without an issue.

"Perfect. Vince will send you all the information you need. Let me know if you have any questions."

"Will do. I'm going to get started."

"Sounds great. Thanks, Dani."

"No problem."

I walk out of his office with my head held high. *I can do this.*

As I walk back toward my office, my internal caffeine meter registers *very low,* so I knock on Maia's office door to see if she wants to grab a cup with me.

"It's open," Maia calls.

When I swing the door open, I find her inside with her husband, Vince. Maia is Leo's younger daughter, and despite being younger than me, is married. Then again, she was a teen mom, so she seems to live a more accelerated life.

"Hey, Dani," Vince says. Vince is the oldest son of Leo's business partner, Noah, and is in his senior year of college, studying architectural design. "I just sent all the specs over to you. Don't let it scare you. Once you get into it, it's not as bad as it seems."

"Thanks. I'm headed to grab some coffee, just wanted to see if you wanted to join me."

Maia smiles brightly. "Yes. I'm in desperate need." She runs a hand over Vince's shoulder. "Want anything?"

"Nah, I'm good. I've got another soda in my bag to hype me up," he says with a laugh.

"Okay." She gives him a quick kiss and walks out of the office with me.

I appreciate the energy here at AB. They don't shy away from showing the depth of the relationships. Noah's wife runs the front of the business, greeting customers and answering phone calls. Maia and Vince share an office and aren't afraid to show affection. It's not PDA, but it doesn't leave you wondering. I love that it's a family business built on respect and love because it reminds me of my family. It's the same way my grandfather would build a business. Then again, in many ways, Leo kind of reminds me of my grandfather.

As Maia and I wait for the espresso machine to brew our espresso and the steamer to steam and froth the milk, we chat about her upcoming college graduation and how it feels more important to her than her high school one. She also mentions that her almost-five-year-old daughter Harper has been having nightmares at three in the morning every single night for the last week.

Friends with kids are the best birth control.

Don't get me wrong, I want kids one day. But not this day. I still have at least half a list of items to cross off first.

Once I'm caffed up, I make my way back to my office and work through the tedious task of setting up all the room dimensions and basic layouts in my design software. By the time I'm done, my eyes hurt and my brain is mush. Not the best time to jump into designing the interiors.

After packing up my laptop, I head out for the day, but rather than going to my apartment, I drive up to my grandparents' farmhouse. Maybe I'm hoping inspiration will hit me there, because for now, I have *nothing.*

"Hey, Sunny," Gram says, smiling brightly when I walk into the kitchen. If I got my sunniness from anyone, it was definitely her. Grandpa's far too much of a troublemaker.

She wraps me in her arms, and I relish the tightness of her hugs. All the women in my family hug similarly, and while Gram's hugs are always comforting, they also remind me of my mom and Olivia.

"Everything okay, sweetheart?" she asks as she lets me go.

"Yeah. I'm good. Just love your hugs. And I'm missing my parents, Olivia, and Weston."

Gram nods in understanding, then tips her head toward the kitchen counter, indicating I better sit my butt down so she can feed me.

"It must be hard being away from them. It was hard for me when your mom moved. She was the one who ran out of town like her hair was on fire. Not to get away, but because she wanted to explore."

"And she hates the cold."

Gram laughs. "Yes. That too."

Gram sets a plate of homemade sugar cookies in front of me and a glass of milk.

"Gram... these are my weakness."

She grins. "I know. I made a batch today, hoping I'd lure you over with them. It seems you knew telepathically, though."

"I'm sorry I haven't been around much," I say after a bite of her decadent sugar cookies. I swear, they're magic.

"Busy with work?" She gives me a knowing smile, telling me that's not all she's asking.

"Yes, but also friends." I swallow down my cookie, debating whether to tell her more, but odds are she'll see right through me. "And maybe dating." I glug some milk as she looks me over.

"Dating, huh? Anyone we know?" Grandpa asks, strolling into the kitchen and looking at me like he already knows the answer. Hell, he probably does. I swear the man knows everything. And if he doesn't, he knows a guy who does.

"We haven't gone *public* yet, so keep it to yourselves, but I've been spending a lot of time with Jesse." I mutter his last name, though I don't need to. They know.

When I look over at them, Grandpa is positively beaming. "Now that sounds about right."

"Why do you say that?" I ask.

He chuckles and looks down at Gram as she looks up at him. "Because you have the type of personalities that are drawn to each other."

I almost choke on my milk. All my life, Grandpa has told the story about how he knew it was love at first sight, but Gram says he's crazy and that he annoyed her at first sight and finally wore her down. *Oh my god.* I know there's that whole Freudian thing about choosing someone like your father, but how did I end up mimicking my grandparents' love story?

I take another bite of cookie. Well, if I'm going to mirror any love story, it might as well be theirs. Fifty years of happiness, love, and building an incredible life and family together. Something to aspire to for sure. Not that we're necessarily at that level, though with each passing week, my feelings for Jesse deepen, and I keep praying nothing tears us apart because I'm positive if anything did, it would rip my heart from my body and leave me an empty shell on the floor.

Well, that's a lovely thought. Moving on.

"He's a good guy. We're still easing into it, though, so—"

"We get it, girly. Our lips are sealed. But whenever you want to make it official, he better be here with you for a family dinner, got it?"

"Yes, sir."

"So, if all that's good, what has you all worked up?" Gram asks.

"I'm not worked up, but I'm a little stressed. Leo and Noah are in the top three bids for that new development they're starting on the south side. I have to come up with four whole house designs by next Monday. So far, I've got nothing."

"How long have you known about it?" Grandpa asks.

"Since this morning."

He chuckles. "Well, give yourself some time, girly. It might take you more than twenty-four hours. Plus, you might need some kind of inspiration."

"I think I do, but I don't know what."

"Ah. That's why you're here. Well, walk around outside, wander around the farmhouse. Anything you need."

"Right now, I think I need more sugar cookies," I say with a big smile.

Gram laughs. "How about a meal before another dose of sugar?"

"That might be good too," I agree.

"Perfect. It's been too long since we've had you here for dinner."

"One condition," I say. "You let me help you."

I hop off my stool and take my plate to the sink. Gram wraps an arm around me. "I suppose I can live with that." She looks at me for a moment, then narrows her eyes, smiling all the while. "You look like yourself again. Like my sunny girl. Ida's been good to you."

I smile back at her. "Yeah, it has. I think I've finally found my place."

# Jesse

"I'm never going to get this done! My stupid brain has apparently forgotten how to be creative, which is kind of important since this is my *job*." Dani growls and throws down her sketchpad.

I set my laptop down and slide over on the couch. "Come here."

She grumbles, but scooches closer. Sweeping her hair over her shoulder, I gently but firmly press my thumbs against her neck, rubbing the muscles in circles. Every muscle I touch is tight. She definitely needs this.

"It's only been two-and-a-half days," I whisper. "It takes time."

"I know but—" She stops short, letting out a little groan. Then she sighs, talking softer now. "I switched to my sketchpad, hoping it was just the computer throwing me off, but nothing. Creatively speaking, I feel like I've hit a wall. It's not just this project. I tried to do some designs for my apartment, just to get myself in a different headspace, and it was all coming out weird."

I continue moving my thumbs, going over her shoulders now.

"You might need a break, or maybe you need a fresh perspective. Something special to jolt your creativity."

She snorts. "Yeah. I don't know where I can just find something special."

I smile to myself. I was going to wait and surprise her tomorrow, but I think she needs to know now. "Good thing I do."

"Oh, really? Where?"

Dropping my hands, I spin her so she's facing me. "The house I'm going to look at tomorrow morning. I'm hoping you'll come with me."

Her eyes instantly light up.

"Yes! Oh my gosh. Of course. Where is it?"

"Right down the street. The for sale sign hasn't even gone up yet. We'll be the first ones to see it tomorrow morning."

"This is amazing. Which house is it? Are there pictures? Show me pictures!"

I laugh and kiss her nose. Her excitement is adorable. "It's the one with the grayish brown wood shingles and the covered front porch. You are not getting any pictures of the inside. They aren't online yet, and I want you to see it in person."

She pouts a little, then says, "Oh, fine. It looks gorgeous on the outside. Spacious, too."

"Well, gotta have space to fill it up with kids, right?" My cheeks heat as I say the words, but I want her to know how I feel about having a family. I've told her I want that, but we've never talked about specifics.

"How many kids do you want?" she asks, sliding her hand into mine.

"I guess I'm not really sure, but I was thinking two or three. I'd be open to more. Really, I just want to be sure I make individual time with each child. I don't ever want them to feel how Joel and I do."

She shifts on the couch, nestling into me.

"Why don't you ask your parents to spend time with you? Come home more? I know you want them here for the NICU fundraiser. Why don't you ask?"

I swallow down the emotion that wells in my stomach. My saliva sticks in my throat, and I hate it. Hate that I feel this way. That my own parents hit my trigger points. Sometimes I think it would be so much easier if they were actually shitty people. Then, at least, I could hate them. I love my parents, and in many ways I respect them. As human beings, at least. As parents, not so much.

I graze my fingers down her back, closing my eyes as I answer. The last thing I want is to see pity on her face. "I don't ask because I don't want to hear them say no. It's one thing for them to not actively choose me. It's another for them to actively *not* choose me. I don't want to feel—"

"Unwanted," she whispers, stroking a hand over my cheek.

I open my eyes and look down at her. She's giving me a soft smile, and there's not a hint of pity to be found on her gorgeous face. Just understanding. Caring. *Love.* We still haven't said it, but whether we admit it out loud or not, we both know it's there.

"Yes."

She nods and rests her head on my shoulder. "I understand that, and I'll never push you, but there's also a chance they could say yes. You won't know unless you try, but that's something only you can decide. I'll support whatever you want."

I kiss her head and pull her closer. "Thank you. Now back to what we were talking about... how many kids do you want?"

"Mm," she mumbles, brushing her fingers under my shirt and over my stomach. I love when she does that. It calms me down and lights me on fire at the same time. "I'll have to see how much I puke when I'm pregnant, but I would like several kids. No more than four, I think, but I'd really like a few. I loved having Wes and Olivia."

Twirling my fingers through her hair, I whisper, "Want to practice?"

She looks up at me, surprised for a second, but then she smiles. It's wild and seductive and has me ready to rip my clothes off right here.

"Always," she purrs, then she tackles me and kisses me deeply.

*What the hell? Might as well do it on the couch. I've already made her squirt here. Plus, it's not like anyone else is ever home, anyway.*

Dani is a ball of barely-contained excitement as we walk up the front porch to meet the realtor, who Dani also knows, since it's the same realtor AB Construction uses.

"Dani, I didn't realize you'd be joining Jesse."

She side-eyes me, wondering what I told her.

"I wanted to surprise her, Ellen."

Ellen laughs and turns toward the door. "Well, it seems like you did that. Are you two looking at the house *together?* I only ask because if you're interested, that will affect how we handle financing."

Again, Dani looks at me, this time with wide eyes. "I'll be the one buying, but I want Dani's opinion." I squeeze Dani's hand, and she breathes out a sigh of relief. I know this is a tricky thing since we haven't been dating long, but I want Dani to feel *at home* in any house I buy. Maybe it's crazy, but I see a future with her. It's still scary to want it and believe in it, but she's put her trust in me. I'm trying to do the same. Either way, I want to see Dani's smile as she walks through this house. From the few pictures I saw, I already love the interior. The old hardwood floors have been well-maintained, especially on the first floor, where there are some designs in the wood. The kitchen and bathrooms have been updated but still fit with the feel of the house. It's large and open. A blank slate to build into my home. Assuming I love it as much in person as I did in the pictures.

Ellen unlocks the door and swings it open. "Since we've already discussed the details, I'll let you two explore. I'll be in the kitchen whenever you need me."

"Thank you," I say as we walk through. I quickly turn and watch Dani's reaction.

Her eyes go wide and light up, her mouth dropping open. Then she makes a little squealing noise as she looks around the huge entryway with a massive oak staircase leading to the second floor.

"This is... oh my god." She grabs my shirt. "I know I haven't seen it all yet, but I can tell... this is going to be beautiful. So promise me you aren't just doing this to inspire me or dream or something. Because if I'm going to fall in love with this house, there better be a good possibility I at least get to visit it regularly."

"I promise I'm interested, Dani. I've been looking for months. Ellen called me and let me know this was coming on the market. Another realtor in her office is the listing agent, so Ellen gave me first dibs. I'm pre-approved, and I have a down payment ready, so if I love this like I think I will, I'm not going to waste any time."

She squeezes my hand, then asks, "Upstairs or downstairs first?"

Knowing what's at the back of the first floor, I say, "Upstairs."

We head up the large staircase, Dani running her hand over the banister as we go. "All this woodwork is stunning."

That means a lot coming from Dani. Not just because she's an interior designer, but because her grandfather was a woodworker all his life. He still does small projects, usually crafting cutting boards, kitchen utensils, and rolling pins for each of his grandchildren when they buy a home or get married.

"It is gorgeous," I say. This house is massive. Five bedrooms and two-and-a-half baths. We check out the four bedrooms up here and the two full baths. The fifth bedroom is downstairs and traditionally used as an office. We end in the master, taking in the large space, and I can see Dani's mind whirling with ideas. She turns and looks at a small nook in the room.

"A crib would fit there perfectly. In my brain, that's how I'd design it. A spot for a crib if it's a couple who are having kids. Otherwise, a little reading or office space." She turns to a wall of windows facing the backyard and overlooking the river. "This is beautiful. I could see some kind of bench or settee there. Where you could sit and look out the window or read a book."

I wrap my arms around her waist from behind and look out the window with her, imagining how we could fill up this bedroom, and envisioning the type of furniture I might want. Ever since I found that old record player cabinet, I have a better idea of what I like, especially when it comes to finishes.

"Come on, let's go downstairs."

I lead her back downstairs, and we walk through the open space. When we stop at the fifth bedroom or office, she pauses in the doorway. I can already see her bookcases and desk in here. *It's too soon*, I tell myself, but apparently, I'm a bad listener, because it's all I can think about.

When she looks over at me, her cheeks are pink. "It's a beautiful room."

I let out a breath of relief because too soon or not, she's thinking the same thing.

"It is. But there are a couple more spaces to see and they're even better."

"Show me."

I take her hand again and lead her into the kitchen. It's updated with dark wood cabinets and light modern countertops. It might be the only thing I don't love here. The cabinets contrast a bit with the floors, in my opinion, but that should be easy enough to change.

Dani looks around and opens her mouth to speak, then suddenly notices what the kitchen opens up into. Ellen smiles as Dani scampers into the three-season room.

"Oh my gosh," she breathes, staring out the wall of windows. They pop out with screens to replace them for use in the summer. It's meant to be a three-season room, but with a ceiling fan and a gas fireplace, it'll be usable year-round. But for bad weather and particularly hot or cold days, there are doors that close it off from the kitchen. "This is amazing." She shakes her head. "If you don't buy this house, I will. I don't know how, but I will."

I chuckle and pull her close, then look over at Ellen. "I have every intention of buying this house."

"Hey, Dad," I say into my phone as I walk down the hallway toward the kitchen of my parents' house. "Do you have a minute to talk?"

"Sure, bud. What's up?"

I probably could've talked with Ellen about this, but when it comes to financial stuff, my dad knows his shit. I'd rather get his opinion.

"I found a house."

"You did? That's great. Where is it?"

"Just down the street." I describe it to him.

"Oh, I've been in there once. Beautiful home," he says, and I smile. It was even more beautiful in person, and as I was hoping, Dani got a burst of inspiration from seeing the house and is sketching away right now.

"It is. I love it, and I'm putting together an offer. We're going in right at asking, which Ellen agrees will probably be perfect for the sellers. My biggest thing is figuring out how much to put down. For a second, I thought about doing it all cash. I know it would make it go faster, but that's almost fifty percent of what's in my trust, and I didn't think that sounded like a smart move. I'm pre-approved for a mortgage, but I'd like for it not to be massive, so I was thinking of doing one hundred thousand down. What do you think?"

He asks me some questions and talks me through it, then agrees that's a reasonable number.

"I'm proud of you, son. You've found a path for yourself. You're building your career, making wise financial decisions, and buying a home is a big step. Congratulations."

My chest warms. I wish his praise didn't make me feel so good, but it does. "Thanks, Dad. I'm excited."

There's quiet for a moment, and I think back to what Dani said the other night. I won't know if my parents will show up if I don't ask. I take a deep breath, finding the courage to ask him, when Dad says, "All right, son. I've got to meet your mother for dinner. She's enjoying wine with a couple of friends she's made. But I can't wait to hear more. Call me if you have any other questions. Or email anytime. Okay?"

I swallow down my disappointment. I'm not sure if I'm disappointed I didn't get a chance to ask or that I'm still too much of a chickenshit to do it. "Sure, Dad. Thanks again."

"No problem, son. Have a good day."

"You too. Bye."

I hang up and quickly text Ellen the specific numbers. She says she'll submit everything soon. If they like my offer, she said they may not even officially list it. I let out a sigh. It's nice that my dad's proud of me for making good decisions. I kind of wish he was here to see them, though.

*Whatever.*

Shaking it off, I walk into the living room to the person who is here and always seems to support me.

She's running her fingers over her sketchbook as I walk into the room. "Whatcha drawing?" I ask.

She slams the book shut and leaps off the couch. "Nothing."

She's jittery, and has the look in her eyes that I haven't seen since we started dating. *Like she's about to bolt.*

Stepping over to her, I gently wrap my hand around her arm. "Dani, what's wrong?"

# Dani

"Dani, what's wrong?"

*What's wrong?*

I don't know.

*Maybe that he's fucking loaded and never told me. Maybe that I thought we were being open with each other. Maybe that I spent the last half hour designing a dream home that will never be mine. Maybe I'm an idiot.*

I mash my lips between my teeth and take a steadying breath.

*Maybe I'm feeling extremely triggered.*

I think back to Jesse's words on my front porch that day. The frustration on his face and in his voice as he told me to talk to him when I feel triggered. This is the hard stuff. Sex is easy.

Caring for him comes naturally. Being open about my fears, especially when they feel a bit irrational, does not.

Gently removing my arm from his hand, I wrap my hand around his and pull him onto the couch with me. "You told me to talk to you if I felt triggered."

"I did," he says, tucking a leg beneath him and pulling me closer. He brushes his hand over my shoulder, caressing the side of my neck with his thumb. "You can talk to me about anything, Dani girl."

I bite my lip, not wanting to sound like an asshole. "Why didn't you tell me you have *money?*" His eyes widen and he opens his mouth, but before he can say anything, I say, "Sorry. I wasn't listening in. I had stepped into the kitchen to grab some water and heard you say the thing about paying all cash."

"Right. I'm sorry. I wasn't keeping it from you. Not intentionally, at least. It's just not something I open up about much with people. I probably should've brought it up, but honestly, I liked that..." He sighs.

"You can tell me anything, too."

He nods. "I kept asking how much the cabin cost when we went for my birthday because I've rented cabins like that before. Usually I was the one paying. Not that I couldn't afford it or I minded, necessarily, but let's just say there's a reason I'm not close with anyone I went to college with. Once my friends figured out I had money, suddenly, when it was my turn to pay, we went to the fanciest restaurant and everyone ordered the expensive shit. It sucked, and as time went on, I started to feel like they liked my money more than me. Sometimes, I even wondered about Carrie. She didn't know when we first got together, but she did when we got back together. You know, obviously G and Evan, Jenna... they don't care. I don't advertise it otherwise, because then everyone wants to be your friend for the wrong reason."

"That makes sense," I say softly.

"It's not that I didn't trust you. It's that I enjoyed money not being a focal point or a second thought. In some ways, having money makes things easier. In other ways, it complicates things. It makes people act differently. And I promise, it wasn't that I thought you'd suddenly be expecting me to pay or wanting fancy things. With you, I was anticipating the opposite. That you wouldn't want me to spoil you or do too much for you, even though I can. I just didn't want to think about it."

I stroke my hand over his cheek. "It's okay. I promise. I'm not mad at you. I can understand why you wouldn't want to bring it up. It's not even the money that got me, it's..."

"What?" he asks, fingers trailing through my hair.

"My ex owned our condo. I didn't find out until the day we broke up that he purposely did that. He used money as power. Looking back, he did that a lot. When I heard you say that, I felt stupid."

I look down, but he cups my cheek, tilting my head back up. His eyes are as soft as his tone when he asks, "Why?"

My eyes jump to my sketchpad, my heart beating faster again. "I was inspired. That's why I started sketching the second we left the house. I got down some sketches for the housing development and jotted down even more ideas, but the inspiration quickly shifted to that house, and I felt like I was designing my dream home." I pause, my throat feeling dry. I hate admitting this. "When I heard you say that, I realized how ridiculous it all was. I was designing a house that isn't mine."

"It's not ridiculous," he whispers, looking into my eyes. "I'm sorry your ex used money as power. It's what plenty of people do, but it's the last thing I want from our relationship. I don't want someone to overpower. I want a partner. I don't know for sure where we're headed, but I know where I hope this goes. And if we end up..." He stares at me, throat bobbing as he swallows hard. "If we end up getting married, I would make sure your name went on the house, too. I hope I get that house and one day you'll live there with me. If you do, I want you to know with certainty that it's your home."

"Damn it, Jesse," I breathe.

"What?"

"When you say things like that... those are always the things that make me roll my eyes because you say it with such a calm confidence that it sounds like a line. Shit my ex would say that he never actually meant."

He shakes his head. "The more I learn about your relationship with your ex, the more your hesitance with me makes sense. There's a difference between someone telling you what you want to hear and someone telling you the truth. They might have the same smooth, refined sound, but the truth is always there. If you ever question that, just look into my eyes. You'll always see the truth in them, and the way I feel for you. Look at me." I meet his gaze, my heart beating rapidly as I do. "What do you see?"

My breath hitches with a mix of excitement and fear. *What if I'm wrong?* "I don't... I don't know."

"Yes, you do. What do you see in my eyes?"

"Love," I whisper.

"Because I love you, Dani. With everything inside me, I love you. I know it's scary, but I promise to keep you and your heart safe, always. I'll protect this with everything I have. I love you, Dani girl."

Tears flood my eyes as my body relaxes. A smile tugs at the corners of his mouth, and he wraps his hand around the back of my neck. I pull him closer, brushing my nose against his as I say the words that have been swirling inside me for weeks. "I love you too." Then I press my lips into his. Our kiss starts off slow but quickly grows deeper as our tongues entangle. I let out a happy moan against his lips, and he pulls away, grinning. A moment later, we're tearing off clothes and I'm pinned beneath him on the couch as he buries himself deep inside me.

## Jesse

We're wrapped up under a blanket on the couch after our second round, intermittently kissing and saying we love each other over and over. Her head is resting on my shoulder as she trails her finger over my chest.

"So..." she begins, eyes dancing. "How much are you actually worth?"

I chuckle at that. "My trust was 750,000. I've spent just under twenty thousand of that. Now I'll be taking another hundred thousand out. Why?"

She bites her lip, holding back a laugh.

"Just wanted to know if I was living out a billionaire romance fantasy." Laughing, she gives me an adorable shrug.

"Sorry. Can't help you there. What do people even do with that much money?"

"Buy planes? Countries?"

We share a laugh, then I give her a gentle kiss. "So, can I see the drawings?" She looks at me, uncertain, so I run my hand down her thigh and say, "Please, baby? Or do I have to beg?"

"Mm. I do like when you beg." She lifts an eyebrow as she smirks at me. She sighs, her smile growing softer. "Thank you for being patient with me."

"Thank you for talking things through with me."

She kisses my cheek, then sits up and grabs the pad.

Leaning back against the couch, I wrap my arm around her as she flips through the pad, going over the few pages she designed so far. She's so fucking talented, and I love seeing her inspired. As we go through the designs, though, I'm excited for a different reason. She wasn't just designing *her* dream home. Her bookcases were there, but so was my record player. A color change for the kitchen cabinets like I mentioned to her as we were leaving the house. The chaise under the window in the master bedroom. She was designing *our* dream home.

I skim my fingers up and down her arm as she excitedly shows me all the little details, and my heart lights on fire for her.

I don't know how I got so lucky that my soul got twisted up with hers, but I never want it to come undone. We're tangled together now; I have a piece of her and she has a piece of me. I hope we never unravel. I hope we stay this way forever.

# 18
# Tell Me You Love Me

## Dani

"Here, babe," I say, handing Jesse a water bottle as he wipes his brow. For the beginning of April, it's hotter than hell. Pushing eighty, despite the fact that it was snowing nine days ago. New York weather is weird.

"Thank you. A couple more boxes, then we'll be done."

"This house is seriously so gorgeous," Amelia says, looking up at the ceiling and then back around the room.

"No kidding," Olivia says. "You bagged a good one."

"Hold on, did you two just agree about something?" I ask.

"Hey," Amelia says, holding up her hands. "I have no issues with little miss drama pants over here."

Olivia squints at Amelia, then lets out a little huff. "I might be warming up to you. You make my sister happy, so I can't completely hate you." She smirks at Amelia, who shakes her head.

Jesse wraps an arm around my back. "What about me? I make her happy, too."

"I already like you. Plus, even if I didn't, I would now with this fancy house."

I roll my eyes, but Jesse just laughs.

Garrett and Evan wander into the room laughing and... *canoodling.*

Jesse stares at them, then steps forward, pointing a finger at them. "Where the hell were you?"

"Nowhere," G says easily as Brett and Jenna walk in and set down boxes.

"No. You were having sex. *Where?* Where in my new house did you have sex?"

"Calm down, we weren't having sex," Evan says.

"Bullshit. You have sex hair," Jesse counters, making Brett snicker. I side-eye my boyfriend and he looks at me, exasperated. "Believe me, I wish I didn't know that."

"Dude. Chill. We didn't have sex."

Jesse glares at him. "Right, because you only consider it sex when one of your asses is involved. How could I forget? So where did you hook up? Tell me now so I can go sage and sweetgrass it to get your gross pheromones out."

Brett is full-on belly laughing now, as I stare down this train wreck, unable to look away if I wanted to.

*I don't want to.*

G smacks a hand on Jesse's shoulder. "There are no gross pheromones."

He and Evan turn toward the front door.

"But if there were," Evan says, turning back, "they definitely wouldn't be in the closet off the kitchen."

Letting out a grumble, Jesse yells after them. "I hate you!"

"No, you don't," G says as they walk onto the porch.

"Well, that was a fun interlude," Brett says. "Back to moving things?"

"Let's go," Jenna says.

Amelia and Olivia follow them to the front door as I turn to Jesse and toss my arms around his neck. "You're very grumpy. You waited six weeks and got through all the paperwork and nonsense to get here. You should be excited to move in."

"I am." He gives me a pathetic pout. "But I wanted to be the first one to have sex here."

I lean in and press my lips to his. "I promise, we will make a list and have sex everywhere in this house we can think of."

At that, his face lights up. He brushes his lips over mine. "I guess I could agree to that."

"Good." I smack a kiss on his cheek, then spin out of his arms and head for the door. He smacks my ass as I walk away. "Think about that list." I wink at him, then head back outside to the truck, leaving him to trail after me.

I'm busy unpacking kitchen stuff with Olivia while the guys continue moving furniture in. We took a quick break for lunch, then Jesse and the guys went to pick up the various furniture items he'd picked out. We figured it was easier than waiting for a delivery time since we had the hands to move it today. Plus, it'll be nice to be settled before we go out of town tomorrow. We're dropping Olivia—who has been visiting for the week—off at the airport, then heading up to visit Rae, Aaron, Joel and everyone else where they go to college about two-and-a-half hours away. Because all of their friends have birthdays in the same couple of months, they're having a big twenty-first birthday celebration tomorrow before they head to Charleston for their spring break.

Olivia bumps her hip against mine as I put the few cookbooks Jesse grabbed at the bookstore yesterday in a row on the counter. Something about having a few cookbooks on display makes things feel homier.

"So…"

I turn to face my sister. "What?"

She looks around to make sure no one else is nearby, but Jenna and Amelia are upstairs unpacking sheets, towels, and bathroom stuff, and the guys are probably still trying to figure out how to get Jesse's couch in the front door.

"You and Jesse are adorable. I know I've told you that multiple times this week. So why haven't you told everyone else yet?"

I shrug, a wave of discomfort lodging in my stomach. "I don't know. We just haven't. Things have been amazing, but ever since we started dating, it's been busy. His birthday, the swim team going to the state finals, the housing development stuff for work, and all this with the house… every free moment we have has been spent in our little love bubble."

"I guess I get that, but if you love him as much as you seem to, you need to think about telling everyone else. Secrets have a way of destroying relationships, even when you're not keeping the secret from your partner."

I stare at her for a moment. A lot of the women in our family take after Gram. Strong, loving, comforting. Olivia has bits of her, but damn if she's not mostly Grandpa. Especially her effortlessly blunt way of calling people—particularly me—out.

There's talking and faint arguing as the guys make it through the front door.

"Yeah," I say softly. Because she's right. I need to stop holding back the best part of my life from the people I love—and I need to stop asking Jesse to do the same. He hasn't pushed me about it, but things *have* been busy. His swim team and then the house have been his focus. Work has been mine. When we're together, we're just *us*. We deserve to be us with everyone, though.

The guys stroll into the kitchen and reach for fresh water bottles.

"Got the couch in," Jesse says with a sigh of relief. "Hopefully, the loveseat will be easier."

"Let's hope," Brett says. "Of course, if someone had listened and not tried to jam the couch through the door..." He looks pointedly at Garrett, who looks up from his phone with a smirk.

"Hey, we made it fit."

"Is that what he tells you?" Amelia asks Evan, strolling into the kitchen.

Olivia and I are fighting back laughter, but surprisingly, Garrett misses the joke.

"Everything okay?" Jesse asks him.

Garrett tucks his phone away and looks at Jesse. "Uh, yeah. That was just Brooks. He wanted to see how things were going."

Jesse plays with the cap of his water bottle. "He could've just texted me and asked."

"He wasn't so sure after how your last conversation went."

"Well, maybe he should have told me sooner that Carrie liked to hit on him. I'm still annoyed, but I'll get through it. I just trust him a little less now." He walks over and leans against the counter, pulling me in front of him and wrapping his arms around my waist from behind. I rest my head against his shoulder and he squeezes me tighter. "Lying sucks."

Olivia's eyes dart to mine.

*Okay, universe. I get it. It's time to woman up.*

Olivia squeezes me tightly as we stand together just inside the airport.

"I miss you already. Can I come back this summer? Maybe stay in that big house with you?"

I push out of the hug and shake my head. "I don't live there, remember?"

She rolls her eyes. "You will."

"We'll see."

She gives me one more quick hug.

"Don't be afraid to tell the world, D. Don't be afraid at all. Jesse's one of the good ones. I can see it in his eyes."

I smile softly at that. "Yeah. Thanks, Livvie. Love you. Have a safe flight and text me when you get there."

"Will do. Love you too." She takes a few steps, then turns back. "Don't be a chickenshit!"

"Thanks for that."

She shoots me a wink and blows me a kiss.

I blow one back, then she walks away, and I turn and walk out of the airport.

When I get back to the car, Jesse smiles softly and gives me a kiss. "Olivia all set?"

"Yep. She said she wants to come back this summer."

"Definitely. She can stay with us."

My eyes widen slightly, but then I smile because he doesn't even realize what he said.

*He's one of the good ones.*

Maybe it's time to come clean.

We get to the lake house that Jesse's parents own—and where Rae, Aaron, Joel and all their friends live while going to school—around eleven. Jesse agreed to come up early to help decorate. I just didn't mention I'd be coming too.

That's perfect. We could walk in together and I could just kiss him in front of everyone. We haven't talked about telling everyone, but I doubt he'd care.

He opens the car door for me and takes my hand.

*Are we doing this?*

We walk up onto the porch hand in hand, but when we get to the door, Jesse glances at me, uncertain. I try to read his expression, but before I can, he squeezes my hand, then lets it go.

*So we're not telling people?*

Whatever. I'll follow his lead, I guess.

He swings the front door open without knocking and we're greeted with several smiling faces.

"Hey, big bro," Joel says as Jesse hugs him.

"Little brother." He smacks Joel on the shoulder as he steps back, then looks toward the kitchen. "Rae Rae. Sarah."

"Hey, Dani," Joel says.

"Happy almost birthday," I tell him as I follow Jesse into the house.

"What are you doing here?" Sarah asks, surprised.

"I told you I was coming," I say, like it's no big deal. Jesse's acting... normal, I guess. I will too.

Rae and Sarah exchange a glance. "You didn't mention you were coming with Jesse," Rae says.

I glance over at him and shrug. Keeping a smile plastered on my face, I say, "We're friends."

Though I don't show it, the words stick in my throat, making me feel like I'm choking. Unable to meet Jesse's glance, I walk past him into the kitchen, desperate for some water. As I go, I feel the heat of his gaze on me, but I'm not sure if it's desire or frustration.

## Jesse

I watch Dani across the room laughing and talking with Rae, Sarah, and a few of their other friends. Goddamn, I want her, even though it was a slight knife to the gut how easily she said we were just friends, but I'm trying to let it go.

We didn't talk about telling everyone we're together before we came, but at the same time, it's been almost three months. I don't want to hide this anymore. It was easy back home. Life was crazy, but I'm moved into the house now. There's still plenty of unpacking and decorating to do, more things to buy, but I want to do it all with her. I hope she'll live there with me in the not-too-distant future. I'm ready for the world to know she's all fucking mine.

*I hope she is. I hope I'm hers.*

Pathetic asshole, party of one.

Maybe that's why I let her hand go before we walked in. I was hoping she'd grab it again.

*Yay for baggage. Maybe I need to go to therapy.*

"So, what's going on with you and Dani?" my brother asks, stepping up next to me.

I glance at him for half a second before my attention turns to her.

"We're friends." *Great, now I'm doing it.*

He chuckles. "Got it."

I turn toward him. "What does that mean?"

He shrugs. "Nothing... I've had a friend like that before. So has Aaron. Worked out pretty well for both of us." He smirks at me like the asshole he is. I have no room to talk. He learned that shit from me. And here I am, following in his footsteps by acting like I'm not with the girl I'm in love with. The cycle of stupidity is complete.

"You're annoying."

"Hey, I get it. I waited a long time for Sarah to be ready, and it was worth every second of that wait, but you don't have to pretend for our sake. We all want you both to be happy. If you want your girl, go get her." He grimaces. "Before one of my teammates tries."

He nods to where the girls were standing. Rae is nowhere to be seen, Sarah is a few steps away talking to Trevor's girlfriend, and Dani is standing awkwardly in front of some tool in a backward baseball cap.

*Fucker.*

Without another word, I stalk over to Dani and wrap my arm around her waist. "Hey, babe," I rumble in her ear, smacking a kiss on her cheek.

She grins up at me. "Hey." Dudebro raises his eyebrows. "I told you I was with someone." *Fuck yes.*

"You didn't tell me he was here."

"Doesn't matter. I'm not a cheater, and you shouldn't be trying to get with girls who have a boyfriend."

He laughs. "That's nice, but a lot of girls don't share your thoughts on that. Have a good night."

He walks away, and she looks up at me. "Thanks for the save."

"You don't have to thank me. It's kind of my job."

Her eyes narrow for a second, and I'm not sure why. It's almost like she doesn't agree, or doesn't believe me. Which I don't understand. She's been sending mixed signals all day. What the hell does she want? The selfish part of me screams, *what the hell do I want?*

*What I want is to stop hiding this. I want to put everything out there. Fuck, I just want her to show me she wants what I do.*

I search her face for another moment. I wrap my arms around hers, looking into her eyes as I lean forward, ready to show this whole damn party she's mine, but before I can get to her lips, her sharp inhale stops me. Her eyes dart around the room, and she looks a little panicked.

"Jesse, what are you doing?"

I lean back at that and let out a bitter laugh. *Great question.* What am I doing? Making the same mistakes all over again? It's starting to feel that way, since she still wants to keep us a secret from some of the most important people in our lives. It makes me wonder if I'm still chasing a girl who doesn't want me as much as I want her.

I step back and shrug. "I have no idea." Her eyes go wide, so I lean in and nod over my shoulder toward the baseball player who was hitting on her. "Maybe you should go back and hang out with your new friend instead."

"Jesse," she gasps, but I turn and walk away. I played this game for years with Carrie. Dani put me through months of hell. I thought we were on the other side of it, but clearly, I was wrong.

I down a shot of whiskey. My third. We were going to go home tonight, but whatever, we can just stay here. I can. Dani can do whatever she wants. Which has mostly been glaring at me from across the room while pretending she isn't.

"Really? You're just going to sit here and ignore me all night while pouting into your drink?" Dani sasses, coming to stand next to me.

"Nothing better to do," I say with a shrug, reaching for the bottle, but she snatches it away.

"I thought you said you didn't play games. Not with me."

"The only one playing games here is you. Just like always."

Her eyes flare. "That's it. We're going home."

"What?" I spit out.

"We're going home. Clearly, we have some things to discuss and I'm not going to do it here. They cut the cake, and we sang happy birthday. They're leaving first thing in the morning to go to Charleston, anyway, so let's go."

"How are we getting home? I can't drive."

She squints at me. That sassy glare that makes me hornier than it should. Especially right now when I don't understand what the hell is going on with us.

"Did you miss the news? Women are actually allowed to drive cars now. We can own property and vote, too."

"You're hilarious."

"I'm driving. Slur your goodbyes, and let's go."

"I'm not drunk."

"You're on your way," she bites back, and the words cut deep. I don't drink a lot anymore, especially around her. I prefer it, and I like making her feel safe. Now, here I am, acting like an asshole. I'm still hurt and confused, but that doesn't make using drinking as a coping mechanism okay. *Fuck.*

Softening, I gently run my hand down her arm. "Okay."

Her shoulders relax for a moment, then she gives a firm nod, and we split up to say our goodbyes.

When I get to the car, she's already sitting in the driver's seat, waiting for me. I pull the passenger door open and climb in, buckling my seatbelt as she turns the car on. It started raining about an hour ago, and it's getting dark now, so everything feels extra dreary.

She pulls out of the driveway and navigates us back to the main road in complete silence. It's the kind of quiet you can feel in your bones. I can tell she's pissed, and I feel bad for going straight to drinking, but I'm also still upset by how she was acting.

*Be the bigger person. Own your shit.*

"Dani, I'm sorry I was drinking."

She whips her head around to look at me as she stops at a red light, waiting to turn onto the highway.

"Do you think that's why I'm upset right now?"

*Ah, crap. This is one of those moments that feels like a test and no matter what I say, I'll be wrong.*

She focuses back on the road as the light turns green and she pulls onto the highway.

"I... assumed."

She sighs heavily. "No, I don't love that rather than talk to me, you decided to go drink. That's not what I'm upset about, though."

"Then what—"

"Shit," she mutters. Then the sound of pounding rain drowns out any other noise.

Dani's breathing picks up and her knuckles are turning white around the steering wheel.

"Pull off at the next exit if you need to," I say softly.

She barely glances at me, but I can see her eyes are filled with both fear and hurt. "No. I'll be fine." It's hard to believe that, though, because a tear slides down her cheek and she sniffs. "I just don't like this kind of hard rain, but it'll be fine. I want to get home. Can you just put on some soft instrumental music? It helps me stay calm."

"Sure," I whisper, feeling like an absolute asshole. I pull out my phone and find the playlist of instrumental music she shared with me—she said it was good to have on in the background while working. Once it's playing, I say, "I know you want to go home, but pull over any time and we can find a hotel, okay?"

Again she glances at me, but doesn't say anything, giving a quick nod instead. I stare at her for a moment, then slowly move my hand so it's resting on her thigh. She bristles when she feels my hand on her, but then lets out a shuddery breath and relaxes into my touch.

*I've still got you, babe, even when we're all messed up.*

The drive home has been exhausting, especially for Dani. The rain barely let up, and it's coming down as hard as ever as she pulls off the highway in Ida. I sobered up on the drive home and offered to switch with her about an hour ago, but she again told me she was fine and didn't want to stop. I wish we would have, though, because the tension between us has only grown, and it's not fun, sexual tension. It's like the shift in the air right before a bomb goes off. I'm scared that bomb will be us. My insecurities are feasting on that feeling and all the uncertainties I felt at the party are back with a vengeance. The car ride from the highway exit to the house is stifling—it's hard to breathe trapped in this car with her, and she must feel the same because her grip on the steering wheel has loosened, and she's wiggling with nervous energy. I'm starting to wonder if when she said she wanted to go home, she meant she wanted to get away from me.

Things were amazing this morning. How did they get so fucked up?

*She didn't choose me?*

I wish I could shut my brain up, but it's raging, nitpicking all the tiny little things that were signs we were headed here. Wherever here is.

Dani pulls into the driveway, but rather than drive down and pull into the garage, she shuts off the car next to the house, flings her door open, and goes running into the rain.

Without a second thought, I follow her, and we end up in the middle of the backyard, letting the rain coming down in sheets pelt us.

She's standing a few feet away, breathing heavily, but not crying. Doing my best to push my insecurities away, I walk over to her and pick up where we left off almost three hours ago.

"Why were you upset with me? Why are you?"

"Are you kidding me? Why am I upset?" she yells over the pouring rain. "Maybe because you just stomped off rather than talk to me after telling me to go hang out with some other guy! That's the exact kind of thing I never want our relationship to be." Her voice drops. "It makes me feel like it's all a game. I never want to feel that way with you. It pisses me off that you think I'm playing games."

I stare at her for a moment, a volcano of feelings ready to go off. "I told you our relationship and you are not games to me. You know that. But when you wouldn't kiss me, it felt just like it did back in October. This girl who doesn't know what she wants, dragging my heart behind you while you figure it out."

She blinks a couple of times, then slugs me in the shoulder. "You're an idiot! You're too wrapped up in your own shit to bother talking to me and just assumed I didn't want to kiss? You surprised me! That's all. I was asking because I was surprised!"

"Surprised?" I shout back. "Why would you be surprised I want to kiss you? That I want the world to know about us. You're the one who told everyone we were just friends when we got there. What the hell else was I supposed to think?" The words fly out of my mouth with no filter. I'm spiraling now, and there's no stopping it. My heart aches as I yell my biggest fears. "It's been months, Dani! And some of the most important people in our lives don't know about us. That fucking kills me, and it makes me feel like you don't really want this—or don't really love me." I'm panting when I finish, water dripping off my hair and over my cheeks, droplets beaded on my eyelids.

She takes a step back, shocked, her eyes brimming with hurt, and I realize what I just said.

"You think I don't love you?" She bites her lip and closes her eyes, holding back tears. She opens her eyes again, tears flowing down her cheeks and mixing with the rain. "I was scared and nervous, and that made you think I don't love you? How—how do you not know..."

I step forward and wrap my hands around her face, my fingers brushing the back of her neck as I look into her eyes.

"I didn't mean that." She tries to shake her head, but I hold it in place, never breaking my gaze. "I meant that it triggered that insecurity in me. That fear that I'm chasing someone who will never love me right. Sometimes I wish I could still be the guy who doesn't give a shit, but that's not me anymore. And that guy wouldn't be worthy of your love." Her eyes bore into me, and I look back with equal intensity, wanting her to know my words are the truth, desperate for her to know how much she means to me and how badly I want her. I brush my thumbs over her cheeks, wiping away both the rain and her tears. "I want to be worthy of your love, Dani. I hope I am." I continue staring into her eyes as I say the words, praying what I see in them is the truth.

# 19
# Rain & Fireworks

## Dani

JESSE SOFTLY CARESSES MY cheeks as he stares into my eyes, heart cracked open, maybe more vulnerable than he's ever been with me. It's so simple, but it's everything. And it's a moment that makes it clear what we have is worth fighting for.

Love is a funny thing. We think we know what it is, and all too often we hold on for too long when we think we have it, only to realize later we never did. Love isn't the big gestures or the right words. Love is random Tuesdays and late nights. It's caring for someone so deeply you can't imagine doing anything else. It's being open and having hard conversations. It's trust. It's saying the wrong words over and over until you find the right ones. It's the tiniest and simplest moments. Love is choosing each other, holding space, and reassurance. And sometimes, it's when your insecurities clash against theirs and you both have to stand and fight because your love is worth it.

I've never known anything more worthwhile than this.

"Jesse," I whisper, resting my hands on his waist. "You've always been worthy of my love. I don't ever want you to doubt that or the way I feel for you. I love you, and I'm ready for the world to know. The only reason I said we were friends was because you let my hand go on the porch. I thought maybe you weren't sure or weren't ready. Then I started worrying about whether I should say it, which spiraled into wondering what everyone else would think or say. That you were with Rae's cousin. That I was—"

"A consolation prize," he says softly, his hands dropping down to my arms.

I nod. "I didn't want anyone thinking or implying or even joking that I was second best. It sounds ridiculous when I say it now because I know I'm not." I shake my head and take a deep breath, then grab his arms, running my hands down them until my fingers twine with his. "I'm sorry. I let my insecurities get in the way and trigger yours. I love you, and I promise I'm ready to shout those words from the rooftops. You're the man I love, the man I want, the one I see a beautiful future with." I swallow as I squeeze his hands. "Remember what you told me? The truth is always there. You can't hide it. Look in my eyes. What do you see?"

He stares at me for a moment more, then threads his hand through my hair.

"Love."

He crushes his lips over mine before I can get another breath out. His tongue possessively sweeps my mouth as his lips swell against mine, claiming me. I'm his. I think I have been since that night at The Rooftop. I just didn't know it then.

He's always been protecting my heart.

I slide my hand up his chest and rest it over his heart. I need him to know I'll protect his.

He breaks our kiss, breathing heavily and cupping my cheeks as he stares intensely into my eyes.

"I see my future in those eyes, Dani girl." He breathes out a sigh and steps back. "I'm sorry I overreacted. I'm sorry for how I acted. For not trusting you."

"I remember my dad telling me once that trust is an action. And sometimes, even though we know and love the people around us, we let our fears get the best of us and our trust falters. It doesn't mean anything other than we're human. He said what matters most is what you do when you realize you've let that fear creep in." I brush my hand over his cheek. "We talk through things. Or sometimes yell, but no matter what, we fight through it. We don't let the trauma from our past win. Every time we push through, we build our foundation a little stronger."

He pushes my wet hair away from my face and softly kisses me. "And a strong foundation helps weather the storms that blow through. I love you, Dani girl. I promise to keep fighting for us."

"I promise, too."

He kisses me again. It's gentle but all-consuming, like he's casting a spell on me. It makes me feel weightless, wild, free. Like I want to run through a field or... I laugh, pulling away from him.

He tilts his head in confusion. Then I smile and go running across the backyard, twirling around, arms outstretched.

*Wild and free like I want to dance in the rain.*

He chases after me, and grabs my hand, spinning me around. "Dancing in the rain, huh?"

"It's on the list. Plus, you said you thought I'd look sexy all wet."

He drags his gaze over my body, and heat swells inside me, fighting against the coldness of the rain.

"Unbelievably sexy." He pauses for a moment, staring at me. "Are we okay?"

I throw my arms around his neck and kiss him. "Better than okay, but let's try talking first next time, okay?"

He laughs. "Deal."

I take his hands and wiggle his arms. "Now dance with me, Wilkinson."

"Anything you want, Dani girl."

We move together, bouncing and dancing, my hand fisted in his shirt so I don't lose my balance on the muddy ground. I've lost track of what time it is or how long we've been out here, but eventually Jesse stops me, pulling me close. He runs his thumb over my chin.

"You're trembling, babe. Let's go inside. We can do this again in the summer when it's warm."

"Promise?"

"Absolutely."

Then he lifts me into his arms and kisses me before carrying me into the house.

## Jesse

I turn the shower on hot, letting steam fill up the master bathroom, then turn to Dani. She looks even sexier than I imagined. Her soaked sweatshirt is on the floor next to her, and the T-shirt she's wearing is soaked through as well and clinging to her. I run my thumbs over her peaked nipples, then claim her mouth in another searing kiss.

Falling in love after being hurt isn't easy, but when you find the right person and they support you while you heal, it's beautiful. Dani and I have our share of baggage, but the love we have for each other outweighs all of that. Wading through the emotions isn't easy, but it's a hell of a lot easier when you know you're safe.

It felt good to be vulnerable, to let my fears out and not have them held against me. I never said those kinds of things to Carrie, even though I felt them, because I didn't think she'd be receptive. She'd mock me or shut me down or it would turn into a fight. Even though it was scary tonight, I knew I could spiral and let my guard down with Dani. I've never had that before.

The freedom of knowing the other person in the relationship will always catch you when you fall makes the free fall a lot less terrifying.

"Jesse," Dani moans. I'll never get enough of her saying my name. It's like crack to me.

I step back and pull her shirt over her head, then unbutton those sexy jeans. They hug her ass perfectly and were driving me nuts all day.

She runs her fingers through my wet hair, and when her fingertips brush my scalp, I go from a semi to hard as a rock.

"Is this where you want to christen the house?"

I kiss her neck as I push her jeans down. "It's a good place to start."

"Such a good answer." She pulls my shirt over my head and drops it to the floor, then presses her body into mine. "I love you, Jesse."

"I love you too, Dani girl."

After stripping naked, we climb into the steaming shower, but we're too busy kissing to get under the water. Pressing her against the wall, I lift her legs and wrap them around my hips, then buck into her. The first few seconds always feel like the first time again. A rush of desire that feels so damn good I have to stop for a second and calm myself down.

It's hot and fast and sloppy, but it fills the immediate needs.

Needs we reawaken as soon as we're under the water and tantalizingly washing each other.

*Hold it together until we get to the bedroom.*

Easier said than done.

After more kissing, we get out of the shower and dry off, not bothering to get dressed because we're both ready to go again.

We kiss our way into the bedroom, then I push her onto the bed.

This is the one thing I cared most about having done and put together. Garrett and Evan helped me get the gorgeous dark oak bed frame put together and then I made the bed up with the sheets I picked and added the throw pillows Dani thought would complement them. It looks like an adult bed. Something I've never had. I was still sleeping on the fifteen-year-old full-size bed at my parents' house. It worked, but it wasn't comfortable.

Dani pulls me to her lips again, kissing me forcefully. I grind my cock between her thighs, letting it rub the outside of her pussy.

"God, you make me crazy. I need you."

I lift my lips off hers and grin down at her. "I can see why you like this begging thing. I think I need a little more of that." I kiss down her chest and abdomen, lifting my lips when I get to her pelvis. "And if we're christening this bed, I definitely need to make you squirt."

"But then we'll have to change the sheets," she whines.

I laugh as I sit up. Yeah, cleaning up after that is a bit of a beast. I paid to have my parents' couch professionally cleaned. I cared a lot less about the old mattress in my bedroom. We put down about a thousand towels at Dani's apartment, since her squirting is now a regular thing. Once she did it the first time, it came more easily to her.

"Don't worry, babe. That's why I got this." Reaching down, I pull a tote from under the bed, open it, and take out the waterproof blanket I got. Expensive, but if you take good care of it, it'll last a long time. "It's a waterproof blanket. I guess lots of people hate cleaning up after..."

She grabs my arm and pulls me to her lips again. "You're sweet. And thoughtful. I love you. Now I won't try to hold back."

"Good. Because I don't ever want you to." I unfold the blanket and lay it over the comforter. "Lift that sexy ass," I say, smacking the side of her butt. She laughs and lifts her hips, allowing me to slide the blanket underneath her. As soon as it's in place, I prowl across the bed, grab her legs and pull her to me, dipping my mouth between her legs.

Her soft moans rile me up, and I'm desperate to feel her come. I lap at her clit as I slide two fingers inside her, pumping rapidly.

"Oh god," she groans. "Fuck..." Her legs clench around me as she fists my hair, controlling the exact position of my head and making sure I'm right where she wants me. I'm delirious as she grinds against my mouth. All the blood in my body is flowing away from my brain. I curve my fingers slightly and pump them faster. Then all at once, she cries out, screaming as she squirts then comes hard. She pushes on my head, but I'm having too much fun, and don't stop until she brings her feet to my shoulders and pushes me away.

Laughing, I slide up her body, lining myself up between her legs.

She groans as I thrust into her. I can't help but smile looking at her gorgeous face.

She smirks back, then hooks her leg around my thigh and pushes me onto my back, giving me that seductive look she always gets when she's in control.

Her hand comes to my neck, and a shiver runs up my spine.

Leaning down, she runs her lips over my cheek. "We need to break this bed in properly."

*Fuck yes.*

I met my match with this girl in every possible way, and I couldn't be happier.

I wake up tangled in Dani's arms, and I thank the universe or fate or whatever higher power there is for bringing us together.

"Morning," she whispers, kissing my neck.

"Morning, gorgeous." And she does look gorgeous. Her amber hair is messily strewn over the pillows and she's wearing a soft smile.

"How was your second night sleeping in your new bed?"

"First night."

"What?"

"I slept on the couch the first night."

Her brow furrows. "What? Why?"

"Because I wanted to sleep in this bed for the first time with you."

She gives me adorable puppy dog eyes. "Aw. Babe. You're cute."

"Mm. I kinda love you, Dani girl."

"I love you too." She rolls on top of me and gives me a sexy good morning kiss.

We're lost in a steamy make-out session when Dani's phone rings. She reluctantly breaks our kiss, but when she reaches for it, I smack her butt.

"Behave, it's my grandparents."

Yeah, that's a surefire sign that I won't.

"Hello?" she answers, shifting back onto the bed. *Straddling me.* But I'm supposed to behave? Yeah, right.

I softly graze my fingers up her thighs and she swats at my hands.

"Hey, Gram. Hi, Grandpa."

Running my fingers the opposite direction, I brush them past her bent knees and down her calves, reaching to tickle her feet. She nearly shrieks and tries to kick my hands away.

"I'd love to come for dinner." She flares her eyes at me. "But only if I can bring my boyfriend."

At those words, I bring my hands to her thighs, my thumbs resting right at her pelvis and I gently push them in, watching as she squirms.

"Yeah," she chokes out. "We're slowly making it public."

I repeat the same movement and she nearly falls over. When she rights herself, she glares at me, then she smirks, and tantalizingly slowly rolls her hips. Her crotch grinds over my dick, causing me to harden.

*Damn, she's good.*

"Absolutely. Can we bring anything?" she asks calmly, repeating the movement of her hips.

I bite back a groan.

"Perfect. We'll see you at six. Love you. Bye."

She hangs up and tosses her phone to the side before stretching her body over mine and brushing her lips across my lips. "Two can play at that game."

I stare at her for a moment, then quickly flip her, pinning her hands next to her head. I repeat the movement she made, brushing my lips over hers. "Two can play at this game, too." Then I thrust into her as she gasps. *My favorite game to play.*

# Dani

Fun fact, Jesse likes edging me. I don't think he knew that before this morning, but he discovered it. His way of punishing me for teasing him while I was on the phone.

Not that it was much of a punishment. I came so hard I couldn't see for a second.

I should not be thinking about any of this right now, but that asshole has been doing the same thing tonight—just a more family friendly version. Touching me in just the right spots at just the right time to get me all riled up. *While we're at my grandparents' house.* He drives me insane in the best possible way.

We had some small talk, devoured dinner, and now that we have coffee and dessert, Grandpa starts in on Jesse.

"So, Jesse Wilkinson, are you taking care of my girly?"

"Of course, sir."

Gram laughs at that and Grandpa smiles widely. "Drop the sir, crap. We both know that's not you, Wilkinson."

"I'm capable of being respectful," he says in mock offense.

A dinner with my grandparents is the ultimate test of any relationship. Whoever any of us picks has to be able to contend with my grandparents. They aren't formidable necessarily, but they see through people, and Grandpa loves to give people a good ribbing. Granted, he knows how to read a room and not push people too hard, but he likes the ones who can take his shit and give it back. Maybe if I'd had dinner alone with them and Jason, I'd have realized what an asshat he was sooner. He was terrified of my grandfather.

"Respect isn't about what name you call me. It's about how you treat Dani. The greatest respect you'll ever give me is taking care of her."

Jesse swallows and meets his gaze. "I will always take care of her." Under the table, he squeezes my hand. "I'll tell you what I promised her before this all started—I'll always protect her heart. I know all too well what it's like to have someone not value you or respect you. I will never take her for granted. I'm a lucky guy, and I know it."

Grandpa gives him an approving smile and nods. "Good."

We talk a little more, then Grandpa invites Jesse out to the back deck for a cigar. He'll probably grill him a little more, but Jesse can hold his own.

I give him a quick kiss, and again he lights me on fire by simply dragging his fingers under the back of my shirt along the waistband of my pants.

He gives me his signature charming smile, then strolls out the back door with Grandpa.

Flustered, I turn to help Gram clean up, though there's not really much to do. We loaded our plates in the dishwasher after dinner, so she makes some tea and we head for the couch in the living room.

"Jesse brings out your joy," she says softly, taking me in.

"He does. He also makes me feel safe enough to let it out. I was pretty guarded after what happened with Jason."

Gram laughs a little. "I remember."

"It was hard for me to open up to Jesse at first. In fact, I was pretty mean to him. I was so afraid he was going to be like Jason and hurt me."

I rest my arm on the back of the couch and she gently puts her hand over the top of mine, giving it a little squeeze.

"Yet, you managed to open your heart to him."

"Something kept pulling me to him. Once I did…" I trail off. Tears well in my eyes as emotion clogs my throat. "He loves so deeply. I've never had that—not romantically, at least. I've never felt as free with anyone else as I do with him. I can be any version of myself and he still loves me."

"That, my dear, is real love. I'm so blessed to get to watch so many of my grandchildren find it. Some had a bumpier path than others." We both laugh, knowing she's alluding to Rae and her roller coaster love story with Aaron. "It's beautiful to watch you all grow into the strongest, best versions of yourselves. You've found more than love this year, haven't you?"

I nod. "I feel like I've found myself again."

I sniff, and so does Gram. She sets her tea on the table and pulls me into her arms. "I'm proud of you, Sunny. Of the woman you've become. I love you, honey."

"I love you too, Gram."

When she lets me go, I snuggle up next to her on the couch as we drink our tea and chat. It's hard living so far from my parents and siblings, but I'm incredibly grateful to have my amazing grandparents so close.

I nestle tightly against Jesse, nuzzling my face into his neck as we cuddle in bed.

He laughs and tickles his fingers down my ribs. "What are you doing?"

"Mm, you're cozy, and you smell good." I laugh at myself. "I read these books sometimes set in what's called the omegaverse. Long story short, there are regular humans and then alphas and omegas. Omegas and alphas are drawn to each other's scents. Omegas, specifically, are extremely comforted by alpha scents and will burrow into their neck or armpits. It sounds silly, but that's how I feel right now. Like I just want to burrow into you. Honestly, you never have to worry about me leaving you," I say with a kiss to his neck. "I'm kind of obsessed."

He laughs again. "I always knew you were secretly my stalker."

I run a hand down my face. "Do you know how embarrassed I was when I liked that picture on your Instagram from like two years ago?"

"I loved it. I was fucking thrilled. And it felt special knowing you were stalking me."

"How do you know I don't stalk other guys?" I tease.

He rolls over and looks at me, eyes dancing. "Is that your kink?" Shaking my head, I laugh, but he grabs my arm. "Seriously, have you done that with anyone else?"

"No, not really."

"Not really? Oh my gosh, were you the girl watching guys you crushed on from behind a locker and following them to their classes?"

I smack his shoulder. "No, you goof. But there was one little boy I was obsessed with. My first crush. I thought of him regularly into adulthood, but that might just have been because I didn't know who he was. It was more of a fantasy."

He squints at me. "Hold on. How did you not know the identity of your crush?"

I rub my forehead. I wasn't planning on revealing this tonight, but sure. "I met him at one of Grandma and Grandpa's parties. It was the Fourth of July and he was in the bunch of kids who were running around with us at the party. He was adorable, but I never knew his name. Later that night, when it was time for fireworks, I was nervous because they really scared me when I was a kid. I tried to be brave, but I got scared and went running for the farmhouse. Knowing my grandparents were near the house, my parents let me go, but then there was a really loud one and I stopped by the barn, absolutely terrified, and started crying. The little boy came out of the house, walked over to me, and took my hand. He told me it was going to be okay, and I believed him. I felt so safe in that moment." I shrug. "But I never found out who he was."

Jesse bites his lip, fighting back a smile, and nods. "Do you remember the first time we met?"

"Yeah. It was a summer gathering at my grandparents' house when we were in middle school. I knew Joel since he was with Rae a lot, but it was the first time I met you."

He brushes his thumb over my cheek. "That might've been the first time we were introduced, but it wasn't the first time we met. For most of my childhood, we didn't go to your grandparents' for the Fourth of July because my dad's friend lived in Pennsylvania and had lakefront property with lots of cottages, so we'd go there. One year, though, we couldn't for some reason, so we went to your family party instead. We were never introduced, but as soon as we got there, Rae scampered over and pointed out you and Olivia and said, *'That's Dani and Olivia. They're my cousins, so be nice.'*"

I laugh at that. That is one hundred percent Rae.

"Anyway," he continues, "later that night, when the fireworks started, I snuck back to the house for another soda, hoping I could drink most of it before my parents caught me." He grins at me. That's very Jesse. "When I came out of the farmhouse, I saw you standing against the barn crying." *Wait. What?* My eyes widen as I stare at him. "When we were playing together that afternoon, you were so joyful and seeing you sad seemed wrong.

I wanted to help." He shrugs. "So, I walked over, took your hand, and told you it would be okay. I kept squeezing a little tighter to try to calm you down. We stayed like that until your grandpa came out of the house and picked you up." He laughs. "He also took my soda."

"It was you?" I breathe. "You're my fireworks boy?"

He runs his thumb over my cheek. "All me."

I can't help but laugh. "At Rae's wedding, I kept wishing I'd meet him again. You were right there all along." I shake my head. It's been him all this time.

"All this time, I've been saying I'd protect your heart. It's because I always have. It's the same reason I never made a move on you when we were teenagers. I thought you were sexy, but I never wanted to risk hurting you. But your joy and happiness always captivated me."

"I guess it makes sense now why I always felt like I was fighting my instincts with you. I was so drawn to you, but then my fears would creep in and try to convince me I was being too trusting. Really, I felt safe with you because I was." I gently kiss his cheek.

He shrugs. "Maybe you recognized my scent."

I laugh and snuggle closer, wrapping my body around his, truly feeling like the luckiest girl in the world. Somehow, without me ever realizing it, the universe gave me my dream boy, and I couldn't be happier.

# 20
## Legacy of Love

## Jesse

I FLOP DOWN ON Dani's bed, wrapping my arms around her. We've both been insanely busy the last week-and-a-half. I'm glad we've only got a couple more days until the weekend, because I need some alone time with my girl. She's been busting her ass designing all kinds of interiors for Leo, plus wrapping up the redesign of G's ice cream shop now turned dessert bar. It looks awesome. Meanwhile, I've been focused on all the last minute details for the NICU fundraiser next month. This is crunch time, plus the season just started, so there's that, too.

I'm exhausted, but time with Dani is worth it. It's weird sleeping in her bed these days because it's so much smaller than my king, but it's better than sleeping in my huge bed alone. I hate those nights when I have to sleep without her. I'm not going to push her, but I'm hoping she'll be willing to move in with me soon.

After a few steamy kisses, she cuddles in closer.

"So, I talked to Rae this morning. Just a quick text to find out how their trip was," Dani says, but her smile is mischievous. I wonder if she told her. Aside from telling Dani's parents during a video chat last week, we haven't rushed to tell anyone else, mostly because we've been so damn busy. I'm waiting until my next scheduled video chat with my parents. They'll be happy for me, but it's not worth an extra call because it's not like they'll be *that* happy.

"Joel said it was good when I talked to him the other day."

"I thought about telling her, but then she told me they're coming home next weekend and she mentioned she can't wait to see the house, so I thought it would be way more fun if they walk into the house and see us making out on the couch." Her eyes are dancing with excitement, and it makes me ridiculously happy.

I laugh. "You're adorable. I love it. I think they all have an idea it could be happening. Joel seemed to, at least."

"If you want to tell him..."

I softly kiss her. "No. I like your plan better. Much better. If I'm kissing you, it's always the better plan."

"Agreed."

My phone goes off and I groan. I've barely seen Dani this week. I *do not* want to be disturbed right now. Plus, it's after ten. Probably Brooks with some new beer idea. We're getting back to how we were before—for the most part. I'll never trust him the way I used to unless he grows up a lot. Grabbing my phone, I see it's a text from my mom.

**Mom: Hi honey, sorry it's late. Just wanted to let you know Dad and I are home. We cut our trip short. I'll tell you all about it when we see you. Can't wait to see your new house. Love you!**

"Huh," I say, staring at my phone.

"What is it?" Dani asks. I show her the message. "Wow. They're actually home. This is the first time since Christmas, right?"

I nod. "Yep. I guess I'll stop over in the morning."

"Want me to come?"

"No. I've got to get up early, shower, and head back to my place for clothes. I didn't feel like bringing a bag over. I'll just stop in and let them know. I'll mention you and invite them to dinner this weekend if you're good with that."

"Works for me. And then we can tell everyone else when they're home next weekend. Can't wait to be obnoxiously in love with you in front of everyone."

I kiss her again, but I'm exhausted and I barely make it through without yawning. "Me either. Right now, though, I feel lame. I don't think I can hang."

She kisses my nose. "I barely kept my eyes open until you got here." She flips off her lamp and rolls against me. "I'm just happy I get to fall asleep in your arms. Love you, babe."

"Love you too." I kiss her forehead. "Goodnight."

Holding her close, I drift off to sleep quickly, excited to finally tell the world she's all mine.

"Nothing ever goes as planned," my mom says with a laugh as she recounts how the friends they were traveling with have very bad luck and ended up losing suitcases on the plane, the wife fell and broke her ankle, and then the yacht they chartered had a massive leak, that thankfully the inspector caught before they left port. Unsurprisingly, they cut the trip short and Mom and Dad decided to as well.

I haven't had a chance to tell her about Dani and me yet because she started telling me about their trip the second I walked in. My mom loves talking about it all, so I let her go. Everything changes, though when the back door swings open, and to my surprise, Joel walks in, looking pale and drained. Given that he should be hours away at school right now, I'm instantly filled with concern.

Since she's making a breakfast sandwich, Mom doesn't immediately notice his demeanor.

"Joel! What are you doing here, honey?"

"Little bro? What's wrong?" I ask, drawing Mom's full attention and causing Dad, who was standing in the corner of the kitchen sipping coffee to walk over to him.

"Son, what is it?" Dad asks.

"Bea passed away last night."

*Dani's grandmother...*

My stomach drops like a rock, and I fumble to pull out my phone. I only left Dani an hour ago, and she didn't know. I don't remember her phone going off last night, either.

"Oh no," Mom says softly.

Seeing nothing from Dani, my stomach turns even more. "Shit," I mutter.

"What happened?" Mom asks as my dad pulls out his phone and steps away.

"She had a heart attack."

"Poor Kara," my mom whispers.

*Does Dani know? Am I going to have to tell her?* Fuck.

Proving that my parents are the kind of people who come through in an emergency, Dad is on the phone with Rae's dad finding out how he can help. For being money-focused at times, my parents are never stingy with it and are happy to help however they can.

"Hey," I say to Joel, thinking of Sarah and Rae, "how are the girls?"

"Rough. They're rough."

*Like Dani is going to be. I need to get to her.*

"I've gotta go. But keep me updated? And let me know when the funeral is. I'll be there." I don't know why I say any of that. Obviously I'll know when the funeral is, but I'm mumbling random words at this point.

"Will do."

I squeeze his shoulder, then walk toward the front door, sending a text to my boss as I go that I won't be in today. I stop on the front porch, then send another text, this time to Jenna, asking her to let her dad know that Dani won't be in. Then I tuck my phone into my pocket and take off running for Dani's apartment.

*I need to get to my girl.*

## Dani

Is this what it feels like to have the air ripped from your lungs? Because I can't breathe. I can't think.

*Gram's gone?*

I just had dinner with her last week. Just talked to her yesterday and now she's...

I'm still clutching my phone as I stagger out of my bedroom.

"Dani?" Amelia asks. "What's wrong?"

"I—I—my grandma died."

My jaw trembles as I say the words. I'm sure to some people it barely matters. Their grandparents get old and they die. It's sad, but they move on. I don't know how to move on from this. How to deal with it. Despite them living ten hours and several states away, I still had a close relationship with them, one that has only deepened since living in Ida.

Amelia wraps me in a hug as I try not to fall apart. "I'm so sorry," she whispers.

I don't know how to do this. I want to curl into a ball and fall apart. I want a hug from Gram. Now I'll never get one again.

Pounding on the door makes me jump. Amelia loosens her grip on me, looking at the door, but doesn't let me go. More pounding. "Dani! It's me." *Jesse.*

Amelia lets me go and runs to open the door. A moment later, Jesse's arms are wrapped around me as I break down, sobbing.

"I've got you, babe. Come on."

He guides me back into my bedroom and sits down on my bed, pulling me down with him. I climb onto his lap, curling into him as I cry.

"I'm so sorry, baby," he whispers, pressing his lips into my temple.

"How did you know?" I mutter against his chest.

"I was at my parents' house when Joel walked in and told us. When did you find out?"

"Just a few minutes ago. Mom didn't want to wake us in the middle of the night, so she waited to call us." I sniff. "Fuck, I need to call into work." I turn to find where I dropped my phone on my bed, but Jesse holds me tighter.

"Already done. I texted Jenna before I left my parents' house. She let Leo know."

His words make me cry harder. How did I end up with such a wonderful, thoughtful man? What would I do without him? That thought makes my tears come faster. I don't ever want to be without him.

He runs his fingers through my hair and kisses my head, letting me cry. My hand is fisted in his shirt—which I'm soaking with tears. He keeps holding me tightly and doesn't move, except to reposition us so he's leaning back, allowing him to cradle me more. He runs his hand down my back, whispering soothing words in my ear, and at some point, I fall asleep.

When I wake up, I'm still wrapped around Jesse, and he's typing away on my phone with one hand.

"Hey, babe," he says softly, kissing my cheek. "Your phone has been blowing up. Lots of people sending love and thoughts and prayers. I only responded to your mom, Weston, and Olivia because they were all worried about you. Weston says to call him when you're ready to talk. By the way, I already told them they're staying at my place. No point in them getting a hotel room when I have so much space."

I blink a few times, then lunge forward and kiss him hard, tears welling in my eyes as I do. "I fucking love you."

He pushes some hair off my face, looking at me tenderly. "I love you too. Oh, um, I didn't text back, but Rae texted you and said everyone's meeting at her parents' house in a little while to talk about funeral stuff. That's where your grandpa is staying too."

Again, it feels like the air leaves my lungs. I can't imagine the kind of heartbreak Grandpa is experiencing right now.

"I need to go."

"If you don't want me to come since not everyone knows—"

"No," I nearly shriek. "I need—" I stop and clear my throat. "I won't get through this without you. I need you with me." My voice shakes as the words spill out.

"I'll be wherever you want me to be," he says reassuringly.

"With me. Don't leave me."

"I won't, babe. You've got me. I'm right here."

"Good."

I lean against his chest again, wishing I could somehow burrow closer. Right now, he's the only thing giving me comfort.

Jesse's hand is wrapped tightly around mine as we walk up the front steps of Aunt Kara and Uncle Charlie's house. It's funny, he's probably spent more time here than I have over the years. He gives my hand a reassuring squeeze as he opens the front door.

The loud conversation drops off when we walk in, as everyone looks at us. I'm sure some people already know. Obviously Grandpa does. I aim for him, giving him a big hug and trying not to cry at the sadness on his face. Rae and Sarah both eye me suspiciously, but I doubt they're that surprised, and frankly, I don't care. I want the world to know how much I love Jesse, and I need his love more than ever today.

Once we sit down, an intense conversation begins again. It's actually more of an argument. Everyone seems to have a different opinion about things, from flowers to catering to where the reception should be held. I look over at Rae and Sarah, who look as uncomfortable as I feel, though they're doing their best to stand up for Aunt Kara. She's been the one here with Grandma and Grandpa for years now and knows their wishes best. She's also bearing the brunt of the emotions.

Finally, she snaps, yelling how things will be before leaving the room. Sadly, Grandpa stands and tells everyone they should be ashamed of themselves before going upstairs.

A moment later, Rae and Sarah leave to check on their mom.

My cousin Mark crosses the room and sits down next to me, dropping his head into his hands. "That went like shit."

"Emotions are high," I say, squeezing his hand.

He nods and leans back in his chair. "I'm glad I've been staying in Ida with Frannie," he says, mentioning his girlfriend, who he randomly met on a flight to South Carolina a couple of months ago with no idea they both had ties to Ida.

"Where is she?"

"She had to check in at work. She'll be here soon." He nods at Jesse. "Normally, I'd give you the *what are your intentions with my cousin* speech, but given the circumstances and that you're Joel's brother, I'll let it slide."

I elbow him as Jesse laughs lightly. Then I lean in closer and whisper, "He's a good one. Trust me."

My phone goes off and I pull it out of my sweatshirt pocket to find a text from Rae.

**Rae: This is a whole lot of chaos. How do you feel about taking a little break and grabbing some ice cream?**

**Me: I like that idea. We'll meet you outside.**

I show Jesse, then Mark. "Do you want to come?"

Mark shakes his head. "No. I'm going to go check on Grandpa."

I nod. "Let me know if you need anything. Or he does."

Though I don't think anything helps when you've lost the love of your life.

"You owe us details," Sarah says, sitting down next to me at an outdoor table at Chewies, a local place that serves ice cream, hot dogs, and french fries. It's not homemade ice cream like G's is, but it's still good.

We're here with Rae, Aaron, Joel and their other two best friends, Miles and Mackenzie. The guys are off to the side talking, probably grilling Jesse and coming up with a game plan to take care of us.

"I second that," Rae says. "Since a week ago you lied through your teeth and told us you and Jesse were just friends. When did this happen?"

Letting out a sigh, I say, "I think it's been happening since the night you announced your engagement." Sarah, Rae, and Mackenzie stare at me wide-eyed. "I know. It's crazy, but there were undeniable sparks that I tried to ignore and push away because I was scared."

"At the wedding Aaron said Jesse told him you hated him," Rae says.

I look down. "I didn't hate him, but I wasn't particularly nice. The things I felt for him... I knew he had the power to hurt me, so I shut it down."

Sarah's gaze swings to Rae.

"Shut up," Rae says with a little smile.

"I apologized and then kinda let myself imagine what it could be like with him. Then in early January, Jenna invited me to go out with her husband and best friend. I didn't realize her best friend was Jesse. That's really where it started. He asked me to be his girlfriend the following weekend."

"Why didn't you tell us?" Sarah asks.

My eyes drift to Rae, who grabs my hand. "You know there's nothing between Jesse and me anymore, right? I mean, there never really was, but—"

"I know," I squeeze her hand. "He told me. There were definitely times I worried I was a consolation prize because he wanted you—then I was worried other people would see it that way. Now I know I never needed to worry about that."

"You're in love with him, huh?" Sarah says, smiling.

"Yeah, I am. He was so patient and supportive while I learned to trust him."

"That's a Wilkinson boy specialty," Sarah says.

"I'm really glad you're happy," Rae says, looking over at Jesse. Tears fill her eyes. "I'm glad he is too. He's a good guy who deserves to be loved right. I know you'll do that." She laughs. "You two really are a perfect match."

I grab her hand. "Oh my god. Did you know he's the fireworks boy?"

Rae's eyes bug out. "What?"

"I second that question," Mackie says with a laugh.

"When we were kids, Dani was scared of fireworks and a cute little boy held her hand and comforted her when she was scared, but she never knew his name," Sarah says, looking at me in surprise. "It was Jesse?"

I nod. "Yep. I only found out a week ago."

"I had no idea. I never even considered him because I remembered seeing him sitting next to Joel."

"He said he snuck off to get a soda—which Grandpa took from him."

"Grandpa had to have known it was him," Sarah says.

I laugh at that. "Oh my gosh, you're right. I wonder why he never told me."

"He was probably waiting for you to figure it out," Sarah says.

"Or waiting to use it as his Hail Mary if you didn't," Rae teases.

"Definitely that one."

"I'm sure Gram knew, too. She always knows," Rae says softly, then catches herself. "I'm not ready for that to be past tense yet."

Sarah, Rae, and I tearfully look between each other. A moment later, the guys surround us and pull us into their arms, trying to take our pain away. They can't, but their presence means everything.

## Jesse

Bea's funeral is exactly what I expect from the Abbott family. A true celebration of life filled with deep emotion. Dani is glued to my side and I have my arm tightly wrapped around her. If I could, I'd pull her onto my lap and hold her close, as I've done every night for the last few days. Even during the day she's been snuggled up next to me, working on her iPad as I worked on my laptop. We've both been working from home the last couple of days. It's been easier with everything going on and Dani's family around.

There's not a dry eye in the house as Rae's dad gives the eulogy, talking about the incredible legacy Bea created, and how it will always be a part of those who knew her—just like she will. I wipe away a couple of tears as Dani sobs next to me. For her, losing Bea is more like losing a parent. I think that's true of all the grandkids. Their grandparents have always been an active part of their lives, helping to shape them into who they are.

It's hard for me not to think about the fact that I wouldn't ever be able to give the same speech about legacy and family regarding my parents. I love them, but they didn't build a family like Pete and Bea did. Their commitment to their family has always been unwavering.

Pulling Dani closer, I kiss her head, wishing I could take this pain away.

Despite the circumstances, I find myself wanting this. Not this moment. The thought of losing Dani is something I don't want to consider, but the love in this room... I want that. I want to build a life like this with Dani. One full of love and warmth and family. I want to help her continue the legacy her grandparents built.

After the service, I wrap my arm around Dani as we join the crowd of people exiting the building. Weston is on her other side, and I have to say, he's great. I think he'd get along well with Evan and Garrett, too, so I'm hoping he'll come for a visit during happier circumstances.

"Dani."

Dani bristles at the sound of her name, stopping in place and spinning around. "Jason. What are you doing here?"

*Jason. Her ex.*

Olivia appears out of nowhere, positioning herself on my other side.

This is it. I can finally punch this guy in the nuts. Or maybe thank him for fucking up so my girl found her way to me. Either way, I already *hate* him.

I get why she was put off by the charming smile I like to give. This guy has that smooth charm, but he also has an asshole vibe which tracks.

"I came to pay my respects."

"Bullshit," Dani snorts, stepping forward and glaring at him. "You don't care. If this had happened when we were still together, you would've made me come here alone."

Weston shoots me a look like I should intervene, but I give a little headshake. I will, but not yet. Dani clearly has some things she needs to say.

"Ah, come on, baby. I never would've done that."

"Do not *ever* call me baby again or I will cut off your balls and force feed them to you. Got it?"

*Damn, my girl is spicy when she's mad. It's hot, but I don't want to piss her off that much.*

"I'm sorry, Dani. I know I messed up a lot of things—"

"No. You didn't mess up. You used me. You treated me like crap. You broke my trust. And you have no right to be here. Did you seriously come up from Virginia for this?"

He looks down. "No. I was in New York. My grandmother told me what happened and said I should—"

"Of course. You do whatever she says, hoping to get more money out of her when she dies. You're disgusting."

"Dani, come on. I didn't just come because of her. I came because I care."

And this is my moment. I step forward and wrap my arm around Dani's waist again, staring dickhead right in the eyes. "I really don't think you care at all, but either way, it doesn't matter. It's not your job to care for her anymore."

He scowls at me. "Who are you?"

"The guy who loves her a hell of a lot more than you ever did. We appreciate you paying your respects, but the funeral is over. It's time for you to go now."

"What. He. Said." Olivia glares at Jason, and man, if looks could kill. Olivia is scary. Then again, I've seen how protective Rae and Sarah are of each other. It only makes sense that Dani and Olivia would be the same way.

Jason puts his hands up. "Whatever. Glad to see you're slumming it now, Dani."

I roll my eyes and laugh, but then Dani steps forward and whispers something to Jason that makes him frown and step back. He grumbles something else, then walks away. *Thank God.*

"What did you say to him?" I ask.

She grins, her cheeks going a little pink. "I told him your trust fund is bigger than his. Petty, I know, but God, it felt so good."

"I love you, Dani girl."

"Love you too," she says softly, looking around. And just like that, the few moments of ridiculousness have passed, and the weight of the day settles over all of us again.

"Come on, let's head to the farmhouse," Weston says.

We all nod and walk toward the exit.

The reception at the farmhouse is a true celebration of Bea's life. It is filled with love and laughter and warmth and many stories about Bea.

I'm on my way back to the living room after grabbing a drink for Dani, when Pete steps up next to me.

"Saw what happened at the funeral home. That bastard is lucky it was you and not me. Thank you for taking care of my girly."

I look over at him. "You don't ever have to thank me for that. If I could protect her from this pain, I would."

Pete nods solemnly, then watches from across the room as a couple of Bea's siblings tell the story of how Pete and Bea got together. I can't help but smile hearing it. He said he knew from the moment he met her. She said he was annoying.

Pete claps a hand on my shoulder. "I always thought you two would make a good match. Maybe because I saw a reflection of my relationship in the two of you." He sighs, then pauses for a moment. When he speaks again, his voice is gravelly and filled with emotion. "Cherish her, and don't waste a second of your time together. It goes too fast, and you never know how long you'll have." With one last squeeze to my shoulder, he walks away. I stay where I am for a moment longer, watching as Dani goes between laughing and crying while listening to Bea's sister talk.

I will do my best to never waste a second of my life with her, and to never take for granted how special what we have is.

# Dani

Today has been both heartbreaking and uplifting, but this is the hardest part. We're standing in a wooded area of my grandparents' property with a small clearing that overlooks a massive field. It was one of Gram's favorite spots, and this is where we say goodbye to her. I'm not ready.

I fidget with the hem of my dress, anxious energy bubbling through my body. Jesse wraps his arm more tightly around me and I bury my face in his shoulder. His fingers brush through my hair, comforting me like he has every night since Gram died. After we were cozy in bed, the tears would creep in, and Jesse would run his fingers through my hair and rub my back, soothing me to sleep. I feel bad that I've barely been to my apartment this week, but I haven't wanted to leave Jesse.

"This spot was Bea's favorite," Grandpa says, standing in front of everyone with Gram's ashes. "She'd come out to watch the snow fall, the stars grow in the sky, or the butterflies flit through the fields. It was where she always found peace." He looks down at the ashes. "This is where you get to rest, Ma. Your forever peace," he whispers through tears.

I'm crying so hard I can barely breathe as Grandpa turns and opens the small wooden box containing her ashes. In gentle movements, he spreads them as we all look on, crying. Gram was our matriarch, the center of our family's love, and the calm comfort we all depended on. Without her, it feels like we're driving blindly through a storm, not knowing where we're going. That's probably a good metaphor for grief. Our pain won't fade when we leave the property today. It'll shift and grow and change as we figure out what life is like without Gram here with us.

When Grandpa is finished, he closes the box, but continues staring at the field, whispering a few words that the rest of us can't hear. As he turns back around, he wipes his eyes.

"Bea had one final request. She wanted this whole out of tune bunch to sing her favorite song—*All You Need Is Love*—my lord, she was obsessed with those damn Beatles. And I think she wants to hear us all sing it as one final laugh, but let's see if we can hold it together for her, huh?"

*Crap.* I clear my throat, wanting to be able to sing this for her the way she did so many times for me. When I was little and we visited Ida, we always stayed at the farmhouse. Gram would insist on tucking us in before bed, and she'd always sing this song. It seemed like it was always in the back of her head. But love was her biggest lesson, so I guess that makes sense. I'm glad she got to see me find the man who truly loves me, even if she won't be around to watch it grow. I know she'll be watching, but it's not the same.

We laugh through our tears as we sing the song. I hope Gram's smiling as she watches. This is all for her. For the love she left.

When we've finished, Grandpa heads back toward the house and the group breaks off. I wait for a chance to walk over to the clearing.

When there's a free moment, Jesse walks over with me as I stare out at the field. "I love you, Gram," I whisper. "I'll try to remember everything you taught me and carry it with me. I need it now more than ever. Love you," I whisper again, then Jesse kisses my head and guides me back to the farmhouse.

"I still can't believe Jason showed up," I say, walking back into the master from the attached bath in one of Jesse's T-shirts.

"Your takedown of him was pretty damn hot."

I laugh as I climb onto the bed, then I shake my head. "My emotions are all over the place right now." Now I'm sniffling. I feel a little crazy, but maybe that's normal.

It's a strange feeling when the immediacy of grief is over. Grief isn't, but the daily conversations about it and the ceremonies are over. Everything feels even emptier than it was before. I don't know what to do with myself now, or how to navigate everything I feel.

"I think that's normal. If you want to talk about any of it, I'm here. If you need more time to process, that's okay, too. Just know I'm here. I'm always here."

Tears fill my eyes again as I curl my body into his.

"I don't want to lose you," I whisper.

"You're not going to lose me," he says firmly.

"You don't know that," I choke out.

He shifts us so we're lying flat, then turns so he's looking into my eyes. Sweeping his hand through my hair, he says, "I love you, Dani girl. I'm going to keep loving you every single day of my life. No one can promise how long we get, but I promise you forever. I will never stop loving you, no matter where I am. And I'm going to make sure I hold you so tightly and love you so deeply you'll always be able to feel my love, whether you're in my arms or not."

I slant my mouth over his in a messy kiss, tugging at his hair and pulling his body flush against mine. I hope we get to have a long, beautiful life together because I know without a doubt, he's it for me, my fireworks boy, the fantasy, and the love I always dreamed of.

# 21
# Not Yours

## Jesse

"You've put together quite an event," Dani's dad, Eric, says to me, looking around the stadium.

"Thank you, sir."

Eric laughs. "How many times have I told you? Just call me Eric. I can't stand being called 'sir.' It makes me feel old and boring."

Beside me, Dani stifles a laugh. She's told me before that her father isn't a particularly exciting person, but he's clearly a loving father.

"We can't have that," Dani's mom, Sylvia, says, walking over with Olivia. I can't believe Dani's parents and sister came up from Virginia for this event. "Wine in a sippy cup? Who'd have thought?" Sylvia laughs.

Olivia shakes her head. "Odds are that'll be helpful when you can't keep the cup upright."

Sylvia rolls her eyes and elbows her daughter.

"Oh boy," Pete says with a sigh. Then he turns to me. "You have done a fine job here. You should be proud of yourself."

"Thank you. I appreciate that."

"You guys should go explore," Dani says. "If you stop by G's ice cream booth or Evan's pizza, just tell them you're my family and they'll give you a freebie."

"Nonsense," Eric says. "They deserve the money. But I agree, let's go explore. We'll find you later." He smacks my shoulder and kisses Dani on the cheek before walking away.

"It was sweet of your parents to come up for this." I say, wrapping an arm around Dani.

She smiles up at me. "They're proud of you and they want to support you. And yes, you should feel special. Every event that Jason ever had, it was pulling teeth to get them there. With this, Mom bought the tickets while I was still on the phone with her."

"Your mom is a little wild."

Dani grins and shimmies her shoulders. "Where do you think I get it from?"

I laugh and give her a quick kiss, but as we pull apart, I'm shocked by who I see walking toward me.

"Mom? Dad?"

"Hi, honey," Mom says, coming in for a hug.

"Hi," I choke out, still surprised. "I—I'm glad you're here."

"So are we," Dad says, giving me a quick hug and a pat on the shoulder. "You've done something remarkable."

"I had a lot of help."

Dad grins at me. "Take the credit where it's due. You were right about this job. It suits you. I'm proud to see you doing great things for this community."

"That's my goal. People have really showed up, especially for this cause."

"Dani told us so much about it all and how important it is to you, and we didn't want to miss it."

I glance at Dani, who simply smiles at me.

"Thank you for coming. I'm glad you're here to see it all," I say, voice thickening with emotion.

"We're always happy to support you, son," Dad says. "And I can't wait to check everything out here. I saw Evan and Garrett both have booths."

"That they do, but it's just the tip of the iceberg."

"Clearly," Mom says, looking around. "I have no idea where to start."

"I'm hearing good things about wine in a sippy cup," Dani says with a laugh.

Mom raises her eyebrows. "Oh, interesting. We'll have to check it out."

"Yes, we're going to wander. We'll check in later. Congratulations, bud. You did a great job."

"Thanks, Dad," I say softly, watching as they walk away.

It means a lot that they're here. It's not a magic button that fixes everything, but it gives me hope that maybe in the future it can be. When I grow a pair and am willing to deal with this head-on. Until then, I'll celebrate this tiny win.

"What did you say to them?" I ask, wrapping an arm around Dani.

"Who, me? I just chatted with them. Told them how fabulous you are and how hard you worked."

"When did you do that?"

"When they were here last month. I also told them how important it is to you." She shrugs. "I know you wanted to ask them but were worried about their response. I figured if I did it for you, you wouldn't have to know if they said they couldn't come, but you'd be happy if they could."

I lean down and kiss her hard. "You are incredible. I love you."

"Mm, I love you too."

"So, what should we do now?" I ask.

She gives me her beaming smile. "Ice cream?"

I laugh and grab her hand. "Ice cream. Let's go."

# Dani

"Okay, Dani. You get to be the first taste tester for this one outside of Evan and Jesse. Ready?" Garrett asks, handing me a spoon. For some reason my eyes have to be closed for this part.

"I'm always ready for ice cream."

"Good. Eat up."

*Don't have to tell me twice.*

Shoving the spoon in my mouth, I savor the flavor, trying to figure out exactly what it is. Realization hits me all at once, and I open my eyes.

"Raspberry cheesecake?" I ask, looking from Garrett to Jesse, whose hands are in his pockets as he gives me an *aww-shucks* grin.

"It's your favorite," he says softly.

Walking over, I give him a big kiss, shoving my tongue in his mouth and giving him a taste of the ice cream.

"Uh, excuse me, I made it," Garrett says, arms crossed over his chest as Evan laughs in the background.

I turn to him. "And you did an excellent job."

He jokingly wipes his brow. "Whew. Thank goodness. That base took me a good five months to get right."

I blink a couple of times, then look at Jesse again. His cheeks are pink now. "Five months?" Grabbing Jesse's hand, I ask, "When did you tell him raspberry cheesecake is my favorite?"

"I didn't tell him that exactly, but I mentioned the flavor to him in November."

My eyebrows shoot up. "November?"

"Thanksgiving." He clears his throat. "What can I say? There was something about you... I couldn't give up hope."

I throw my arms around his neck and squeeze him tightly. "You're very sweet." I lower my voice. "And such a good boy."

"Ew," Garrett says.

"Mm. Do I get a reward for being good?"

"Keep behaving for the rest of the day, and we'll see."

"Okay. How about we put some more ice cream in that dirty mouth of yours. Maybe cool you off a little," G says with an eye roll.

"You have more?"

"Of course. I even packed a little half pint up for you. It's in the freezer."

Clapping my hands, I run over and climb inside the truck, digging through the small freezer off to the side until I find what I'm looking for. I'm grabbing a spoon when I hear someone say Jesse's name.

Garrett freezes in his place, and I peek out the opening of the truck, looking down at a girl with blonde hair and lowlights, who has just walked over to Jesse.

"Carrie," he spits out, and my eyes widen. "What the hell are you doing here?"

His witch of an ex. I laughed when Rae told me what she changed Carrie's contact info to in her phone. She does seem like a witch though.

G elbows me in the side. "What are you still doing in here, crazy girl? Go claim your man."

"I want to let him say anything he needs to first. He did that for me."

Garrett nods, and we both watch from the edge of the service window.

"I heard about this from one of our college friends. Someone had an extra ticket, and I thought I'd come. Knowing you planned all this... I wanted to see it in person and support you."

"I don't need your support, Carrie. I stopped needing it a long time ago."

She looks down. "I know I messed up, okay? But you forgave me once, and we got through it. I promise I'll never talk to another guy. You could check my phone every night. I—"

"Enough," Jesse says sharply.

She steps closer and puts her hand on his arm.

*Oh, fuck no.*

I shove the ice cream into G's hand and walk out of the truck as she says, "Come on. We were good together."

"No, we weren't. If we were good together, you never would've chosen someone else over me."

"I was confused. I was figuring things out."

Jesse pulls his arm away. "You might've been figuring things out, but you weren't confused about what you wanted. You just didn't want me."

"I did, but—"

"Stop," Jesse says. "There aren't any buts here. You broke my heart twice. Left me for someone else *twice.*" He squints at her. "That's it, isn't it? When did things end with Dean?"

I'm glued to the side of the truck, watching.

She looks down. "A few weeks ago."

"Yep. There it is."

"Because I realized it was wrong. You were on my mind—"

"Well, you weren't on his." I walk over and wrap my arm around his waist. He smiles softly and drapes his arm around my shoulder.

"Who are you?" she sneers.

"The woman who loves him and appreciates him for the wonderful man he is. I'm sorry if you're hurting or second-guessing your decisions, but this isn't your place anymore."

"Jesse..." she says, looking hurt, and I do feel a bit bad for her. It's clear she doesn't know herself enough to know what she wants or needs.

"She's right. I've healed and moved on, and I'm happy. I'm sorry if you aren't, but regardless, I would never be able to fix that. You need to take a break from relationships and figure your own life out, Carrie. I hope you do, and I hope you find the right person for you one day, but it won't be me. It never was. Feel free to hang out and enjoy the event, but this conversation is over. Take care."

With that, he turns away and guides me back to the truck. She looks up at Garrett, who gives an awkward wave, then she rolls her eyes and walks off.

Evan appears at the back of the food truck. "Damn, that was intense."

I run my hand through Jesse's hair. "How are you doing?"

He smiles softly. "Might need some of my favorite ice cream, but otherwise, I'm fine. She doesn't hold any power over my heart anymore." He runs his finger down my chest. "That all belongs to you. I mostly just feel sad for her."

"And grateful you dodged a bullet," G says.

I smack his arm as Evan says, "Well, at least it only grazed you."

Jesse chuckles at that. "My heart didn't make it out unscathed, but at least I found the right person to heal it."

"Gross," G says.

"Whatever you say," Jesse says with a grin. "But please note that Ev is the one with sex hair." Snickering, he turns to the cooler and pulls out a half pint of his favorite ice cream, then wraps his arm around me. "Come on, Dani girl. Let's go have some fun."

"Yes, sir."

"Am I still a good boy?" He asks as we stroll across the field together, looking at the many tents and trucks.

I loop my arm through his as I say, "The best one I know. Love you, babe."

"Love you too, Dani girl. Always."

He pops a kiss on my head, and together, we enjoy the fantastic event he created.

# 22

## Ours

## Jesse

"Last box?" Dani asks, sticking her head into the living room as I set the box I'm holding down.

"Yep. Why?"

She smiles flirtatiously and scampers over to me, wrapping her arms around my neck. "Mm, I was just excited to kiss you."

"Well, I'm all yours."

"Perfect."

Slowly, she presses her lips into mine, teasing her tongue over my bottom lip.

I fist her hair and guide her backward until she's pinned against the wall in the entryway. Tangling my tongue with hers, I grind against her.

"Where first?" she asks, briefly lifting her lips off mine.

I cock an eyebrow. "What do you mean?"

"What spot should we break in first?"

"I think we've fucked in every room of this house," I rumble, lips pressing into her neck.

"Now that I'm officially living here, we have to do it all over again."

*Well, I'm not going to complain about that.*

I kiss her hard again, teasing her with my tongue as she moans against my mouth. Wrapping my arms around her, I walk backward toward the stairs. The first place we need to start is the bedroom. She was the one who picked out the chaise by the window and it needs to be broken in.

Dragging my hand up her side, I cup her breast, roughly running my thumb over her nipple. Even through the fabric, the contact makes her moan.

"Fuck," I growl as we start up the stairs. Still twisting her tongue around mine, she slides her hand inside my exercise shorts, stroking me.

*Fuck the bedroom.*

I stop in place and lean her backward against the stairs before dropping my shorts and yanking hers off as well.

"Jesse," she gasps.

"This is where we're starting," I rumble, pressing into her and fucking her on the stairs.

I never made a list like Dani's, but if I had, this definitely would've been on it.

"I can't believe you never got throw pillows," Dani says, shaking her head as she places the ones we just got on the couch. "I can't believe I didn't make you."

"Well, I had the few that came with the couch. They sufficed."

"These add so much more to the room, though."

I wrap my arms around her waist from behind, squeezing her tightly. "I know they do. There was a reason I never picked out any pillows or blankets or accessories. I wanted you to pick them out. I've figured out my style to some degree, but you are the one who fills this house with warmth. This is your home, Dani. I hoped it would be since the first time we saw it. I waited on all the little things so this house would have pieces of you."

She spins to face me, eyes wide. "Really?"

I chuckle and kiss her nose. "Yes, baby. I told you if you moved in here it would be your home too. I want to feel your warmth and happiness in this space. In fact, I have something to show you. G, Evan, Amelia, and Rae came over while we were gone and got this all set up." I lead her through the downstairs and over to the office. Swinging the door open, I pull her inside.

"Oh my god. Jesse... all my books... everything. It's amazing."

"It's us."

She walks into the center of the room and takes in the far wall lined with her bookcases. Amelia and Rae put all her books there, but I know she might want to reorganize them. On the opposite wall is my desk and a bookcase filled with records and a few of the Lego builds I made and kept pristine over the years. There's also a large bulletin board over my desk, which I use when I'm working through ideas. On the wall opposite the door, Dani's desk sits beneath a large window.

On the floor is a beautiful throw rug Dani had book-marked on her phone. It's soft but durable with a confetti pattern featuring warm earth tones.

She spins around and throws herself into my arms. "Thank you," she whispers.

"Thank you for wanting this, for seeing a future with me and fighting for it. I was afraid to believe in a forever for myself after getting my heart crushed, but you walked in and pulled me into the eye of the storm. It was terrifying and exhilarating, and it led me to the best part of my life. I never imagined I'd get as lucky as I got with you. I will spend every second trying to make sure you feel the same."

"I already do." She brushes her lips over mine, then looks around the room again. Squinting, she walks over to my desk. "What's on the bulletin board?"

I smile softly as she pulls down the blank sheet of paper. "That's for our list."

She raises her eyebrows. "Our list?"

Nodding, I walk over to my desk and sit down in the large chair, pulling her onto my lap. "We've crossed off most of the things on your list, other than a couple of places to travel, so I think they should be the start of our list. The things we want from our future together."

I jot down the two things from her list that I have every intention of fulfilling.

*-Drink espresso at a café in Paris*

*-Drive across the country*

Then we spend the next half hour coming up with more ideas for the list. Everything from continuing to be naked regularly to making babies. I guess those two kind of go together.

When we've written down everything we can think of, Dani reads it all aloud. A pulse of excitement shoots through me. This list is just the beginning of our forever, there's so much more we couldn't even imagine right now.

"Hm, there's one thing missing," Dani says, grabbing the pen from my hand and scribbling one last thing.

*-Live happily ever after*

I pull her to my lips. With those words, she's encompassed all those things yet to come. It might not always be easy. It won't be happy every second, but as long as we're together, it'll be everything.

In the past I was always a little unsure of my future. I knew what I wanted, but it all seemed hazy and uncertain—like I didn't know how to get there. Now when I look ahead, there's no uncertainty. I look at her face and I see my future—our future together. A forever worth fighting for.

# Epilogue
# Like Sunshine
## 10 Months Later

## Jesse

"It's about time," Garrett says, doing a slow clap.

"Thank you, that helps."

"Why are you being such a sourpuss? You're going to ask Dani to marry you. That's big," G says.

I let out a sigh, running my hand through my hair.

*Of course it's big. That's why I called this meeting of the minds. I'm nervous as fuck and I need help.*

"Aw, he's nervous," Aaron teases.

"Literally all of you here have proposed," I say, looking around the room at Aaron, my brother, Garrett, and Evan. "You know this shit is nerve-racking."

"Yeah, but you don't usually get nervous," Evan points out. *So helpful.*

"No, I don't. But I need to get this right. It's a big deal. Especially because it's right this time."

"Whoa, hold on," Joel says. "Did you just say 'this time?'"
*Fuck.*

Everyone is staring at me, eyes wide. "Yeah."

"Wait. Did you propose to Carrie and not tell us?" Evan asks.

I let out a sigh. "No. I never proposed. But I had a ring. It should've been fucking obvious that it was wrong since I was afraid to tell anyone in my life about it. I had no idea what kind of ring to get and it just felt weird. It doesn't feel weird this time, but I want it to be perfect, especially since Dani's been proposed to before. That starts with the perfect ring. I know Dani's general taste, but I have no idea where to start."

Aaron and Joel exchange a look. "It's a good thing you asked us to help," Aaron says, smiling mischievously.

"What is that look for?"

"We have some good news," Joel says. "You don't have to pick out a ring."

I narrow my eyes at the two of them grinning like idiots. "What the hell are you talking about?"

Joel nods to Aaron, and he looks at me seriously. "You might not know this, but Bea was obsessed with rings. It was really the only sort of jewelry she wore, so every year starting with their tenth anniversary, Pete bought her a special ring. Before she died, she started setting them aside for each of the girls in the family. Obviously, she was still alive when I got the one for Rae."

"And Pete took me aside at Bea's funeral and gave me the one for Sarah. He'll have one set aside for Dani, too."

My mouth drops. "Seriously? And this is just passed down in whispers or what?"

"Well, I think the idea is to talk to her family first and then you find out."

I shake my head. "I was going to talk to them *after* I had a ring, and—wait. If that's how this works, wouldn't Dani already have the ring? What about her ex?"

Joel and Aaron raise their eyebrows at each other. Joel clears his throat. "Yeah, uh, I think the ring is reserved for someone Pete approves of. Or believes is the right match. I don't think anyone in her family liked her ex."

"But they like me?" I ask, hoping I'm not going to have to pass a series of crazy tests to get this ring.

"Dude, you're an idiot," Aaron says.

Garrett chuckles at that, and I shoot him a glare. "What? Even I know the answer to that."

I blow out a breath. "So, I need to talk to Pete?"

"I'd talk to her parents soon, too, but yeah. We can go with you, if you want," my brother says.

I smile at that. Crazy that I'm going to propose to the cousin of my little brother's fiancée—soon to be wife. I definitely didn't see that coming when my life fell apart a couple of years ago. Surprisingly, what makes me more emotional is knowing that Aaron and I will be family now, too.

"Well, it seems like you're in capable hands," Evan says as he and G stand up. "Let us know if you want to bounce proposal ideas off us, but let's face it, we suck at them. We were lying in bed and we looked up and proposed to each other. Not exactly the fanciest proposal ever."

G takes Evan's hand and looks at him lovingly. "No, but it was perfect for us."

Evan looks at G like he hung the stars, then they share an emotional kiss. I pick on them a lot about their PDA, but I love how happy they are.

"Hey, why didn't you invite Brett and Jenna to this shindig? He went up big for her," G says when he and Evan step apart.

"Have you met Jenna? She can't keep a secret to save her life. For that matter, neither can Brett. He barely managed to propose to her without giving away the secret. I want this to be a surprise."

Garrett puts a hand on my shoulder. "Whenever you do it, however you do it, it'll be perfect for her because *you* are perfect for her. Remember that, okay?"

"Yeah. Thanks."

"We'll see you later. Text us pictures of the ring," Evan calls as they leave.

Blowing out a breath, I look over at Joel and Aaron, who are smiling again.

"Ready to go see Pete?" Aaron asks.

"What the hell? Let's do it," I say, nervousness hitting me all over again. Normally I'm perfectly content going toe to toe with Pete Abbott and letting him give me some shit, but this is different. I'm asking him for one of his late wife's rings to ask his granddaughter to marry me. This is a big fucking deal, and I am appropriately scared as shit about that.

"Well, well," Pete says, swinging open the door to his apartment. He moved out of the farmhouse a few weeks ago, and transferred the property over to Aaron and Rae, who live in the farmhouse, and Joel and Sarah, who are moving into the log cabin on the property after they get married in a couple of weeks. "To what do I owe the pleasure of a Cooper and two Wilkinsons?"

Joel and Aaron both look at me. I swallow hard, then open my mouth to speak, but before I can, Pete grins at me.

"Ah, that's about right. Well, come on in and tell me your intentions with my granddaughter."

We follow him inside and sit down around the small kitchen table. I'm surprised that he's not being snarky. He's serious but relaxed.

"I want to propose to Dani," I blurt out.

"Smooth," my brother whispers as Aaron chuckles.

Pete smiles widely. "I got that, son. When do you plan to propose?"

"She's taking off for the week of her birthday. I'm going to propose the Saturday before. Then Sunday we're going to fly to Paris for a few days to celebrate. She thinks we're going to Montréal."

"You've thought this through."

"I want it to be special for her. She's wanted to go to Paris for a while, but I wanted to save it for the right time."

Pete nods knowingly. "Have you talked to her parents yet?"

"No, not yet. I was going to talk to them when they're up for Joel and Sarah's wedding."

He nods again. "Good. All right, well, let's get the ring."

I stand up, confused. "Wait, that's it? I don't have to state my case or pass a test or—"

Pete turns to me and puts a hand on my shoulder. "I'm not one for bullshit or wasting time. I've known for a long time how you care for my granddaughter, and that's all that matters to me. You care for her, make her happy, and bring out the best in her. That's all I want for anyone I love—to find a partner who cherishes and respects them. It's clear you do that with Dani." He swallows, his eyes growing misty. "And I know Bea loved seeing the two of you together as well."

"Thank you," I say softly.

"Follow me, boys," he says, leading us down the hallway to a small bedroom. There he goes to a jewelry box and opens it. "Bea didn't specify a ring for each of our granddaughters, but she had an idea. She did, however, have a specific one set aside for Dani. Even if she didn't, I would've known." He pulls a ring from the box and holds it up. "This is a round cut, two carat, bright yellow sapphire on a white gold band. As you might know, Bea always called Dani 'Sunny' and when she was little would often tell Dani she was her sunshine. When I gave Bea this ring, Dani would've been six or seven. She smiled and told me it made her think of Dani, which made the ring extra special. Vibrant, just like her. It's only right that she have this ring now." He hands it to me, letting me look it over. It is beautiful. And perfectly Dani. Timeless but with a pop of color. "Make sure she knows the ring is passed on with all the love of her grandmother and me."

I swallow hard as he takes the ring and puts it in a small box for me. "I will. Thank you. I know this will mean a lot to her. It means a lot to me, too, that you're trusting me with it."

He meets my gaze and says, "You deserve to give her that ring as a symbol of your love. Thank God Sylvia and Eric knew not to send Jason to me for a ring. Not that I think he would've wanted it anyway, but Bea wouldn't have parted with her rings for anyone who wasn't worthy of her granddaughters. I'm simply carrying that out now in her stead. Keep taking care of my girly, and make sure you send pictures when she says yes."

My heart stutters in my chest at that thought. Me down on one knee. Her saying yes. Holy shit. I'm really going to do this. I'm going to propose to the love of my life.

"Hey, babe. How was guy time?" Dani asks as I walk into the kitchen.

She finishes putting a few dirty dishes in the dishwasher, then rinses her hands and comes to give me a kiss.

"It was good. How was your time with the girls?"

"Spicy," she says with a smirk. "We were talking about romance books, then the conversation turned to vibrators, and—"

"Mm, more toys to add to our collection? I'm game."

Do we have a specific dresser drawer set aside for just sex toys? Yes. Am I ashamed of that? Hell fucking no. It is fantastic.

She laughs and the sound shoots through my body in waves, heating me up, filling me with desire for the gorgeous girl in front of me.

"I added them to my Amazon Wishlist," she says, wrapping her arms around my neck and kissing me deeply.

I run my hands down her ribs, then break our kiss, staring at her tenderly. "I love you."

She tilts her head and smiles, brushing some hair off my forehead. "I love you too. Everything okay?"

I nod. "It's perfect. Just having a moment of gratitude for how lucky I am that I ended up with you."

"It's pretty special, huh? I never understood what love could be before. Now that I do, I understand what people mean when they say it's easy. Life isn't easy, but we are. The way we love each other comes naturally. I'm so grateful I get to do life with you." She gives me another kiss. It's softer and more tender than the last, but it's filled with the depth of our love. I kiss her back with everything inside me, needing her to know how intensely

I love her and how grateful I am to have found her amid the chaos.

After everything I went through with Carrie, it was hard to continue to imagine a forever with anyone, but I held on, unaware that the universe was about to drop my dream girl in my lap. Even though it took us some time to get here, it was worth it. Every complicated, messy step was worth it to have a forever far better than what I dreamed of.

Now I need to nail the proposal.

## Dani

This is my new favorite spot.

When the weather broke in the spring this year, Jesse had a swinging bench put in at the back edge of the property overlooking the river. Though it's not the prettiest river in the world, it's still gorgeous to sit out here at sunset and watch the changing sky color the river. Hell, if I'm honest, I sit out here just about any time of day, enjoying the combination of quiet solitude and the distant noise of traffic and the downtown hustle and bustle. It's even more beautiful after the sun has set and the stars are out and the world gets a little quieter.

Tonight, I'm enjoying the sunset, waiting for Jesse to join me with some strawberry lemonade. He always makes sure to have lots of fun beverages in the house for me, so if he wants to sip on a beer, I have something tasty to drink, too. His thoughtfulness truly knows no bounds.

I'm beyond excited to get on the road tomorrow as we start our road trip to Canada, something Jesse has been planning for my birthday week for quite a while. I can't believe I'm about to turn twenty-five. It's crazy how much has changed in the last two years. All for the better.

"Hey, babe." Jesse kisses my cheek and sits down next to me, handing me my glass of lemonade. I'm surprised to find he has some too.

"No beer tonight?"

"Nah, I want to be clear-headed for our trip tomorrow. Sometimes beer keeps me up."

I nod as I push my feet off the ground, sending the bench moving back and forth. Jesse sets up some music on the Bluetooth speaker he brought out. Then he wraps his arm around me, and I snuggle against him, tucking my feet under me and letting him rock us as we sip on our drinks.

When the sun has nearly set and the colors in the sky are at their most vibrant, Jesse turns to me and kisses my forehead. He pulls the empty cup from my hands and sets it on the table next to the bench.

"How cheesy will I sound if I say I love watching the sunset with you?"

I laugh a little. "Hm. Pretty cheesy. But it's cute, too." I lean in and kiss his neck. "This bench was an amazing idea. I could sit out here and watch thousands of sunsets with you."

He kisses my cheek, then slowly untangles his body from mine. "That's the plan, Dani girl."

I look up at him as he rises from the bench, then he gives me that sexy, lopsided, melt-my-panties-off smile. I can't believe it ever irritated me. Maybe because I know what it means now. And I also know I'm the only one he ever uses it on.

"What are you doing?" I ask.

"Something important." Then he drops to one knee.

One knee!

*Oh my god. It's happening.*

I squeak as I sit up straight, staring at him. He takes my hand as he looks up at me, eyes filled with love.

"Dani, the day you strode back into my life changed everything for me. I was lost and hurting, hopelessly believing that I could still have the future I dreamed of. Only it wasn't hopeless after all. It took a girl with wildcat eyes, a feisty personality, and a smile like sunshine to make me see everything I'd been missing. It took a little time and patience..." I laugh at that, squeezing his hand as he smiles at me. "But it was worth it. Worth it to find the love of my life, who fights with me to make our relationship the best it can be every day. I love your brightness and the way you add more color to everything—especially our life together. I love your patience and kindness and willingness to be open with me. I love that you watch *Stranger Things* to unwind after a long day, *Pride and Prejudice* when you're in a bad mood, and *Frozen* whenever you're sick. Most of all, I love you and I love us, and I want to make that official. Will you marry me, Dani girl?"

"Yes," I whisper, then slide off the bench and pull his lips to mine for a kiss. "Yes." Another kiss. "I love you."

He captures my lips in another slow, soft kiss, then with a shaky breath, he opens the ring box.

Tears flood my eyes. "Oh my god."

"I know you know whose ring this is. She set it aside for you because you were her—"

"Sunshine. This... this is..." I snuffle on my tears, unable to get any words out.

He kisses me again, then slides the gorgeous ring on my finger.

"Your grandpa said to make sure you know this ring comes with all of his and your grandmother's love."

I nod, still crying. "I will cherish this forever." I rest my hands over his cheeks. "Just like I'll cherish you." I press onto my toes, wrapping my hand around the back of his neck as I kiss him deeply, my tongue tangling with his as I lean into him. God, I love this man.

He slides his fingers up the back of my neck, twisting them through my hair as he dips me back. I laugh against his lips as he dips me even lower.

Pulling me upright again, he grins at me. "Did I do good?"

"You did amazing." I tousle his hair. "You were a very good boy."

"Good." He pulls me into his arms, dancing slowly to the love song playing in the background. "I thought about proposing on vacation, but figured it would be more fun to spend vacation celebrating."

"Oh my gosh, yes. I didn't think of that. Six days of celebrating us sounds perfect."

He gives me a cheeky smile. "I was hoping you'd say that, especially since we'll be celebrating in Paris."

I stop moving and take a half step back, looking up at him to figure out if he's serious. "Wait. Paris?"

He gives a little shrug. "It's on your list."

"It—yeah. Oh my god. How long have you been planning that?"

"Since I first mentioned we should go on vacation for your birthday. I picked Montréal because it's out of the country and has similar weather to Paris this time of year."

I stare at him for a minute longer, then jump into his arms. "Oh my god. You're perfect."

"Oh, I'm going to remember you said that."

I slide down his body and look up at him reverently. "As long as you remember how *incredible* I am, that's fine with me."

"You're more than incredible, baby. You're my everything. I love you."

"I love you too."

He pulls me flush against him, and I rest my head on his shoulder as we dance in the backyard to a playlist of love songs.

I don't know how long we've been dancing when *Forever After All* by Luke Combs comes on.

"I love this song," I breathe.

"So do I. It makes me think of you and us. You made me believe in a love that could last forever."

I glance up at him, then rest my head on his shoulder again, tickling my fingers over the hair at the back of his neck. "That's what we're going to have."

I told Olivia and Weston I wasn't going to fall in love again. I don't think I fully believed it myself, but I didn't think I'd fall this hard again so soon. It wasn't easy, but Jesse broke my locks, tore down my walls, and gave me a safe place to heal while showing me what real love is.

I came to Ida to find my vibrancy again, but I found so much more. My fireworks boy, my forever love, and a happily ever after better than anything I could've imagined.

## *The End*

# A Note from Bethany

Hey y'all! Thanks so much for reading Jesse and Dani's story. I hope you loved all the snark, banter, sweetness, and steam. Jesse is a favorite of mine from his freckles to his sarcasm to his heart of gold. He *might* be my favorite Wilkinson boy (don't tell Joel!).

If you want more of Jesse and Dani, you can grab a sweet and steamy bonus chapter on my website.

If you want to know more about Jesse, his *flirtationship* with Rae, his friendship with Aaron, and his relationship with his little brother Joel, be sure to check out the *Friends Like This* series. Outside of the six besties in that series, Jesse is one of the most prominent characters. You'll also get plenty more from Gram and Grandpa. You can find *Friends Like This* on Amazon and Kindle Unlimited.

Looking for the next book in the Ida Heartthrobs series? You can find Trevor Matteny's story in *The Perfect Love*.

And if you want to know more about the Barone/Ardito families, check out the *Freaking Love* series also on Amazon and Kindle Unlimited.

Thanks for reading!
XO
Bethany

# Bethany's Books



## Friends Like This series

Friends Like This
Falling Like This
Broken Like This
Love Like This
Married Like This
*(a Friends Like This bonus novella)*
Together Like This
Heartbreak Like This
Family Like This
Future Like This
Nothing Like This
Trust Like This
Always Like This

## Ida Heartthrobs series

The Forever Fight
The Perfect Love
The Future Play

## Freaking Love series

First Love
Real Love
Forever Love

## Baker Girls series

The Last Lie
The Last Key

## Ida Romance series

Reckless for You
Faking It for the Holidays
Waiting for Your Heart
*(free novella)*
Everything for You
Running Back to You
Caught Up In Your Love

## Lacy Creek series

Finally Yours
Always Mine
Only Ours
Complete Trilogy

# The Forever Fight Playlist



- Babe- Sugarland (feat. Taylor Swift)

- Jordan Davis- One Beer In Front Of The Other

- Heart to Break- Ryan Griffin

- Heat of the Summer- Young the Giant

- Cruel Summer- Taylor Swift

- Give Your Heart a Break- Demi Lovato

- Takes A Breakup- Chris Ruediger

- Too Hurt to Fall in Love- Lauren Spencer Smith

- Sucker- Jonas Brothers

- CWJBHN- Jake Scott, Josie Dunne

- Wanted- Hunter Hayes

- More Than I Know- Jordan Davis

- First Times- Ed Sheeran

- Run- Matt Nathanson, Sugarland

- Wreckage- Nate Smith

- Used to This- Chris Moreno

- What It's Like Loving You- Maddie & Tae

- Baby I Am- Dalton Dover

- The Good Ones- Gabby Barrett

- What My World Spins Around- Jordan Davis

- I Don't Dance- Lee Brice

- I Just Love You- Roo Panes

- The Last Time- Tenille Townes

- Like I'm Gonna Lose You- Jasmine Thompson

- We'll Figure It Out- Smithfield.

- She's The One- Brantley Gilbert

- Forever After All- Luke Combs

- I Choose You- Forest Blakk

# Abbott Family Tree

**A QUICK GUIDE TO THE ABBOTT FAMILY...**

- Pete & Bea Abbott
  - Chris (Cynthia) Abbott
    - Mason (Taylor) Abbott
    - Cole (Justine) Abbott
    - Andrea Abbott
    - Mark Abbott
  - Sylvia (Eric) Malone
    - Weston Malone
    - Dani Malone

- Olivia Malone

○ Darren (Lindsay) Abbott

  - Cassie

  - Lincoln

  - Kyle

  - Tori

○ Kara (Charlie) McKinley

  - Rae (Aaron) Cooper

  - Sarah McKinley

# About the Author

Bethany Monaco Smith is a writer-mom. When she's not busy hanging with her boys, she's writing beautifully messy love stories.

She loves happily-ever-afters and cries at every emotional moment, whether reading, writing, or watching. When she's not mom-ing or writing, you can find her binge-reading on Kindle Unlimited, supporting fellow indie authors, and having sushi dates with her SIL. Bethany survives on coffee, rewatching the same TV shows over and over, and her KU subscription. She lives in the Southern Tier of NY with her husband and two sons.

For more about Bethany and what she's working on, follow along on Instagram (@bethanymonacosmith) or on her website, www.bethanymonacosmith.com. Stay in touch by joining Bethany's exclusive Facebook group, Bethany's Book Nook & signing up for her newsletter.

# Acknowledgements

To Cassie for keeping me organized and semi functional! LOL I love you and can't thank you enough for all you do to support me.

To Lacey for taking such good care of my book babies, fixing all my commas, and being the incredible friend you are.

Shani, for constantly supporting me, being there to chat about anything and everything, and wowing me with all your amazing creations!

To the BOD squad for your endless support, cheering me on, and lifting me up. You are THE BEST. All the hearts.

Jenni, thank you for your friendship and for letting me steal your characters on occasion & for loving mine in return. Aaron will always be yours.

To my supremely awesome ARC/Street team, THANK YOU. You ladies are the absolute best and I could not do all this without you!

To the incredible author/bookish community I'm lucky to be a part of, thank you. You have been a source of camaraderie, support, and hilarious memes that keep me going on the rough days and celebrate with me on the awesome ones. Y'all are the best!

Finally, to all of you for picking up this book, reading this story, and (if you've read this far) hopefully falling in love with these characters. I appreciate every one of you!